Evie Undercover

Evie Undercover

Liz Harris

Where heroes are like chocolate – irresistible!

Published 2015 by Choc Lit Limited
Penrose House, Crawley Drive, Camberley, Surrey GU15 2AB, UK
www.choc-lit.com

A CIP catalogue record for this book is available
from the British Library

ISBN 978-1-78189-240-4

Printed and bound by Clays Ltd

MIX
Paper from
responsible sources
FSC® C018072

For my sister, Diana
Thank you

Acknowledgements

Evie Undercover was a highly enjoyable novel to write as much of it takes place in a part of the world I've come to love – Umbria, Italy. I would like to say a heartfelt thank you to my sister, Diana, for introducing me to the area in which the novel is set and for the many hours of enjoyment I've had in Casa Torre, a beautiful house in a beautiful location.

I owe my husband, Richard, too, a huge thank you. Without his encouragement and his willingness to do all of the real-life things I'm always too busy writing to do, this novel would never have seen the light of day.

Finally, I'm immensely grateful to the Romantic Novelists' Association, whose friendship, support and advice helped me enormously when writing the novel, to Choc Lit and their Tasting Panel (Melanie A, Nadine K, Avril M, Sonya B, Betty, Sally T, Liz R, Trudy O and Clare C) for taking Evie to their hearts and publishing her story and to the Choc Lit authors for being such fabulous friends.

Writing is a solitary occupation, but with family and friends such as these, it's never a lonely one.

Chapter One

A hotel bedroom in Umbria, Italy

'Will you sleep with me?' Evie Shaw stood on her dishevelled bed, spotlit by a sliver of moonlight that fell from the unshuttered window above her. The man who'd just started to walk out of her bedroom stopped sharply. He turned to face her. 'Please sleep with me,' she repeated, wriggling toes that were tipped with scarlet and holding clenched fists in front of her mouth.

She lowered her head to let her long auburn hair fall across her face. Strands of hair drifted across eyelashes caked with thick black mascara, and stuck there. Damn! That wasn't meant to happen. She raised a hand and tugged lightly on the wayward strands. A second, more forceful, tug freed the hair. The sharp pain made it easy to work a tremor into her lower lip.

Leaving the bedroom door wide open, Tom Hadleigh took two or three steps back into the dimly lit room. He pulled the belt of his white towelling robe more tightly around him and cleared his throat.

'I'm sorry, Evie,' he began, his voice firm but edged with embarrassment. 'Attractive though you are, I don't sleep with the people who work for me. It's just not a good idea. In fact it's a bloody awful idea and I'm sure you can appreciate that. Though of course I'm flattered you asked me,' he added quickly.

She opened her eyes wide, her face a picture of astonishment. She wrinkled her nose questioningly at him, then startled surprise gave way to dimpled amusement. Cute, dimpled amusement, she hoped.

'Oh, I don't mean sleep with me, as in *sleep* with me. I certainly don't want to sleep with you like that. God forbid!' She threw back her head and laughed. 'No, I just want you to lie next to me. Nothing more than that. Good Lord, no.' She let the smile fade from her face. 'It's the scorpions.' She made an exaggerated show of looking nervously around the hotel room. 'There might be more of them hiding in here.' She managed a theatrical shudder.

One of the shoestring straps of her short nightdress slipped off her shoulder. Result! She left it there.

Tom Hadleigh took another step into the room.

'The scorpion's gone, Evie, and I'm sure there aren't any more.' He gestured around the room. 'You saw the staff thoroughly search the place before they left. There's nothing for you to worry about, so why don't you get down from the bed and let me go back to my room?'

What was wrong with the man!

OK, she was being a bit full on – well, maybe a little more than a bit, and that could be seen as a turn-off – but in the circumstances she was entitled to expect that she'd get more of a macho response to her quivering plea for help. So much for last week's article in *Glamour Puss* which said that no man on earth could resist a damsel in distress; she seemed to have found the one man who could.

She gave an inward sigh. She was just going to have to work harder to break down the barrier he seemed determined to keep between them. Their four days in Italy didn't give her much time in which to find out what she needed to know, and although she'd be working for him for two more weeks once they were back in London, those two weeks would be a dead loss – he'd be in his Chambers all day and she'd be alone in his house. No, it was now or never, and the best way to make it now was to get him into her bed.

Just between the sheets: nothing more.

Him being next to her when they woke up in the morning would get them talking conversationally, and that was when tongues were more likely to loosen. His tongue, to be more precise. That was Plan A, and it had to work – there was no Plan B.

Rearranging her features into fearful anxiety, she stared intently at the wooden beams of the roof rafters, which were throwing long, dark shadows across the whitewashed walls.

'They're in those beams.' She shivered and hugged her arms across her chest. 'I know I'll never get to sleep – I'll keep on thinking that something horrible's going to fall from the ceiling and land on my head.' She turned frightened eyes back to her boss, pleading with him. She'd audition for the National Theatre when she got back to England, she decided.

'You'll be fine, really you will.' He sounded weary. 'It's past midnight and all good scorpions are in bed by now. As we should be. But not together,' he added hastily. 'Now, won't you let me help you get down?'

He moved closer to the bed and held his hand up to her. Ignoring the outstretched hand, she jumped down and landed lightly on the stone floor, her short nightdress flying up. The second shoestring strap slipped down.

'I'm not worried about the good scorpions, Mr Hadleigh,' she said, inching one strap back over her shoulder. 'It's the bad ones that frighten me, the ones that curl their little black tails in my direction, thinking evil thoughts. If you were next to me, I wouldn't feel afraid.'

If ever there was a time for a tear, this was it.

In her head, she frantically conjured up the last few moments of *Ghost*, when the yummy dead hero said a final goodbye to the distraught wife he adored and left her forever, slowly walking into the glittering stars that were leading him into the heaven for good guys. Her eyes filled with tears. Success!

'How can you be so scared of them?' he asked, his amazement unmistakably tinged with irritation. 'You must be used to them – the agency said you were part Italian.'

So much for chivalry and damsels in fear and distress. The man had a heart of stone. She was going to have to try another tack, and fast.

'Only a tiny part,' she said. She followed her words with a slight smile. 'My grandmother was Italian. It's the English bit of me that's scared of scorpions.' The smile became stronger, more cajoling. 'Please, Mr Hadleigh, or I'll never get to sleep.'

He gave a loud sigh: loud and frustrated. 'I suppose I could stay in here until you fell asleep – if you didn't take too long about it, that is.' He glanced around the room. 'Look, there's a chair over there. I can sit there till you've dropped off.' He raised his arm and pointed to a cane chair in the corner of the room. His towelling robe fell open above his belt and Evie saw a line of dark hair snaking into the belt.

A rush of adrenaline shot through her, and her stomach jumped.

She tore her eyes away and fixed them on the chair. Being turned on by him wasn't part of the plan. He was a job and nothing more. Nothing else was on the cards. No way!

Biting her lower lip – a sure sign of deep concentration – she fixed her eyes on the chair and tried to look as if she was considering his suggestion.

'No,' she said at last. 'I'm sorry, but I don't think that would help. Deep down, I'd know that you were going back to your room as soon as I fell asleep, and that'd kill any chance of me dropping off.'

God, what a wimp she sounded – she couldn't keep this up for much longer. If she didn't get a result soon, she'd have to give up. In desperation, she tried out a range of different expressions, hoping that one of them would strike a chivalric nerve.

Apparently immune to the panoply of performances being played out before him, Tom Hadleigh sat down heavily on the edge of her bed and sighed wearily.

'Just remind me why I employed you, will you?'

'To do some interpreting for you, and to help you with paying bills and sorting things out in London – the sort of personal things you wouldn't ask your work secretary to do.'

'Exactly. You are meant to be helping me, not the other way round, and the best way you can help me at this precise moment is to let me get some sleep. Which I can't do until you get back into bed. It's not as if I'm miles away – I'm only in the room opposite. You shouted out for me before, so if necessary you could shout out again.'

What a man! She'd have one last shot at trying to find a streak of gallantry somewhere deep inside him, and if that failed, she'd go to bed alone and spend the night working on a Plan B.

'I know I'm being a nuisance and I'm really sorry, but I know that I won't be able to get that scorpion out of my mind. I'm worried that if I don't get some sleep, I'll forget all the Italian I know. If you were next to me, I'd fall asleep at once.'

'How highly flattering,' he murmured dryly.

A giggle escaped her and she quickly smothered it. 'I didn't mean it like that.'

She stared at him, widening her eyes with hope. Annoyingly, they began to water and she was forced to blink.

'Oh, all right then. I suppose I'll have to if I want to get any sleep before tomorrow – and I do. I don't seem to have much choice in the matter.'

Eureka!

'Thank you,' she said, her voice shaking with relief. And no wonder – she'd totally run out of ideas for simpering helplessly. She directed a heartfelt smile of gratitude towards her boss for rescuing her plan from the jaws of defeat at the eleventh hour.

He stood up. 'I'll go and lock my door.' He crossed the room in long strides and went out into the corridor.

She stared after him, her heart beating fast. This could turn out to be the worst plan she'd ever had in her life – and she'd come up with some pretty dire plans in her time – or it could turn out to be the best.

Tom leaned back against the door of his room and slowly released his breath. How the hell had he let himself be manoeuvred into sharing a bed with Evie Shaw?

He hadn't often been lost for words in his life, but as he'd stared across the room at the girl he'd hired the week before, her white nightdress translucent in the moonlight, it had been one of those rare occasions.

And that had only been the start of the rapid downhill slope. Things had speedily gone from being downright awkward to bloody impossible, with the result that he was now about to spend the night in an employee's bedroom. Entirely her choice, not his. For someone who prided himself on always being in control of the situation, he hadn't managed things too well just now. Somehow or other, Evie Shaw had wrong-footed him.

Muffled by the thick stone walls, he heard the sound of Evie moving around in her room. He went quickly to his chair, picked up his boxer shorts and stepped into them.

Sleeping naked as he usually did was not an option. He pulled his robe around him again and tied up his belt as tightly as he could.

She'd seemed such a good secretary, too. Admittedly she'd only been with him for a week, but she'd got to his house on time every morning, and she'd always succeeded in getting through the list of things he'd left her to do whilst he was in his Chambers. He'd swiftly seen how efficient she was, and had been able to concentrate on bringing his junior up to speed about his ongoing cases and making sure that the junior would be able to deal with anything that came up in his absence.

And her Italian was excellent. On her second morning, he'd asked her to phone the hotel in Italy to confirm their reservation, and he'd hung on at the house in case there were any problems. As soon as she'd started talking to the receptionist at Il Poggio, the small hotel he used whenever he visited the Italian house he'd bought a few months earlier, he'd known that her Italian was as good as the agency had promised.

It had been a massive relief that the agency had been able to find an Italian speaker at such short notice. His regular interpreter had pulled out of the trip a week before they were due to leave as his wife had had to go into hospital. He'd thought at first that he might have to postpone his visit, which he was desperately anxious to avoid doing. He had a high-profile libel case beginning two weeks after his return from Italy, so he wouldn't have been able to reschedule his trip for any time in the immediate future.

The restoration of his house was almost complete. He was going to be free for the whole of August and he wanted to spend the month at the house. What's more, he hadn't seen his parents for a while and he'd invited them to come for a couple of the weeks that he would be there. If he left it any longer to order the furniture, it would be impossible for any of them to stay there.

Finding Evie had been a godsend as it meant that the planned trip could go ahead.

Ideally, she could have been easier on the eye – thick-rimmed glasses and a severe hairstyle, along with downright dowdy clothes, didn't really do her any favours. But her appearance was irrelevant. What mattered was that on his first visit to Umbria he'd fallen in love with the place and had bought a house on a whim. No one in the area spoke English, and he didn't speak Italian. Evie did.

And there was another good thing about her – she wasn't the sort of woman who spoke merely for the sake of saying something. She hadn't attempted to force a conversation during the flight from Heathrow to Rome Fiumicino, nor on the journey from the airport to Umbria. Instead, she'd been content to stare out of the window, occasionally exclaiming in delight at the views.

Admittedly he hadn't tried to start up a conversation with her. If he remembered rightly, 'Lunatic drivers!' was about the only thing he'd said during their one-and-a-half-hour drive to the hotel. Nevertheless, unlike Evie, a lot of women would have found it virtually impossible to hold their tongues in check. Uncontrolled tongues made him a great deal of money every year, but he wouldn't have wanted one in the car with him.

They'd reached Il Poggio with time only to wash their hands before the evening meal, and although she'd made one or two general comments while they were waiting for their food to be served, she'd soon fallen silent, respecting his unspoken need to check his emails.

When he'd wished her goodnight after dinner, he'd gone to his room and congratulated himself on having hired a female who wasn't totally superficial and self-obsessed. She was a plain, but pleasant, woman, who wouldn't make a fuss about a broken nail, and who'd be an excellent interpreter for the week.

So where had the other Evie come from!

The Evie who'd screamed in fear at the sight of a tiny insect halfway up her wall; the Evie without glasses, whose hair hung gloriously about her face; the Evie who'd stood on her bed looking ...

He stopped himself. He wasn't going to go there. He didn't want to remember how she'd looked. Suffice it to say, her behaviour over the scorpion had shown a very different side of her, and he'd been put in an impossible position. He must keep that in the back of his mind and be more alert in the future, but for the moment, all he was going to think about was getting through the night as quickly as possible, or what was left of the night.

He picked up his watch from the wrought-iron bedside table, walked out of his room and closed the door firmly behind him.

Evie was lying in the middle of the bed, holding the sheet up to her chin, when Tom came back into her room. There was a look of grim determination on his face.

'You can have whichever side you want,' she offered.

'I'm usually on the left,' he said, and he walked to the far end of the large iron bed, his eyes firmly on the floor in front of him.

'I didn't realise you were married,' she said, shifting to the right-hand side of the bed.

'I'm not.'

'Oh.' She stared up at the ceiling, her heart thumping. This was more embarrassing than she'd thought it would be. Much more. Plan A hadn't gone into trivial details like the sides of the bed and what it'd actually be like when he lay down next to her.

And suppose she reached out unconsciously for him during the night, forgetting in her sleep that this was strictly a non-sex thing. *Aargh!* Just thinking about it was scary. She slid deeper into the bed and fervently wished it was morning. And by the look on his face when he'd come in, so did he.

Out of the corner of her eye, she saw him drop his towelling robe on the floor and pull back the corner of the sheet, making sure that he didn't uncover so much as an inch of her body. She turned her head and looked towards the door. The mattress moved beneath her as he slid into the bed and immediately rolled on to his side. She surreptitiously glanced at him – his back was towards her and she could only see the side of his face.

'Right,' he said. 'Sleep. Goodnight, Evie.' He closed his eyes.

'Goodnight, Mr Hadleigh.'

He opened them again. She quickly looked away.

'I really don't think you can "Mr Hadleigh" me when I'm in bed next to you, even if I *am* only here as a sort of sleeping pill. I'm sure it won't hurt us to drop some formality whilst we're in Italy. You can call me Tom. But only whilst we're here.'

'Goodnight, Tom,' she said, and she smiled at the dark rafters above her.

Chapter Two

In the scheme of things ...

The rays of the early morning sun slanted through the small window in the ceiling and fell on Evie's face. She stirred. Still half asleep, she turned over and buried her face in the pillow next to her. Her cheek met with hard muscle, and a male scent filled her nostrils. Her eyes flew open. Ohmigod, that was no pillow.

She rolled on to her back and breathed in deeply. She'd done it. She'd actually done it, and after only two small glasses of red wine. She'd found the courage from somewhere to ask Tom Hadleigh – hotshot barrister Tom Hadleigh – to get into bed with her, and he'd agreed. Well, perhaps agreed was a bit too strong for the position she'd put him in, but the result was the same. Wow!

It had been an inspired plan, if she said so herself, and it just showed how keen she was on keeping her job – her real job.

Within two days of working in Tom's house, she'd realised that she was never going to uncover the proof her editor wanted by looking through Tom's files and in his desk drawers. No one would leave full details of their affairs, complete with times, dates and places, lying around to be read by every nosy temp.

Her only hope of finding out what he'd been up to socially – well, sexually, to be more precise – in the previous couple of months was going to be the week in Italy.

The first stage of Plan A had been to get things on to an informal footing by getting him into her bed – she glanced across at the sleeping back and smiled in satisfaction – and the second stage was to encourage him to start talking as they lay side by side.

Getting him to start talking was going to be far from easy. The habit of watching his words in court had clearly extended to his private life, and although he'd always been courteous and polite when they'd met, he'd firmly kept his distance. Perhaps more of a distance than he would have kept if she hadn't gone quite so overboard in following the editor's instructions about her appearance.

'You'll need to keep a low profile, Evie,' he'd told her when he'd called her into his office at *Pure Dirt* less than a week after she'd started working for the magazine. 'Be smart but unobtrusive.'

As he'd been speaking, his eyes had been travelling down from the auburn hair that was piled carelessly on top of her head; to the unnaturally long black eyelashes; to the bright green sweater, cut very low, that clung to her curves and barely reached the waistband of her short black skirt; to the expanse of long, fake-tanned leg that ended in emerald green spiky-heeled sling-backs.

'Unobtrusive,' he'd repeated. 'We don't want to scare him, do we?'

Minutes before, he'd told her that one of his contacts at an employment agency had rung earlier in the day to tell him that Tom Hadleigh urgently needed an Italian speaker. The person had to be available to go to Italy with him for a week, and if he or she had secretarial skills, too, the contract would be for a month – a week working at his Hampstead house, a week in Italy, and then two more weeks back at his house.

As he'd only just hired Evie, the editor remembered her listing fluent Italian on her CV. Unable to believe his luck, he instantly dug deep into the magazine's pocket and paid his contact to courier Evie's CV to Tom, along with a personal recommendation from the agency saying that she was fairly new to their books but that she'd made a highly favourable impression on her first placements for them. His contact had got back almost at once to say that the job was Evie's.

Normally the lawyer would have interviewed her first, the agency contact told the editor, but he was extremely busy, and it would be difficult to find the time to do so. He'd used the agency for several years and was prepared to take their recommendation on trust. However, he'd look upon the first week in London as a probationary period. If she proved unsuitable, he'd terminate the contract, no matter the difficulty that caused him.

'Fuck probationary periods and all that crap,' the editor concluded. 'All I'm interested in is the proof that he was screwing the so-called morally blameless Zizi Westenhall. Get me that, and I'll sue her for the shitload of money we had to pay her. And I'll make that lawyer look bad, too, for screwing a client whilst he was trying to screw us. I don't care how you go about it, just get me the fucking lowdown.'

'Why are you so sure they were an item?'

The editor rifled through the pile of papers on his desk and pulled out a photo. He waved it in front of her. 'That's why. Just look at them both – you can almost smell the sex. A paparazzi mate of mine came across them and he took it when they didn't know.'

She picked up the photo. Tom Hadleigh was gazing across a candlelit table into the eyes of a very beautiful woman.

'That's Zizi Westenhall. Mrs Rich Bastard. And she had the fucking cheek to say we libelled her for fooling around behind her idiot husband's back. Huh! You look at that and tell me she's not having it off with her lawyer.'

'They certainly seem to be very close.'

'Tell me about it. Well, we've well and truly got him now.

He sure is gonna regret the times he's deliberately twisted our words and made us look like incompetent fools and liars. It's up to you now, Evie. Together we're gonna shaft the bastard.'

Scared witless and giddy with excitement at having been given such an important first commission, she'd turned to leave the editor's office, but he'd stopped her.

'If you fuck up this assignment,' he'd said steadily, 'your first job at *Pure Dirt* will be your last, and you'll never again work on any other magazine if I can help it. But you know that, don't you?'

The next day, she'd tied her hair tightly back in a bun, left her false eyelashes on the bedside table, put on the tortoiseshell spectacles she'd bought in the market and a drab beige suit, and presented herself at Tom Hadleigh's house. She'd nearly spoilt it all by giggling at the expression on his face when he saw her thick glasses and sensible shoes.

The week in London had gone smoothly, and he'd seemed pleased with her work. So far things had gone well in Italy, too – after all, in fewer than twenty-four hours, they were calling each other Evie and Tom. But there was no time for her to rest on her laurels – she had to step things up a notch in double quick time, and she couldn't expect the black scorpion to do it for her again.

The moment she'd caught sight of the scorpion in the corner of an empty hearth on her way back to her room after dinner, she knew she'd found the inspiration she'd been looking for. With wooden beams everywhere, there was bound to be a black scorpion somewhere in her room. All she had to do was find it, wait for the right time, jump on the bed and scream as loudly as she could. Which is what she'd done, and very successfully, too, as testified by the legal head on the pillow next to hers.

She glanced sideways at the object of her thoughts. He

was asleep, half lying on his back. She propped herself up on her elbow and leaned slightly over him to get a better look at his face. Her eyes slowly traced his features and slid down his throat to a mat of rough chest hair. She moved closer still and followed the line of hair until it disappeared into a tangle of white linen.

Holy crap, she thought, and she fell back against the cool sheet – he's absolutely gorgeous.

She closed her eyes tightly. She wasn't going to look at him any more. He was a job, and nothing else. She pressed her eyelids harder against each other.

'So, Evie, which of us is going to move first – assuming a) that you've finished your physical examination of me and b) that you don't need to be rescued from any other insects prior to moving?'

She gasped and opened her eyes.

Tom had raised himself on his elbow and was staring down into her face. 'Well?' he repeated.

'Huh?' she squeaked nervously, trying not to look at the broad chest in front of her.

'With reference to a), you've just given me a thorough once-over, but if you haven't finished, I could lie still a little longer. It's as you wish. With reference to b), as far as I can tell, I seem to have been a successful bug deterrent, but despite you not wearing your glasses at present, you might be able to spot something I've missed.'

She felt herself going scarlet. 'I was just wondering if you were awake.'

'I see. And there was I, thinking you were scoring me out of ten. Silly ol' me.'

'No, I wasn't.' Her voice ended in a high-pitched croak.

He sighed deeply. 'Ah, Evie. I've spent too many years watching people in court not to know when someone's telling me porkies. So what was the score?'

She looked up and saw laughter in his eyes.

'Well, then,' she said, breaking into a smile. 'Since I wouldn't want to disappoint my boss on this beautiful Tuesday morning, I'll quote my father – although he used to say it in Italian – every beetle is a beauty to its mother.'

He threw back his head and laughed. 'I deserved that. All I can say is, I hope you don't feel about beetles as you do about scorpions or we're going to have a difficult few days ahead.' Still laughing, he fell back against the pillow.

Evie started to laugh with him, and they turned at the same moment to look at each other across the pillows.

'Well, then, Evie,' he said, his laughter dying away. 'What comes next?'

'Nothing comes next,' she said quickly. Even she would baulk at flinging herself on top of her employer's muscular body and demanding immediate action. No, although Plan A had worked – he was where she'd wanted him to be – he didn't look likely to start spilling the beans, and she was clearly going to need a Plan B after all. Maybe something involving hot sun and plenty of wine. When he wasn't as physically close to her, she'd be able to think more clearly.

'Then I'll be a gentleman and get up first, shall I?'

Without waiting for an answer, he swung his legs over the side of the bed, reached for his robe and put it on. He stood up and made his way across the room to the door. When he reached it, he started to turn the handle, then he paused and glanced back at her.

'I'll see you on the terrace in half an hour for breakfast. After that, I think we ought to buy something to deal with any insects that might threaten our future comfort, don't you?' he said cheerfully, and he opened the door and went out.

'Holy cow.' She groaned inwardly as she heard him close his door behind him. 'What *does* come next?'

16

Chapter Three

Their first morning in Umbria

Perhaps it hadn't been such a brilliant idea to wear her grey trouser suit, she thought, coming out from the hotel into the bright morning sun. It was amazingly warm for the beginning of June. She wriggled uncomfortably in her jacket, pushed her glasses more firmly on to the bridge of her nose and looked around the terrace, but there was no sign of Tom.

She hesitated a moment, then made her way towards one of the small iron tables next to the balustrade that ran round the edge of the terrace. The jacket would have to go, she decided, and she started to unbutton it as she walked. It was going to be much too hot to be all starchy and formal. She slipped it off as she sat down. And it was much too hot for glasses she didn't need. She took off her glasses, put them in the centre of the table and reached up to adjust the tortoiseshell barrette that held her hair back from her face.

God knows what he was going to say when he turned up for breakfast, which would be at any minute – it must have surely been a first for him that an almost naked woman practically forced him into her bed. Looking back on the night before, she wondered how she'd had the nerve. She groaned aloud. She couldn't even bear to think about it in the light of day.

Yes, he'd seemed OK about everything when he'd woken up that morning – in fact he'd seemed almost amused by what had happened – but that was then and this was now, and by now he'd have had time to think about it some more. Instead of going one step forward after their night together between the sheets, they might have just gone two steps back.

But she wasn't going to panic; no, she wasn't. She'd deal with the fallout when it fell out and not before. Hopefully, her formal get-up that morning, softened by a slightly more relaxed hairstyle, would strike the right note and things wouldn't be too embarrassing between them.

Anyway, she wasn't going to give him another thought.

Taking a deep breath of lavender-scented air, she turned to stare at the slopes that swept away from the terrace towards distant hills that were a rich green and purple in colour. On top of one of the hills, a small town shone brightly in the clear light.

She wondered whether she should still call him Tom.

'It's a lovely view, isn't it?'

The sound of his voice made her jump. She glanced at him as he sat down opposite her. He nodded towards the distant town. 'That's Todi. You can also see it from my house. Obviously, it's a different outlook, but the view from the house is stunning, too. The scenery around here is one of the reasons why I fell in love with the area.'

'It certainly is beautiful, Mr Hadleigh.'

'I thought we'd agreed on Tom for the week. But if you'd prefer to be more formal ...' His voice trailed off and he gave a slight shrug.

She shook her head. 'I don't do formal if I don't have to.'

'I'd rather guessed that,' he said dryly. 'Ah, here's the waiter with the coffee.'

What on earth did a girl talk to her boss about after a night like the one they'd just had? She bit her lip anxiously as she watched the waiter fill their cups. Handy Hints for Investigative Journalists didn't exactly cover that situation. She was going to have to wait until he started a conversation and then take the lead from him.

'The system is to help ourselves from the buffet,' he said, standing up. 'There's always a selection of cold cuts and cakes. Come on, let's go. I'm starving.' And he moved off in the direction of a table at the far side of the terrace. She quickly got up and followed him.

'The main thing,' he began when they'd returned to their table having helped themselves to slices of the cheeses and cold meats, 'is to make sure that the house stays in perfect harmony with its surroundings. Every piece of furniture has to be in keeping with the age of the property and its environment.' He paused in the middle of cutting a piece of *prosciutto* and looked across at her. 'And that's where you come in, Evie. I need an exact translation of everything I tell the surveyor, or perhaps I should say *geometra*, since we're in Italy. There must be no mistakes.'

'I'll do my best, Mr Hadleigh … Tom.' She gave him a bright, confident smile. This was safe ground.

'I'm sure you will. Now, I think I'll go and get some cake. Can I get you something, too?' He stood up, pushing back his chair.

'No, thanks. I've had as much as I want.'

'I didn't think I'd ever get used to breakfasts like this, but I have and I like them. If you catch the waiter's eye, you could get us some more coffee. And obviously whatever you want for yourself – I hope that goes without saying.' He gave her a quick smile and began to move off in the direction of the buffet.

Her eyes followed him as he wound his way between the tables.

It was a mega relief that he'd put the night's events totally behind them and was focused solely on the day ahead. He didn't seem at all mad at her, and they were still Tom and Evie. So far, so good. Plan A might not have resulted in the hoped-for pillow talk but it had still been a step in the right direction. Now all she had to do was learn as much about the contents of his life as she was going to learn about the contents of his house, ideally keeping all of her clothes on this time, and her editor would be one happy man.

She wasn't sure that she'd be one happy woman, but she wasn't going to go down that path. She'd no choice but to do what she'd been told to do, and that meant that she had to come up with some ideas. That had got to be her focus, and nothing else.

Another shot of caffeine was a must.

'*Un altro caffè*,' she called to the waiter. '*Per noi due.*'

While she waited for their coffee to arrive and for mind-blowing inspiration to fill her head, not necessarily in that order, she idly glanced across at Tom. He'd just bent over the breakfast bar and was reaching for a plate. His forearm gleamed in the rays of the morning sun. Her eyes dropped to the stone-coloured chinos fitting smoothly over his buttocks. He could win rear of the year, she thought, and leaned slightly forward.

A dark shape stepped in front of her, and cut off her line of vision. Damn!

She looked up and saw the waiter standing in front of her, coffee pot in hand. Impatiently she waited for him to fill their cups and move on, but by the time he'd done so, Tom was already on his way back to the table.

'So, Evie,' he said in an easy, conversational tone as he sat down and started to cut up his cake, 'apart from something to deal with scorpions, and possibly even beetles – we've yet to establish your thoughts about beetles – is there anything else we need to buy in order to ensure that we sleep in our own beds tonight?'

Bloody— The events of the night weren't totally behind them after all.

'About yesterday evening,' she began, twisting her features into an expression of tortured regret. 'I'm truly sorry about everything. I don't know what came over me, but whatever it was, it won't happen again. I've always been terrified of scorpions.' She put her hand across her heart and leaned forward, sincerity shining from her eyes. At least she hoped it was. 'I should have thought ahead and brought some spray with me. It was unforgivable of me to put you in such a difficult position.'

'At least that's something we agree on,' he said with a wry smile. 'I suggest that we buy that spray today and then put the whole sad episode to bed. Ooops, I'm sorry!' His hand flew dramatically to his forehead. 'An unfortunate choice of expression. But you get my drift, I'm sure.'

'Indeed I do get your drift,' she said stiffly. She sat back against her chair and picked up her cup. She was the one who was meant to be playing high drama, not him. 'Why don't we drift on to a different subject?'

'What an admirable play on words, Evie. With such a talent, you really ought to consider becoming a lawyer or taking up journalism.' Her cup clattered to the saucer as she choked on her coffee. 'Hey, you've gone bright red. Are you all right? Do you want me to thump you on your back or perform the Heimlich manoeuvre? If I have a choice, I think I'll go for the first option.'

'I'm fine, thank you,' she croaked. 'It's just that I used to dream about being a lawyer when I was a child, so what you said hit a nerve.'

'Well, all I can say is, with the nerve you've already exhibited and your ability to achieve your desired outcome in the face of adverse odds, it's a great loss to the legal profession that you didn't pursue your childhood dream.'

'I thought we weren't going to mention last night again: not directly, not indirectly.' She cleared her throat a couple of times in an effort to bring her squeaking voice down by several octaves.

'You're right. I'm sorry about making the comment. It was meant as a joke, but I can see that it was a pretty poor one. Being in your bed is no joking matter.'

She bit her lip. Was that good or bad? She glanced anxiously across the table and their eyes met. His face broke into a warm smile.

'OK, enough is enough, I'll let it drop.' He leaned back and gazed around him in satisfaction. 'I must say, one way or another this has been a most unusual start to a visit to Italy, but that's by no means a bad thing – it's all been very entertaining. But you're right, sufficient has been said on a certain subject and it's now time to move on. So, what shall we talk about?'

'How about what we're doing today – apart from visiting the supermarket, that is.' She gave him a wide smile – yup, it had been one step forward, and no steps back.

'First of all, we're going to the house. We're meeting the *geometra* there at about eleven. It'll take us roughly forty-five minutes to get there.' He looked at his watch. 'In fact, we can set off at any time now. How long do you need to get ready?'

'No time at all – I *am* ready.' She swivelled round in her chair and started to pull her jacket towards her.

He leaned forward. 'Yesterday morning, I would have agreed with you, Evie. Yesterday morning, I wouldn't have expected you to be wearing anything other than a suit or a skirt and blouse. But that was yesterday morning. Last night I saw a slightly different Evie, and I think that the Evie of last night would choose to wear something more comfortable on what's going to be a very hot day. I'm right, aren't I?'

'I suppose you are.' She gave a short laugh that suggested

embarrassment. 'About the geeky clothes I was wearing last week, it was just that I wanted to look older and more secretaryish so that you'd feel confident I could do the job. I knew that I was on probation. But I suppose that sounds very silly to someone like you.' Cringing inwardly, she attempted a Pathetic Little Woman expression.

'Not at all,' he purred. 'I'm sure it's quite understandable. At least, I think it is. Shall we say fifteen minutes, then?'

'That'll be fine. I'll put on a dress – it'll be much cooler.' She stood up and started to move away from the table.

'You've forgotten your glasses,' he called after her. 'Unless, of course, you no longer need them. The trauma of a recent, unmentionable event may well have effected a miraculous improvement in your vision. I'm sure that such things have been known to happen.'

As she went back to the table to pick up her glasses, she saw that he was grinning broadly as he raised his cup to drain the last of his coffee.

Damn, she thought.

Chapter Four

Getting to know you ...
Getting to know all about you ...

'Here.' Tom leaned across from the driver's seat and handed Evie a leather case. 'You'll find the house plans in one of the pockets and also some rough sketches of furniture. Obviously I need to see the house again before I decide on anything for certain. The *geometra*'s got some ideas as well.' He threw the four-by-four into gear. 'Having a woman's touch wouldn't be a bad thing, either, so feel free to chip in with any suggestions.' He put his foot down on the accelerator. 'The dress is an improvement, by the way.'

She beamed at him. 'Thank you. And thanks for suggesting that I change my clothes. This is much more comfortable.'

'My pleasure. And indeed, it is my pleasure: you were a veritable eyesore in some of the things you wore last week. And before you decide to sue me for that non PC comment,' he said, throwing her a quick smile before returning his eyes to the road, 'you should know that a legal defence to the charge of slander is that the statement tells the truth. "Evie Shaw looks much better in her yellow dress and without thick glasses, M'Lud; and that's the truth."'

Ohmigod, she was going red again! A bright red face so did *not* go with auburn hair.

'I love planning rooms and furniture,' she said in a rush. 'It's fun.' She buried her head in the case and pulled out the photos and drawings. 'And I like co-ordinating colours.' And she did. The purple walls of her room in the Camden Town house she shared with her best friends, Rachel and Jess, made a real statement. Everyone said so.

So he was into beautiful houses and scenery, was he?

She stared with unseeing eyes at the photo of the Umbrian house on her lap, and tried to imagine the expression on her editor's face if the highlights of her exposé were the revelations that Tom Hadleigh was mad about an old stone house, appreciated stunning landscapes, was thoughtful and had a cool sense of humour. All she needed to set the seal on her instant dismissal was to discover that he loved children and dogs and wanted to bring peace to the world.

'I want you to get everything you can on that lump of pig shit,' her editor had said as he'd handed her a wire to wear if necessary. 'But it's got to be provable – times, dates, places, and so on – not some old smut that would be kicked out of court as hearsay. And there'll be a bonus if you can show that he and Zizi Westenhall were into something kinky – people like that always are. Find me something I can nail him with, Evie, or don't bother to come back.'

Well, she wasn't going to find kinky – she'd spent more than enough time with Tom to know that – and she'd no intention of making something up: she was a reporter, not a fiction writer. But that didn't mean to say she wouldn't get her story – she would, but it wouldn't be nasty.

Her job at *Pure Dirt* was the start of her dream coming true and she wasn't going to throw away her chance. Her dream had begun when she was ten years old and had seen her name in the local newspaper under the story about the friendship between her dog and a piglet, and it had still been her dream when she'd left school. She'd gone straight from school to Lake Garda for a year to get her Italian up to scratch, and had sent a weekly article about life in an Italian hotel back to the local newspaper. On her return to England, she'd gone to work full-time for the paper.

Not even the less-than-riveting subjects she'd covered – the school achievements, weddings, local fêtes, disputes between neighbours over the height of a hedge – had dampened her burning desire to work for a top magazine. Two years later, it was clear to her that the local paper had taught her everything it could, and she'd left Suffolk and gone to London with the aim of getting a job with *Glamour*, *Glamour Puss* or *Cosmopolitan*.

Her and all the rest. A lot of other girls had the same aim, she'd soon found out, and she hadn't even been able to get a job making tea for anyone in any of the top magazines. Finally, after more than a year of temping while applying to magazine after magazine, she'd been offered a post at *Pure Dirt*.

A gossip rag wasn't the path she'd have chosen to go down if she'd had any choice, but she hadn't, and she'd grabbed the opportunity with both hands, seeing it as a stepping stone that could lead to one of the big magazines. She'd heard of a girl who'd gone straight from *Pure Dirt* to *Glamour Puss*, and if it could happen to that girl, it could happen to her.

Rachel and Jess had been horrified when she'd told them where she was going to work. OK, she'd agreed in the face of their appalled shrieks, the magazine *was* a bit in-your-face and did sometimes go over the top, but it had to be like that if it was going to stand out from the hoards of other gossip magazines that lined the shelves. They knew how hard she'd tried to find work on a magazine, and they knew it was the only offer she'd had.

And just because *Pure Dirt* was a bit close to the mark, she'd added – well, miles over the mark, if she was truly honest with herself – it didn't mean that she had to sink to the lowest level. She was going to be one of the good guys. She'd uncover the truth and tell it like it was, but nothing more than that. That had to be possible, even at *Pure Dirt*.

'Think *Pure*,' she'd told them. 'Not *Dirt*. A story doesn't have to be invasive and malicious to be a bloody good read.'

'Oh, yeah!' they'd chorused.

'It's still dirt,' Jess had said, standing up, 'but it's clean, honest dirt. So that's OK, then.' And she and Rachel had gone off to their rooms, leaving waves of disapproval in their wake.

Since that conversation they'd been quite shitty towards her, and it had been a real relief to get away from their caustic comments for a week. But once the magazine had published her article and they'd seen that she'd worked on a matter of public interest, they'd know that they'd been wrong about her job and things'd go back to the way they used to be.

But public interest or not, it was going to take quite a lot to do something to someone else that she wouldn't like done to her. However, if Tom Hadleigh had been telling the court something about Zizi Westenhall which he knew to be untrue, then it was right that he was found out, and she wasn't going to let the fact that the guy was cool and fun to be with get in the way of her telling the truth. She was a journalist, and journalists were above being influenced by superficial things like a person being dead sexy.

She looked up from the photos in her hands and saw that the four-by-four had just finished going round the bottom of the hill on which an old town stood, half hidden behind an encircling grey stone wall. That must be Todi, she decided. The road they were on was leading them away from the old town and through an area of more recently built houses and shops.

She quickly leafed through the photos, slid them back into the leather case, sank down into her seat and surreptitiously looked across at Tom. He was concentrating on the road ahead, his left arm casually resting on the frame of the open window while he steered the wheel with his right hand.

He really was mega attractive, she thought, and he

seemed a genuinely fun guy, light years away from the cheating, lying bastard her editor had said he was. Suppose her sod of an editor had got it wrong and there was nothing for her to come up with? She felt a sudden twinge of panic, and turned away to look at the road.

'Aha!' Tom exclaimed a few moments later. 'There's the sign pointing to Massa Piccola. It won't be long till we're there. I've already told you, haven't I, that the house is on the side of the mountain just behind Massa Piccola? You'll like Massa – it's a very pretty small Roman town.'

'I think you did.' She slid back up in her seat and stared out of the window at the lines of ripening grapes and groves of olive trees that were flashing by. Every so often, they passed a pale grey stone house, set against the backdrop of hills and a clear blue sky. 'What's the *geometra* like?'

'A bit oily, I suppose, but he obviously knows his job. He's more than just a surveyor, though. He's very artistic and he's taken a great deal of care over the restoration. Obviously the bathroom and kitchen fittings are modern, but everything else in the house is original fourteenth or fifteenth century, restored to the highest standard. Sometimes I think he loves the house as much as I do.'

'It sounds like you were lucky to find him.'

'I certainly was. But you'll be able to make up your mind about him for yourself – you'll see quite a bit of him over the next few days. I've asked him to make himself available for the week. It's worth the outlay. I'm only here for a very short time and every second's got to count.'

'What's his name?'

'Eduardo di Montefiori. He's from Umbria. One of the lesser nobility, I believe. But talking of family, Evie, what about you? Have you got family in Italy? You said your grandmother was Italian.'

'No one that I know of. My gran married an Englishman

and they lived in London, but she was useless at English, and when Dad was born, she spoke to him in Italian only. They went to Italy a few times when Dad was young, but not a lot, and we sort of lost contact with the Italian side of the family over the years. Gran died soon after I was born, and it was my dad who taught me Italian – really to stop himself from forgetting it, I think.'

'He did a good job. You speak the language like a native.'

'That's because I worked in a hotel near Lake Garda when I left school. I wanted to keep the Italian up as I thought it might be useful one day. And I was right, wasn't I?' She smiled at him. 'It *has* come in useful – I'm here now, aren't I?'

'Indeed you are. And what's more, it's been a strikingly original presence so far, if I may say so.'

She laughed. 'I'm not going to rise to that.'

'So where do your parents live now?'

'Believe it or not, Australia. Two years after Italy, I left Suffolk and went and shared a house in Camden Town with Rachel and Jess – my mates from school. Mum and Dad decided to emigrate to Australia. They'd wanted to go for ages – friends of theirs went years ago and love it there. They must have been there over a year now. I haven't been to visit them yet, but when I'm able to go, they'll send the money for a ticket. They sound really happy, and good luck to them, I say. I've got Rachel and Jess and my other friends so I'm not exactly alone.'

She leaned back against the seat, and smiled to herself. That was nice of him to show an interest in her family. A sense of relaxation crept over her in the warmth of the day and her eyes started to close.

Holy cow! Her eyes flew open and she sat up fast. This was her moment and she'd almost missed it.

She'd been getting so comfortable that she'd almost

forgotten why she was there. The minute he'd asked her about her family he'd opened the door to her learning something more about him other than whether he took milk with his coffee. She could now put the same personal question to him without it looking like she'd overstepped the employer/employee line. Oh, joy unbounded!

'It's your turn now, Tom,' she said brightly. 'I've told you about my family. What about yours?'

'My parents live in Devon, where I was brought up. I don't see them as much as I'd like to, but we'll catch up when they come over in August. There's not much more to tell you, I'm afraid, and if there were, there wouldn't be time – welcome to Massa Piccola, Evie. We're here.'

To hell with Massa Piccola!

She'd been on the verge of delving into his background, and now she'd have to stop. Why couldn't they have reached the place a bit later?

Biting back her frustration, she stared fixedly through the windscreen ahead of her as Tom drove up to the small *piazza* that was obviously the centre of town and turned right. As he started up the hill leading away from the town, she glanced to the left and caught a fleeting glimpse of mustard yellow and terracotta houses through an arch on the far side of the *piazza*.

She sat back. What mega bad timing! Now she'd have to wait for another suitable moment to arise, and almost certainly she'd have to be the one to bring up the subject of family, which wouldn't be nearly as good.

'It's a pity that you won't be able to see much of the view,' Tom said as he turned off the hill on to a narrow, unpaved road which wound up the side of the mountain, 'but the trees block the view on both sides for most of the way up. You'll get a chance in a few minutes, though.'

'I can't wait,' she said, staring dejectedly through the

windscreen at the pebble-strewn track ahead of them. She gave herself a sharp mental kick – if she didn't get a grip on herself, she'd blow the whole thing. She switched on a look of eager anticipation. 'I'm dying to see it.'

He gave her a quick smile and she saw the excitement in his eyes.

A massive wave of guilt swept over her.

Yes, a promising moment had been nipped in the bud, but so what? Even if Tom *had* had an affair with his client, he was a nice man, who'd been very pleasant to her, and he deserved better from her than he'd been getting. She was in danger of becoming so obsessed by why she was in Italy that she wasn't giving a moment's thought to his needs as a person. She could do better than that, and she would.

He turned sharply to the right, and she glimpsed the sky ahead through a gap in the trees at the top of a steep stretch of track. He lowered the gear and they started to climb the slope.

'We're not far off now,' he said. 'You'll be able to see the house at any minute.'

Just before they reached the gap in the trees, the road curved sharply to the left. Tom swung the wheel hard into the turn and brought the car to a shuddering halt on the brow of the hill. 'Look to the right, Evie.'

She turned her head and stared across sweeping golden fields and olive groves to a grey stone house that sat on the side of the mountain. A square tower rose from the back of the roof of the house, its small windows looking out across the countryside.

'My God, what a fantastic spot it's in! And the house – it's awesome, Tom.' She turned back to him. 'Really, it is. No wonder you like it so much.'

'It *is* something special, isn't it?' He glanced at his watch. 'We're a little early. With luck, Eduardo won't be here yet. I'd like to show you the garden and pool myself.'

He started the car up again and drove along the uneven track until they reached two large wrought-iron gates flanked by stone gateposts. The gates were wide open.

'Oh, he's already here.' There was disappointment in his voice. 'Shame. I'd have rather enjoyed wandering around by ourselves for a bit.'

As he drove through the open gates into the parking area, Evie caught sight of a tall, slim man wearing tailored black trousers and a black open-necked shirt. He was leaning casually against a sleek black convertible parked under a pergola on the right of the drive.

Tom drove past the man and pulled up opposite the convertible. He switched the engine off and opened the car door. The man in black immediately straightened up and came towards them, arms outstretched in welcome, the heavy silver buckle on his leather belt glinting in the sunlight.

'*Il mio amico, Tom. Benvenuto in Italia.*'

A row of perfect white teeth rivalled the sheen on the silver buckle.

Evie stared at the crown of gleaming black hair, at the perfectly sculptured face, at the thin Roman nose, the sensual red lips.

'*Mamma mia,*' she breathed, and she took a step forward. 'That's not oily, that's divine.'

'Stop drooling, Evie,' Tom murmured. He brushed past her as he went to greet the man. 'It's not a pretty sight.'

'Maybe not,' she said, and her lips curved into a broad smile as a thought burst into her head like a ray of shining light. 'But that is.'

Chapter Five

Thank you, Guardian Angel!

Eduardo di Montefiori leaned over in a low, graceful bow and brushed the back of Evie's hand with his lips, his eyes never leaving her face.

'*Bellissima*,' he murmured. Straightening up, he gave her a look of undisguised admiration. '*Assolutamente bellissima.*'

OK, maybe a little oily. Definitely not her cup of tea, but a situation offering possibilities. If she could play it right.

'That means—' she began brightly, turning to Tom.

'I think I can just about manage that,' he cut in cheerfully, and she saw that he was trying not to laugh. Her lips began to twitch, too. She quickly turned away and graced Eduardo with a radiant smile, then reined it in a little – she shouldn't be too obvious.

'*Venite*,' Eduardo said with an elegant flick of his right hand. Embracing Evie with his inviting gaze, he moved to Tom's side, took him lightly by the elbow and started to lead him past a row of slender cypress trees towards a path flanked by white rose bushes that led to the house.

Evie followed hot on their heels, her mind racing. Could she work on two fronts at the same time?

If she played up to Eduardo, she might learn something from him about Tom's affair with Zizi. He obviously wouldn't know the full details – he and Tom couldn't talk to each other and there was a limit to what sign language could say – but it was quite possible that Tom had phoned Zizi on one of his visits to Italy, or that she had called him while he was with Eduardo. If that had happened, Tom would have said her name and Eduardo might have heard him.

Or Eduardo might have seen a photo of them together. Tom could have pulled it out of his pocket to look at it, assuming that men did things like that – she wasn't sure if they did. She didn't expect a photo of him and Zizi in the act – that would be too much to hope for – but something that helped to date their affair would be brilliant.

She felt a stab of guilt at the thought of using Eduardo like that, but she'd been stuck on how to move her relationship with Tom to the next base – an emotional base, not a physical one; there was a limit to what she'd do – and the moment she'd seen the gleam in Eduardo's eyes as he'd looked at her, she'd known that her guardian angel had sent her a backup plan. If she was reporter enough to go along with it.

And she was.

Successfully squashing the niggly feeling of guilt, she felt her spirits start to rise. Thank you, thank you, guardian angel, she bubbled inwardly, and she beamed at Eduardo's back, which was swaying from one side of the path to the other every time that he threw his hands in the air to point out the newly planted trees and shrubs.

She'd flirt with him for a bit, which would be easy enough – last night had shown her that she could do anything she put her mind to – and then she'd encourage him to talk about Tom. OK, it was a tall order to work on two men at the same time in the hopes that at least one of them would open up to her – a dauntingly tall order – but she could do it. She had to. Her only chance of breaking into the world of magazine journalism was at stake.

They started to go down the terracotta-tiled steps to the front door when Eduardo suddenly stopped to draw their attention to the roses and purple clematis growing around the stone pillars on the corners of the porch. She slipped into the gap between the men; she was there to translate for them, after all. So far, it had been pretty obvious what Eduardo was saying, what with his facial expressions and gestures, but Tom just might need her help at any minute.

Eduardo finished with the subject of the flowers and produced a large iron key with a flourish. They went down the last couple of steps to the porch and he put the key into the lock of the heavy wooden door. After turning it several times, he pushed the door open, stepped back and slipped a hand under Evie's elbow. At exactly the same moment, Tom slipped his hand under her other elbow.

'*Perdono!*' Eduardo said hastily, seeing Tom's action. He dropped his hand, gave a small bow and stood back.

No one said it was going to be easy, she thought, and she stepped into the small entrance hall at Tom's side.

From that moment on, Tom needed her to translate for him.

As she followed the two men through the ground floor rooms it was all she could do to keep up with Eduardo's rapid delivery as he explained the things that had been done since Tom's last visit. Tom was clearly delighted with what he saw, and when they went through the arched doorway leading from the sitting room into the kitchen, and saw the pale peach-coloured units above and below a granite worktop that spanned the back wall of the kitchen, he stopped abruptly.

'It's stunning. Absolutely stunning. Eduardo was right about the colour bringing out the tones in the stone walls. Will you tell him that I thought the kitchen looked good in the shop, but this is way beyond anything I ever imagined?'

She translated Tom's words, and Eduardo inclined his head in acknowledgement. Smiling with pleasure, he led them back through the sitting room into the hall and up the wide stairs to the upper floors.

'*Questa è la camera principale*,' he announced as they entered a large room leading off the first landing. '*C'è posto per un molto grande letto*.'

'This is the master bedroom,' she translated, turning to Tom. 'He says that there's room for a very large bed.'

Their eyes met.

Her thoughts flew back to the night before. His look of sudden amusement told her that his had, too.

She felt herself starting to go red. Hell's bells and curses galore on her auburn hair – any minute from now she was going to look like an overboiled beetroot. She blamed her mother. Behind them, she heard Eduardo walk across the room, open a door and call for them to join him in the *en suite* bathroom, and she all but ran to him.

When they'd finished looking at the bathroom and the two small rooms in the tower, they went back down to the sitting room and Eduardo began to tell Tom how to work the lights for outside the house and the pool, showing him which switch was responsible for which area.

She shifted from one foot to the other. Hopefully, they'd soon move on to something else and she'd have the chance to make a subtle move on Eduardo, the emphasis being on subtle – Italian men liked to feel that they were the ones who were calling the shots. That had been one of the first things she'd learnt in Lake Garda.

She sneaked a glance at Eduardo and wondered if she could ever fancy him.

A lock of jet black hair had fallen over his forehead and his dark eyes were blazing with enthusiasm. He had amazingly long lashes for a man. They were so long that they were actually casting shadows on his high cheekbones. Without doubt he was gorgeous, the sort of gorgeous that Rachel and Jess went for in a big way.

And as for his body ... Her eyes ran down the length of

his frame. Although slighter in build than Tom and more graceful, he looked quite strong.

Her gaze returned to his face. Yes, he was definitely a dish – a sleek, beautiful dish – but he wasn't the dish of her choice. He might be charming, but he just wasn't her type.

She knew she was going to like him, though, and it was going to be fun flirting with him, provided that she could stop herself from laughing every time he went into his Latin lover routine. What's more, he was bound to have got kissing down to a fine art – a bonus if she ever had to go that far to be convincing. As for bed, well, she was sure he'd be brilliant at that – there'd be no rolling on, and rolling off three snorting minutes later – but she wasn't going to be checking that out.

'Evie!' Tom called.

She jumped, and turned towards him. He was standing next to Eduardo, who had his finger on one of the wall switches, waiting for their full attention. When he was sure that he had it, he flicked the switch and looked up. They followed his gaze. Through the clear glass that formed half of the high ceiling, they saw the illuminated tower rising up at the back of the roof, seeming to look down at them.

Tom gave a sigh of deep satisfaction. 'This is something we've got to see at night at least once before we go back to England, Evie. That's for sure.'

The two of them alone in the house at the dead of night, a time when souls were bared and secrets tumbled out.

'It certainly is,' she said fervently.

The demonstration over, Eduardo switched off the light and led them out through the arched glass doors on to a vine-covered *loggia* that ran along two sides of the house.

An expanse of grass stretched from the *loggia* to a green slope covered with lavender bushes and rosemary, whose musky aroma filled the air. On either side of the slope, paved stone steps led down to a large infinity pool. Beyond the pool, sloping groves of olive trees were set against a backdrop of shadowy distant hills. On one of the dark green hills far away to the right, the town of Todi glistened in the late morning sunlight.

'Bloody hell, what a view!' she exclaimed.

'It is, isn't it? Will you tell Eduardo that I'm very pleased with everything he's done?'

She did, and Eduardo bowed low in Tom's direction.

'Aha,' Tom said, moving closer to Evie as Eduardo bent to examine the white roses growing around one of the stone pillars. 'You're not the only one to get the continental treatment. It's funny, though – I don't remember Eduardo being quite so Italian before, but then I guess my translator wasn't as eye-catching before.'

Eye-catching!

Eye-catching was good, very good. He must be feeling even more relaxed with her than he'd been at breakfast to make a personal comment like that. Tongues loosened when people relaxed. Thank God she'd had the nerve to take that gamble the night before. Who dares wins, and all that.

She watched Tom as he reached up and pushed a vine tendril away from one of the bunches of tiny green grapes hanging from the top of the *loggia*. The sun shone brightly through the gaps between the leaves, bathing his face in dappled light. He really is a knockout, she thought, and her heart gave a sudden lurch.

His hand still on the tendril, he turned slightly and grinned down at her.

'You could make wine,' she said quickly. '*Château* Hadleigh has a good ring to it.'

The corners of his eyes crinkled when he smiled, she noticed.

She beamed back up at him. Yes, she'd get her story – she

had to – but she'd find a way of doing it that didn't hurt him.

'Time's moving on, Evie,' he said, abandoning his attempt at redirecting the vine. 'We'll have to get going or the shops will have closed for lunch. Can you ask Eduardo what we're doing about the furniture?'

After a short discussion with Eduardo, she turned back to Tom. 'He's got to get back to Todi now, so he suggests that we – you and me, that is – go and order the beds and bedside tables from a place just outside Massa Piccola this afternoon, and then come back here, decide what other furniture we need and measure up. He'll collect us from Il Poggio tomorrow morning and take us to one of the furniture co-operatives in Città di Castello. He said you'll get just about everything you want there.'

'Does he have to come with us tomorrow?'

'Oh, yes, definitely,' she said. Spending time with Eduardo was an absolute must if she was going to make any headway with him. 'They know him there and he'll make sure that you get a good price for what you want. And you said yourself he's artistic, so it's worth having his advice. He's sorry about having to go now, but he's leaving us the keys. Is that OK?'

'That sounds fine to me.'

She turned to Eduardo. '*Tutto va bene, Eduardo. Allora, ciao.*'

Eduardo inclined his head towards Tom, then turned back to Evie and took her hand in his.

God, not more bloody gallantry, she thought. She was about to snatch her hand away when she suddenly stopped herself. What on earth was she thinking of? Here was A Golden Opportunity to send a come-hither signal to Eduardo ahead of a day that they were going to be spending with him, and she'd been about to blow it. Memo to self – keep your focus on the all important task at hand.

She forced herself to stand very still as he lightly ran the palm of his hand along the length of her fingers, then bent low over her hand and pressed his lips against her skin for the second time that morning. Straightening up, he gazed intensely into her face, his dark eyes smouldering into hers.

'*A domani, Eduardo*,' she said. Not seductive enough for someone trying to show they were gagging for their meeting the following day, she decided. She lowered her voice until it seemed to come out of her sandals. '*A domani*.' He bowed again at her.

She absolutely must not start laughing.

Out of the corner of her eye, she saw that Tom was leaning against one of the pillars, staring at them, his expression thoughtful. She wondered what he was thinking about. No, she wasn't – she was focusing on Eduardo. She smiled fixedly at the top of Eduardo's glossy head, which was still bent low in a deep bow.

Eduardo rose to his full height and caught the tail end of her smile. His eyes shone. '*Ciao per il momento, Evie. Si, a domani.*'

Turning away from her with an expression of deep reluctance on his face, he gave a slight wave in Tom's direction and made his way back to his convertible. She gazed fixedly at him until he'd got into his car, driven through the iron gates and turned left down the mountain road. When he was completely out of sight, she wandered over to the top of the grassy slope and stared ahead of her, her eyes on the view, but her mind elsewhere.

She hoped she hadn't made a mistake in pressing for Eduardo to come to Città with them. By doing that, she'd missed out on the chance to be alone with Tom all day. Having Eduardo when they went to the furniture co-operative was clearly the right thing to do, whatever her motives, but it wasn't going to make for an easy day. If she was going to keep both men happy, she would need all of her wits about her.

But that was tomorrow. They still had the rest of today ahead of them, and it would be just her and Tom. Just the two of them alone. She turned round and went over to him.

'What's next?' she asked brightly.

Chapter Six

Getting warmer ...

Evie and Eduardo. Tom lounged against one of the pillars and watched them together, Eduardo's dark head bent over Evie's hand as he took his never-ending leave of her, and Evie clearly loving every nauseous, sick-making minute of it.

He shouldn't really be surprised that Eduardo was bowing and scraping in that ludicrous manner – she had a quirky sort of appeal: she wasn't beautiful, but she had a lively face and her hair was a wonderful colour, even if it never stayed exactly where she put it – but personally, she wasn't his type. She didn't have the sleek, sophisticated look that he went for, but he could see that a lot of other men might find her attractive, and Eduardo was obviously one of them – he was acting like a rampant dog in heat.

No, as far as he was concerned, he went out of the way to avoid women like Evie; he only dated women who were emotionally uninvolving. He had absolutely no intention of losing his senses over anyone, not now, and not for many years to come, if at all.

Instinct developed over years of studying the people who'd come to court for one reason or another told him that girls like Evie could be a threat to his emotional stability. Girls like that, with an indefinable spark about them, could get under your skin before you knew it, and the way to guard against that was to give them a wide berth. He had to do so for his own protection.

Time and time again, his barrister friends who specialised in divorce law would tell him about their clients, many of whom were women out to get what they could from husbands who were seen by their wives as the male equivalent of a milk cow. He'd listened hard and learnt his lesson well. It was all too easy for a naïve, gullible man to succumb in all innocence to the wily charms of a manipulative woman, marry her, and then, in the blink of an eye, find himself forced to accept a divorce settlement that screwed every last penny out of him.

Well, he wasn't naïve – far from it, thanks to his friends – and he wasn't gullible. He had no intention of being cheated out of the fruits of years of hard work by a woman's all-consuming greed, and the best way to protect himself from such a fate – in fact, the only way – was to avoid dating any woman who had the potential to draw him in emotionally. Maybe one day he would see things differently, but if so, that day was still a long way off, and until that day came, if ever it came, the Evies of this world were strictly a no-go area.

He watched as she smiled down at Eduardo, who was bending so low that his nose was almost touching the ground.

It was true that she didn't look grasping or devious – on the contrary, she seemed to be good fun and unusually open and honest – but then you wouldn't expect a successful con man to look like a con man. His defences were going to stay up.

Not that she seemed the slightest bit interested in making a breach in them – her interest clearly lay elsewhere. That was pretty clear from the way she was staring after Eduardo as he walked towards his car. He couldn't see her eyes so he didn't know if she was gazing at the retreating back with longing, but he wouldn't be surprised if she was. Not that it mattered, anyway.

He'd seen Eduardo's eyes, though, as he'd turned

away from Evie and given him that silly wave, and what Eduardo thought of Evie was pretty clear from the slobbery expression on his face. It was almost enough to make you throw up. He'd never seen him look like that before.

Obviously that was a good thing as far as he was concerned, he thought hastily – God forbid that he should ever be the object of his *geometra*'s soulful gaze – but it strongly suggested that Eduardo had fallen for Evie in a big way from virtually the first moment that he saw her.

And there was a degree of evidence to suggest that Evie felt the same about Eduardo. In addition to the way she'd been gazing at him, she'd been very quick – unnecessarily quick, he'd thought at the time – to stress that Eduardo should come with them on the furniture expedition the following day, and that could only mean that she wanted to spend as much time with him as possible.

Until the moment he'd suggested that he and Evie go alone to get the furniture, he hadn't known he was going to say that, but the minute the words had left his mouth he'd realised how much he wanted it to be just the two of them.

Not for any particular reason. He'd just thought it would be fun to go off on their own. She was easy enough to be with, had a good sense of humour and there'd be no risk of overdosing on Mediterranean gallantry. He'd been quite disappointed when she'd insisted that Eduardo come too; in fact, he was surprised at how disappointed he'd felt. Eduardo and his over-the-top gallantry must be getting to him more than he'd realised.

But she was right, of course. Eduardo would be a great help at the co-operative. And it wasn't as if he'd need to join them every day.

He and Evie might decide to visit some places of interest in the area, and they'd do that by themselves. Thinking about it, he really ought to take her around – it'd be doing her a real favour to show her as much as possible while they were there as she might not get to Italy again for ages. It was the very least he could do, given how ably she was helping him.

The loud roar of the convertible broke into his reverie. He looked up and saw a cloud of dust where Eduardo's car had been standing. As the sound of the engine faded away down the side of the mountain, she walked over to the top of the grassy slope.

His eyes fastened themselves to her as she stood there staring at the view. Her hands were clasped behind her head, and her short cotton dress had lifted slightly with her raised arms. His gaze was drawn to long bare legs that ended in scarlet-tipped toes that peeped from her sandals.

There was certainly nothing sleek and sophisticated about Evie, he thought wryly, and actually that was quite nice for a change.

She was coming towards him. He pulled himself upright.

'What's next?' She'd come to a stop in front of him, and was smiling up at him. Her deep green eyes were flecked with gold in the bright sunlight.

Very nice, in fact.

He pulled his gaze away from her face. 'You choose. Shall we get the beds first or are you hungry?'

She bent slightly to look at the watch on his wrist. 'I doubt if we'll have enough time to get the beds before the shops close for lunch,' she said. 'If you want, we can go to the supermarket, pick up something to eat, come back here and have a picnic on the grass. I love picnics. After that, we can measure up and think about the furniture you need. Then we can go and order the beds at about five, when the shops have opened again.'

'That sounds like a good plan. Right, the supermarket it is. It's funny, Evie,' he heard himself say as they started to stroll towards the parking area, 'but beds seem to have featured a lot in our visit so far, and we've not even been here for two days.'

He opened the passenger door of the four-by-four, stood back and wondered why on earth he'd come out with such a comment. It was a leading remark of the worst sort as it could take them down a very unwise path. Given that he was keen to keep a safe distance, it had been really stupid of him.

'Haven't they just.' Her bare arm brushed against his forearm as she climbed up into the car, and he quickly stepped back.

'Which reminds me, Evie. We mustn't forget to pick-up that scorpion spray.'

'That was fab.' She pushed the empty food wrappers into a heap at her side. '*Prosciutto*, melon, tomatoes off the vine, pecorino cheese, juicy yellow peaches, and gallons of white wine – everything I like most in the world. What more could anyone want!'

'What more indeed?' he asked dryly.

Out of the corner of her eye, she saw him watching her. Good.

She kicked off her sandals, leaned back on her elbows and stretched her legs out in front of her. Just as well that they were sitting down, she thought, staring down the slope at the pool; sprawling on the grass was about all she was good for. That wine had certainly hit the spot. And if it had done that to her, God knows what it had done to Tom. He'd had twice as much as she'd had.

'You can tell me to mind my own business, Evie, but how come you're working for an agency? I've had a lot of agency help over the years and I can say categorically that you're not the typical agency girl, not even in a severe grey suit, with your hair in a bun and whopping great glasses. Yet you obviously are a temp.'

Oh, joy! She couldn't have created a better chance to Move Things On A Bit if she'd written the script for him. But she must tread carefully. If she tried to go too fast, she could lose her story once and for all as he'd never again be able to relax with her.

'It's complicated. I went to Italy when I left school and got a job in a hotel. After a year, I came home, moved in with my parents and—' Crap! Probably not a good idea to mention working for a paper … 'And, um, got a job in a pub. I wasn't sure what I wanted to do with my life and it gave me time to think. Two years passed and I still didn't know what I wanted to do, but I knew that I was bored stiff with the job and with living at home, especially after living on my own for a year.' Not all lies … She *had* been bored stiff working at the local paper and *was* going stir crazy at home. No need to feel guilty, she told herself. 'My friends suggested I join them in London, so I did. I had to do something for money – there's a small matter of rent, and all that – and I'd had enough of working evenings and weekends so I joined the agency. Temping's OK and it's given me a bit more breathing space.'

She smiled across at him – a playful smile, suitable for harmless banter. At least, she hoped it was that and not the grimace of a hungry journalist. 'But I could say the same thing about you, Tom.'

'You could? Well, yes, I suppose you could, and I think you'd be right in a way.' He sounded as if he was really thinking about what she'd said. 'Being attached to a set of Chambers isn't generally likened to working for an agency, but there are certainly similarities between the two. We both have a varied clientele, for example, and we generally perform just one function for the client and move on. Yes, you may well have hit upon something there, Evie. It's true that in some respects, a barrister's work has much in common with that of an agency temp.'

Shit! She hadn't meant that at all.

'Maybe so.' She sat up and started to twirl a piece of grass between her fingers. 'But what I actually meant was that just as you don't think I'm a typical agency girl, well I don't think you're a typical lawyer.'

'Is that so? You do intrigue me. What's a typical lawyer like, then?'

'Stuffier than you.'

'So I'm not stuffy, am I?'

Thank God he was grinning – she hadn't gone too far. Not yet anyway. But she must be careful not to push for too much too soon.

'No, not at all. I thought you were stuffy at first, but I was wrong.'

'Aha, there are two lines for exploration here. We'll start with the negative aspect of your comment. So you thought I was stuffy at first, did you? And your reasons for this?'

'I suppose it was your clothes, and the way you almost ran out of the house as soon as I arrived each morning. And also, all day long I was surrounded by files and by briefs tied up in ribbon – everything looked stuffy and dry so I thought that you must be stuffy and dry, too. As I'd always assumed that lawyers were dull, it was only what I'd expected to find.' She gave a girlie little laugh.

Yuk! She sounded totally pathetic, but at least she'd got the conversation back to where she wanted it to go. Now the ball was in his court.

'I see. And now to the more flattering part of your statement – at least, I'm assuming that you consider a lack of stuffiness to be a positive characteristic. May I ask what caused you to revise your opinion?'

'For a start, we wouldn't be sitting here like this if you were stuffy. After last night, you would have been cold and unfriendly. Instead, you've been quite cool about the fact that I wrecked your night and put you in a dead embarrassing position. You've let us move on. So whatever you are, you're not stuffy.'

'I'm flattered. At least, I think I am. I'm now not sure exactly what you mean by "whatever you are".'

'I just meant that we all have different sides to us – some we show, some we don't. That's life. I'm sure there's another side to you that I can't see, but the side that I can see isn't stuffy.'

Thank you; thank you, God! She'd got them on to the right path, and she'd done it so neatly, too. She was a star.

'I see what you mean, and I think you're right, Evie. In fact, it's probably true of both of us. I'll pick up on something you've just said to me. You said that my clothes and behaviour led you to think that I was one sort of person, and then you found out that I was another. I could say the same thing about you – your clothes and behaviour led me to see you in one light, but now I see you in a completely different light.'

'You do? A good-different light or a bad-different light?'

She sat back. Holy cow! She'd let him take back the lead and turn the spotlight on to her again. She must get the conversation back to him as quickly as possible. He was the specimen on the petri dish, not her.

'Put it this way, Evie – a few minutes ago, you listed pecorino cheese, melon, tomatoes, peaches, and so on, as the things you most liked in the world. I can believe that they topped Santa's wish list for the Evie of last week, but I doubt that anything gastronomic tops Santa's wish list for the Evie of this week. Or wouldn't you agree?'

Huh. Where was he going with this?

Her mind raced. She watched him pick up the bottle and pour the last of the wine into their plastic glasses. She took a sip of her drink; she needed time to think. It looked as if he was trying to take their conversation down a very interesting path, one that she hadn't bargained upon – or certainly not so early in the week – and she needed to play things very, very carefully.

'No, I'm not sure that I do agree,' she said, after giving herself as long a time to think as she thought she could get away with. 'I can't imagine any sort of Evie rating anything above a perfectly ripe, juicy peach. Surely there isn't anything in the world that could score higher than that. Or is there?'

She stared at him above the rim of the plastic glass, her face a picture of innocence. Fingers crossed that he was into clichés.

'Are you challenging me to come up with something, Evie?'

Spot on! And she liked the almost seductive tone of his voice. On second thought, she wasn't sure there was any 'almost' about it.

'Because if you are, you should know there's nothing I like better than a challenge, as many courtroom opponents have found to their cost.'

'Oh, I do believe you.'

And she did. She finished her wine in double quick time, lay back on the grass and waited.

Don't do it, his inner voice screamed at him.

He was furious with himself: it was entirely his own fault that he'd got himself into the situation he was in. She'd picked up the baton that he should never have dropped, and now she was teasing him with it. Worse still, he seemed to be letting himself take the bait.

He glanced across at her. Her skin was creamy smooth in the afternoon sun, and her lips were parted in an inviting sort of way. It would be very easy to lean over and kiss her, and probably quite pleasant – all in all, it could be a diverting way of killing time. And what harm could it do? He found himself turning slightly towards her and lowering his head towards her mouth.

The inner voice screamed at him again, louder this time, more insistent.

It was a voice that he'd first heard years before, a voice that he'd then ignored, and had regretted doing so ever since. He'd turned a deaf ear the first time that he'd heard it and he wasn't going to ignore it a second time. Only fools failed to learn from the lessons that life threw at them. He wasn't a fool and he wasn't giving in to temptation. Not this time.

Abruptly, he straightened up.

Making a move on Evie was fraught with potential disaster. He didn't get involved with people like her. To have a casual dalliance with her would be both unprofessional and foolhardy. Theirs was a friendly working relationship, and that was the way it had to stay. He scrambled to his feet.

'We'll tidy up now, and then get off to Massa. Up you get, Evie.'

Turning round, he walked away from her.

Chapter Seven

Help! There's a spanner in the works

From her table in the corner of the *piazza* in Todi, Evie watched Tom stroll across the square and start to climb the stone steps leading to the cathedral. The weathered marble walls of the cathedral shimmered pink in the light of the dying sun. She helped herself to a handful of nuts from the small bowl in the centre of the table. Why had Tom changed towards her? Because change he certainly had.

It wasn't that he was acting coldly towards her or anything like that; it was little things she couldn't really put her finger on. She'd been certain – absolutely certain – that he'd been about to kiss her the day before when they'd been mucking around on the grass after lunch, but he'd suddenly pulled back and things hadn't been the same ever since.

They'd ended the afternoon by ordering the beds and bedside tables as planned and had arranged for them to be delivered to the house on the Thursday morning, and then they'd had a nice dinner at Il Poggio, but at the end of the meal he'd made it clear that he didn't want to hang around and they'd gone off to their separate rooms as soon as they'd finished their coffee.

She'd had a burst of hope when there'd been a knock on her door soon after they'd parted. She'd rushed to the door, pulled it open and found him standing there, a can of insect spray in his hand. Her hope had faded fast. The pre-picnic-lunch Tom would have cracked a joke as he'd handed her the can; the post-picnic-lunch Tom had made do with, 'In case there are any problems. Good night.'

The day in Città di Castello had gone well and they'd ordered everything Tom needed.

He'd seemed quite relaxed all day, and hadn't even appeared to be the least bit put out when he'd learnt that the furniture would be delivered over a period of a couple of weeks – he'd just told Eduardo that he could get someone to stay in the house during that time if it made things easier for him. Nevertheless, he'd kept firmly to his side of an invisible wall all day.

This had been even more obvious after Eduardo had returned them to the hotel once all the furniture had been ordered and had gone home to change. True, before Tom had disappeared into his room to have a shower he'd suggested leaving early and stopping for a drink in Todi before they met up with Eduardo at Casigliano for a celebratory dinner, but as she'd stood on the terrace and stared after his departing back, she hadn't seen any sign of a real thaw.

This was a mega big headache. If she didn't know what had caused the change in him, she couldn't work on getting things back to the way they were. She didn't have long in which to act – the week was flying by at a scary speed – so she had to come up with something fast.

Inspiration struck – she'd call Rachel and ask her advice. Rachel always knew what to do in every situation. She pulled her mobile phone out of her bag and flicked it open. It was high time she called her friends, anyway.

'It really is a perfect evening, isn't it?'

She looked up. The focus of her frantic concern was standing next to the table. She snapped her phone shut.

'Don't let me interrupt you,' he said, signalling to the waiter as he sat down on the chair opposite her.

'You're not. I was only going to phone Rachel and Jess – they're the girls I share a house with – but it can wait. I wasn't really in the mood, anyway.'

'Feel free to phone them, if you want to. I promise not to listen.'

'I don't want to.'

'As you wish. Ah, here's the waiter. *Una birra, per favore.* And what would you like, Evie?'

'*Un bellini, per favore,*' she said, and the waiter moved off. 'I think it's my favourite drink of all. Sparkling white wine and peach purée is a marriage made in heaven.'

'Aha, something else to add to your list of favourites. And what's more, it's made with one of the items already on your list. A double whammy, one might almost say.' He grinned at her and reached across to the nuts.

'Why, so one could.' She gave a little laugh.

A frisson of excitement ran through her; he hadn't forgotten their conversation of the day before. She hadn't a clue why he'd suddenly referred to it after the way he'd been acting all day, but it was one hell of a gift horse and no way was she going to look it in the mouth. But slow and cautious would be her watchwords – she mustn't send him scurrying back into his shell by jumping in too quickly.

'I didn't think you'd be back so soon. I thought you were going to look round the cathedral.'

'And so I was. However, if I may quote you, I wasn't really in the mood. I'll go another time, there's no urgency.'

'So what are you in the mood for?'

Shite! That was hardly slow and cautious. One swallow didn't make a summer, and one reference to her list of favourites didn't mean that they were back at their pre-picnic stage. God, would she ever learn to think before she spoke!

'It'd probably be easier if I told you what I was *not* in the mood for,' he said as the waiter put their drinks in front of them, along with a small dish of black and green olives. 'I'm not in the mood for Eduardo this evening. Don't get me wrong, Eduardo was a great help today and I'm very grateful to him for everything he's done – you were absolutely right to insist that he come along with us – however, a little Latin bowing and scraping goes a long, long way, and I could do without any more of it this evening.'

She smiled at him. 'I know just what you mean. But he's good company, all the same.'

'Which he'd also say about you, I'm sure – only he'd put it more strongly than that and each word would be accompanied by a low bow and some suction on the back of your hands.'

She burst out laughing and took an olive.

'He's obviously fallen for you in a big way. The man positively drools every time he sees you, and you love every slushy minute of it. And why not? He's perfect for you. He's a good-looking fellow, wealthy, artistic. Divine – wasn't that how you described him?'

She took another olive.

So Tom thought she fancied Eduardo, and the underlying vibes she was picking up suggested that he wasn't about to give them his blessing. Could he simply be pissed off with her for getting involved with Eduardo when she was in Italy to do a job for him? That would certainly account for his change in behaviour towards her.

She was faced with a stark choice: risk alienating Tom in an attempt to learn about his affair from Eduardo, or stop flirting with Eduardo at once and abandon any hope of getting information from him. It was a no-brainer – she must stop playing up to Eduardo. He was only the side order: Tom was the main course. She'd have to put all of her eggs into that one basket.

A huge feeling of relief swept over her that she didn't have to flirt with Eduardo any longer. It hadn't been one of her guardian angel's better ideas.

She would hate to hurt him, and if he thought she'd fallen for him and he was really keen on her, which Tom seemed to think he was, he could get badly hurt in the end. She'd have to subtly let him know that she liked him as a friend, but not in any other way.

But, hey, she was getting ahead of herself. Tom was wrong about her feelings for Eduardo, and he could be wrong about Eduardo's feelings for her. She should be picking up on what Tom said in his last comment and running with it. She helped herself to a few more nuts and sat back in her chair.

'Really, Mr Hadleigh,' she said in a tone of mock severity. 'Women are always accused of being matchmakers, but listen to you! And you make a pretty bad matchmaker at that, if I may say so. Eduardo isn't interested in me any more than I'm interested in him.'

'The evidence of my eyes says the opposite.'

'Everyone knows that witnesses always give different accounts of the same event – you'd know that better than anyone else. Eduardo's just being friendly, that's all.'

'Fair enough, Evie. But we'll see who's right in the fullness of time.'

'Now that sounds almost like a challenge.' She took a black olive from the dish and popped it into her mouth. 'But it's a challenge I'm going to ignore.'

'You'll ruin your appetite if you're not careful.'

'You sound just like my mother.'

'Ouch! That hurt. From matchmaker to mother in the blink of an eye. I think we'd better drink up and go before I do any more damage to the sophisticated image I aspire to.' He picked up his glass and finished his beer.

'Do you want me to get the bill?'

'No, not this time. I'm going to ask for it in Italian. It's something I should be able to do by now – I've heard you and Eduardo say the words enough times.'

He caught the waiter's attention. '*Il conto, per favore.*' The waiter nodded back at him, and he turned to her, a triumphant smile on his face. 'There you are.'

She laughed. 'You look like a schoolboy who's just found a huge conker.'

'At least you're comparing me with someone of my own gender this time,' he said with a grin. 'That's got to be progress of a sort.'

She smiled up at him. The few days in the sun had bleached his hair and lightly tanned his skin.

This would be so much easier if he were ugly, she thought.

Evie followed Tom and the waiter across the stone terrace of the restaurant in Casigliano. Her steps slowed as she neared the balustrade that ran round the edge of the terrace and saw the panoramic view of the valley beneath them.

The sun was setting in a fiery ball that streaked the sky. Hints of a sparkling rosé gradually darkened into deep claret, bathing the valley and terrace in a warm, rich glow. Above her, fairy lights glittered in the canopy of vine leaves that grew in abundance along the top of the pergola. From somewhere inside the restaurant, the soft strains of a violin floated on the scented evening air.

Wow, she thought. What a romantic place. If only it was going to be just her and Tom at dinner that evening.

'Ah, look, there's Eduardo.' Tom's voice broke into her thoughts. 'He's beaten us here.'

Eduardo looked up from the menu as they reached the table. His face broke into a wide smile and he promptly pushed back his chair and rose to greet them.

'*Buona sera, Tom.*' Eduardo clasped Tom warmly by the shoulders.

Tom gently extricated himself from Eduardo's grip. '*Buona sera, Eduardo.*'

'*E la divina Evie*,' Eduardo sighed. In an elegant action, he bowed towards her, his hand across his heart.

Pointedly ignoring Tom's I-told-you-so grin, she clasped her fingers tightly behind her back and stared at the slender hand that covered Eduardo's heart. Her eyes narrowed: she'd used that same hand-across-the-heart flourish herself in the past. Urgent note to self – delete said action from her mental List of Alluring Gestures. It was much too cheesy.

'*Assolutamente divina*,' Eduardo murmured to the floor.

He slowly raised himself upright, his eyes sliding up her short, strapless lime-green dress to her face and to the cloud of auburn hair that hung loosely around her face. His lips curved into an appreciative smile. Taking his hand from his heart, he gestured towards the table. '*Si accomodino.*'

'Eduardo wants us to sit down.'

'I'm not too sure about the seating plan,' he remarked as he sat down next to her and saw Eduardo taking the place opposite her. 'The sight of Eduardo gazing slavishly at you is likely to play havoc with my digestion. And I'd rather look at you than at that empty chair.'

'You certainly do know how to flatter a girl,' she said brightly.

He threw back his head and laughed. 'You know what I mean. Anyway, how come there's a fourth place set when there're only three of us. Ask Eduardo, would you, please?'

Evie relayed Tom's question.

'*Ah si!*' Eduardo exclaimed, and he broke into a stream of rapid, excitable Italian, which ended with him looking at his watch, shrugging his shoulders and raising his hands to the darkening sky.

'His sister, Gabriela, is going to join us. She lives in Florence, but her job's taking her to London very soon. She'll be there for about a year. Apparently, as soon as she heard that you were over this week, she asked if she could come and meet you. I think she wants to talk to you about London and get your advice about things. According to Eduardo, she's very clever and very ambitious.'

Tom nodded his understanding to Eduardo.

'Oh, and she's late. They've hardly seen each other since she moved to Florence a couple of years ago, so Eduardo suggested that she come early so that they could catch up before we arrived, but she's late, as you can see.'

Tom shook his head sympathetically across the table to Eduardo. 'That's women all over for you.'

'*How disappointing for you*,' Evie translated.

Eduardo smiled gratefully at Tom, then raised his finger to call the waiter.

'*Un aperitivo?*' he suggested as the waiter approached the table.

'*Per favore*,' Tom replied.

'*Bravo, Tom!*' Eduardo clapped his hands. '*Molto bene. E tu, Evie?*'

'*Si, per favore.*'

'*E per me, Eduardo.* And for me, too,' came a husky voice with a strong Italian accent.

'Gabriela!' Eduardo cried, looking up at the slender, beautiful woman with jet black hair who stood at the side of their table, smiling down at him. Jumping up, he kissed her warmly on both cheeks, then he turned to introduce her to Tom and Evie.

'*Mia sorella*,' he said with obvious pride. '*Gabriela.*'

Evie stared up at Gabriela in dismay. Eduardo's sister was the last word in elegance and sophistication.

Not so long ago, Tom had joked about aspiring to an image of sophistication. Maybe he also aspired to having an image of sophistication in his arms, and worse still, in his bed.

What frigging luck!

Chapter Eight

If looks could kill …

Tom rose to his feet at once. 'I don't need a translation for that.' He leaned across the table to shake hands with Gabriela. 'You're obviously Eduardo's sister. There's a strong family likeness. It's a real pleasure to meet you.'

'It's my pleasure, too,' Gabriela murmured, her voice deep in her throat. She held Tom's eyes for a moment, then glanced down at Evie. 'And you must be Evie. Eduardo has told me much about you. It's lovely to meet you, too.'

Evie half rose from her chair. Gabriela's dark eyes swept appraisingly over her. 'We are going to be friends, I feel, Evie,' she said, and she turned back to Tom. 'I was so wanting to meet you, Tom. Please forgive me for inviting myself to join you this evening.'

'There's nothing to forgive. Please do sit down.' He went swiftly round the table and pulled out the chair opposite him. Gabriela gracefully slid to the seat, and Tom returned to his place. 'We're delighted to have the opportunity of meeting you,' he said as he sat down.

While Eduardo was giving the order for their aperitifs, Evie surreptitiously watched Gabriela settle in her seat. She put her slim black leather bag on the table beside her, twisted her body slightly and crossed one long leg over the other. It was hard not to watch her; Eduardo's sister was stunning. She glanced sideways at Tom. He obviously thought so, too. And he'd complained that Eduardo had drooled over her. Huh! Tom couldn't take his eyes off Gabriela and his tongue was all but hanging out.

Glamour Puss would put Gabriela in the category of vamp, she decided.

Her crimson sheath dress fitted her super slim body like a sheet of cling film. Her glossy black hair had been expertly coiled at the nape of her neck, and not a single strand of hair had escaped the coil. Thick bands of silver hung around her neck and arms. Her mouth was the same shape as Eduardo's, but hers was a vivid red gash, dramatic against her pale olive skin.

Yes, definitely vampish. And sophisticated.

For an awful moment she thought she was going to burst into tears. What on earth was wrong with her!

She stared down at the table and swallowed hard. So what if Tom did fall for Gabriela; what he did was his own affair and nothing at all to do with her. He was good-looking and fun to be with, but the bottom line was that he was a job, and no more than that. Yes, Gabriela's arrival might have pushed things in a direction that they weren't meant to be going, but that was no reason for her to get all tearful.

Which she was.

She blinked furiously. She was losing the plot. Whatever the two of them got up to was nothing to do with her, unless it involved a story. And since 'Successful Bachelor Lawyer Screws Beautiful, Unattached Woman' was hardly the exposé her editor was looking for, what he and Gabriela did or didn't do was never going to be any of her business.

She blinked again.

She was probably feeling emotional because she could see that if Gabriela and Tom got together, it would make it harder for her to get her story. The closer he got to Gabriela, the further he'd move away from her, and it would be to Gabriela that he'd whisper his confession, not to the investigative journalist at his side. That was what it must be. It was the sort of setback that would make anyone feel like howling.

She glanced across the table at Gabriela, who was laughing at something Tom had said. The huge silver hoops hanging from her ear lobes were to die for.

She heard Tom say the word England, and felt a rush of relief.

How stupid of her! Gabriela would almost certainly be going back to Florence the following day. When she'd gone, she'd have Tom back to herself, and by the time that the two of them met up again in England – which they would probably do – she'd have moved on to another story and Tom would be completely out of her life.

Panic over. Relieved, she sat back in her chair.

Her blurred vision cleared and she saw an aperitif on the table in front of her. She'd been in such state she hadn't even noticed the waiter putting it down, nor that the others were holding their glasses in the air, waiting for her to join them in a toast. You've gotta get a grip, she told herself, and she picked up her glass.

'*Salute!*' She forced a broad smile to her lips, and glanced around the table.

'*Salute!*' they all chorused.

Gabriela took a sip and put her aperitif back on the table. She leaned across to Tom and seemed to be asking him a question. He smiled warmly at her and began to answer.

She felt Eduardo's eyes on her, and inwardly groaned. She'd have to say something to him, but all she really wanted to do was eavesdrop on Tom and Gabriela.

Was he satisfied with the way the day had gone, was the best she could come up with in her distracted state.

Happily, it was good enough for him.

'*Si, si!*' he exclaimed, beaming, and he began to extol their day's purchases.

Leaning slightly to the side, she strained to hear what Tom and Gabriela were saying, but she couldn't make anything out. She edged still closer to Tom, but it was no use – they were talking too quietly.

Eduardo had stopped speaking, she suddenly realised. '*Interessante*,' she swiftly said, hoping that whatever he'd said could be described as interesting.

'*Grazie mille.*' He smiled warmly at her, and to her great relief, started talking again.

She was just beginning to wonder whether she dared move even closer to Tom or if it would look like she was trying to sit on his lap when it dawned on her that Eduardo's tone of voice had changed. Blast, she thought, and turned her attention back to him. How did someone with such striking red hair come to speak such perfect Italian, he wanted to know.

She groaned inwardly. So much for her finding a way of butting into Tom and Gabriela's conversation. She'd never be able to get away with the occasional *interessante* now.

Making a massive effort to swallow her annoyance at having to answer Eduardo rather than listen to her neighbours, she fixed her eyes firmly on the silver chain visible through his lilac open-necked shirt and began to rattle off the details of her family background and the year she'd spent in Lake Garda.

If she'd had any hope of bringing the conversation to a speedy conclusion, they were dashed the minute she heard the excitement in Eduardo's voice at her mention of Lake Garda. His family had a house on the edge of the lake, he exclaimed in delight, and he used to go there all the time when he was younger. To her misery, he started listing all the places they both might know.

As she verbally ticked off the places on his list, her gaze kept on straying to Tom and Gabriela. They were bent close to each other. He clearly wasn't bothered about keeping any kind of wall between him and Gabriela, she thought tetchily – if either of them moved an inch forward, they'd bang their heads together. And serve them right, too.

She forced her attention back to Eduardo. His dark eyes were staring intently at her face. She shifted uneasily in her chair under his gaze. His eyes moved to Tom, then back to her, and they stayed on her, gradually softening with understanding. And deep regret.

Oh, hell! He'd got hold of the wrong end of the stick and he thought she was keen on Tom. He'd mistaken her professional concern about Tom getting close to Gabriela for an emotional fear of losing him to another woman. She should have been much more guarded in the way she'd behaved. She'd intended to make it clear to Eduardo that they'd never be any more than good friends, but she hadn't wanted him to come to that conclusion by himself, and for the wrong reasons. Damn!

'So you think that English food is the bees' knees, do you?' she heard Gabriela ask, laughing in disbelief as she picked up her menu.

She stared at Gabriela for a moment, and then turned to Eduardo and asked how Gabriela came to speak such perfect English when he didn't know a single word.

He giggled. Gabriela had been a good girl at school, he told her, a mischievous glint in his eye, and he had been a very naughty boy. Drawing plans for houses was much more fun than learning how to say 'I am; you are; he is', so he drew houses while Gabriela learnt to say 'I am'.

He *had* picked up a little English along the way, no matter how hard he'd tried not to, he admitted with a shy grin, and he'd left school able to say a few words. But as he hadn't spoken English since then, he'd forgotten just about everything he'd ever learnt.

However, with the Americans and English buying houses

in Umbria, he knew that he really ought to be able to speak to them himself and not rely on the help of someone else, charming though that person might be, and he was going to ask Gabriela to help him. She would be staying with him at his place near Todi for the rest of the week so he could make a start at once.

So Gabriela would not be heading back to Florence the following day. Damn! Damn! Damn! She'd bet any amount of money that Gabriela planned on hanging around them for the rest of the week. Her chance of getting the lowdown from Tom about his affair with Zizi Westenhall was fast disappearing down the proverbial tube.

Her hand tightened around her glass.

There was a slight pressure on her arm. She looked up and saw Eduardo's eyes on her again. He gave her a rueful smile, gently removed the glass from her hand, picked up his menu and indicated that she should do the same.

'You were very quiet on the way home,' Tom said as they sat over a *grappa* on the spotlit terrace of Il Poggio. 'And you're very quiet now. That's most unlike you, Evie. Are you cold, ill or dreaming romantic dreams that would need to be heavily censored before they could be told to another person? If it's the last of the three and it would help you to unburden yourself, I'll mentally fortify myself and you can share the uncut version with me.'

That was a good opening, and she must rise to it. If only she didn't feel quite so depressed.

'The temperature's just fine, thank you, Tom, and I'm in the best of health. As for relaying the content of my dreams, you can relax – I wouldn't risk any damage to your delicate sensibilities, fortified or not.'

'I'm not convinced that those sensibilities you rate so highly would be averse to a little bit of damage. Try me.'

She laughed. 'Dream on. I'm afraid you'll have to rely on your imagination to help you out with your masochistic tendencies.'

'Masochistic, indeed! That's a long word for this late at night.' He paused for a moment. 'So, tell me truthfully, Evie. Did you enjoy the evening?'

'Of course, I did. Gabriela and Eduardo are both very pleasant and the food was great. What's not to enjoy?'

'I agree, it was a good evening. It was certainly better than I'd expected. Gabriela's English is quite amazing. I can talk to her almost as easily as I can talk to you.'

And that was the problem in a nutshell. With Gabriela around to translate, she wouldn't be needed in the same way, and that would make it much harder to get any closer to Tom. Frowning, she turned towards the dark hills outlined against the distant horizon. Why couldn't Eduardo's bloody sister have stayed in Florence?

'What's up, Evie? Please tell me.' She turned back to Tom and saw that he was looking at her with genuine concern. 'You've not been yourself all evening. I know you like Eduardo – even a blind man could see that – so is it that you don't like Gabriela?'

'Of course I like her. There's nothing not to like. She seems very nice.'

'Well, that's what I thought.'

'Which would be equally obvious to that same blind man. It must have been brilliant for you to be able to talk to an Italian without having to get me to translate for you,' she hastily added.

'I suppose you're right, although I did rather miss you being stuck there in the middle of my conversation.'

'How come? What would I have added to it?'

'Tut, tut, Evie. Could it be that you're fishing for compliments? You're not prepared to indulge my masochistic tendencies, yet you expect me to fulfil your inner need for praise.'

'Of course, I don't.' He raised his eyebrows to her, and she giggled. 'That came out all wrong. Obviously I don't mean that I expect you to fulfil my need for praise – I mean, I don't need to be praised by anyone. Although now that you come to mention it, it's not a totally bad idea. Go ahead, I'll have that compliment after all.'

'Well, then, here goes. While I enjoyed talking to Gabriela, who's a clever woman, she can be quite intense, and to be honest, I rather missed the light-hearted touch that you would have brought into the conversation.'

'Is that a lawyer-like way of calling me an airhead?' she laughed. 'If it is, you can try your hand at a second compliment. See if you can improve upon calling me thick.'

'What I meant is, as you well know, that you're quite good fun to be with. I think you'd accept that, wouldn't you? In fact, you have to accept it – I'm the boss.'

'Didn't I read somewhere that the word "boss" has a second meaning? Doesn't it also mean "stud"? Are you bragging?'

He leaned back against his chair. 'I rest my case.' They smiled at each other across the table, and their eyes met. Both instantly looked away.

'What are we doing tomorrow, Tom?' she asked after a short pause.

'The beds are being delivered in the morning. We need to be there in good time to tell the deliverymen where to put them, and then I thought we could go and see something of the area. Perhaps we'll drive up to Montefalco, which is about forty minutes from the house. It's a really pretty little place, and it's got some wonderful murals in the church there. Well, it's not actually a church any more. It's a cross between a museum and an art gallery.'

She pointed her finger to her head. 'Airhead. Remember?'

'And then we can get some lunch, accompanied by the thing that Montefalco's famous for.'

'Which is?'

'Red wine. While we're there, we'll get a few bottles to take with us when we go up to the house in the evening to see the tower and pool lit up. We'll play it by ear as to whether we go to the house tomorrow night or on Friday.'

'I can't believe how quickly the week's gone by. It'll soon be Saturday, and that means England. What about Friday? Is there anything else we have to get for the house before we leave?'

'Nothing that can't wait.' He paused for a moment. 'Friday's rather been taken out of my hands, I'm afraid.' His words came out on a rush. 'Gabriela's going to show us Perugia on Friday, and Eduardo's coming, too. Believe me, I'd have liked to have got out of it if I could have done, but they mean well and I don't want to upset them.'

Oh, hell! Yet another lost opportunity for her and Tom to do something on their own.

'I expect we'll have a nice time,' she said flatly.

'I'm sure you're right, but that's not how I would have chosen to spend our last full day. However, Gabriela was very insistent. I've promised to help her with any problems in London and she wants to say thank you by showing us Perugia, which she loves. She went to university there.' He paused a moment. 'Are you sure that's all right with you?'

'Of course it is.'

'Look on the bright side – it may be a bit of a hectic way to spend the last day, but at least you'll have another full day with Eduardo.'

'I think I'll go to bed.' She stood up. 'Goodnight, Tom.'

'Goodnight, Evie. Sleep well.'

He stared into the black night beyond the terrace.

What on earth was the matter with him? He'd just spent the evening with a charming woman, who was exactly the sort of woman he chose to go out with in London – beautiful, smart, sophisticated; not someone he'd ever fall in love with, but someone he would, under normal circumstances, have found a stimulating companion – yet instead of thoroughly enjoying every minute of the evening, he'd spent the whole time trying to do what women always did - listen to more than one conversation at the same time.

Despite knowing that he wouldn't understand a word of what Evie and Eduardo were saying to each other, he'd rather hoped to be able to pick up some idea about their mutual feelings from the tone of their voices. But he'd been singularly unsuccessful in doing so, and that was entirely because his conversation with Gabriela had continually got in the way.

They had obviously spent some of the time talking about places in Italy. He'd picked up the words Lake Garda more than once, and he'd wondered if Eduardo had been suggesting that he go with Evie to visit the places she'd got to know when she worked there. That was fair enough – they were free agents, after all.

So why did that idea irritate him? Because irritate him it clearly did. Evie was a pleasant employee and Eduardo was excellent at his job. Good luck to them both, was what he said, or what he should have been saying.

And there was something else. He was mystified as to why he'd missed her contributions to the conversation that evening. Yes, she was amusing, but he could listen to any of his Billy Connolly collection if he felt the need of a good laugh, so why had he found himself wishing that he was talking to her and not Gabriela?

He really couldn't understand himself, but his mood was disconcerting. Whatever the reason was for the way he felt, he very much hoped that it would soon pass and he could get back to his normal state of pleasant detachment.

Unfortunately, getting back to normal in the immediate future was a bit of a forlorn hope. The next morning, for example, could be tricky, given the funny mood he was in.

The beds were going to be delivered in the morning, and he and Evie would be at the house by themselves when they arrived. The fact that they'd be alone shouldn't matter at all.

As they were leaving the restaurant after dinner he'd actually thought about suggesting Eduardo come up to the house before the beds arrived, but in the end he hadn't done so. Thinking back on it now, though, it might have been a sensible thing to do. Once the beds had arrived, he and Evie could have said goodbye to Eduardo and gone off to Montefalco on their own.

It wouldn't have mattered if he'd asked Eduardo at such short notice – it had already been agreed that he would be at their disposal for the week. He had no doubt that Eduardo would have readily come and joined them, if for no other reason than that it would have been a chance to spend more time with Evie.

True, being a minute longer than was absolutely necessary in Eduardo's company wasn't an attractive proposition – far from it – but for reasons that he wasn't clear about, he rather felt that the advantages of having Eduardo there outweighed the disadvantages.

Fortunately, it wasn't too late to ask Eduardo. Obviously it was too late to ring him that evening – and Evie had gone to bed, anyway, so she wasn't around to do the talking – but he could ask her to ring Eduardo at breakfast the following morning and suggest that he get to the house for ten thirty. Yes, that's what he would do. It had been stupid not to have sorted this out earlier on, but at least it wasn't too late to do the wise thing.

He stood up. He felt better already.

Chapter Nine

And so to beds ...

'That's done, then.' Evie stood under the porch in front of the house, shielding her eyes from the glare of the sun as she watched the green delivery van gradually disappear behind the trees lining the dusty track that ran down the side of the mountain.

'Many thanks for your help, Evie,' Tom said, dropping the last piece of cardboard on to the pile of used packaging that was heaped up in the corner of the porch. 'It couldn't have gone better. It all looks very good now.'

'Just think, the next time you come to Italy, all the other furniture will be in place, too.'

'I'm glad you said that. It's reminded me that I need to make sure Eduardo knows where the furniture's got to go when it gets here – after all, he'll be the one who's here when it arrives. We'd better do a rough plan that we can give to him in Perugia tomorrow.'

'I half wondered if you'd ask him to come along this morning, just in case there were any problems.'

And she *had* half wondered, while at the same time she'd hoped like mad with the other half that he wouldn't.

There was no point in her spending any more time with Eduardo. He knew perfectly well that she wasn't interested in him in a romantic way. If she'd needed any more proof than the sympathy she'd seen in his eyes the night before – sympathy that was obviously based on his misreading of the situation – she had only to think back to the moment when he'd said goodbye to her as they left the restaurant.

They'd all stood and waited while he bent very low over

71

her hand, but only she had seen that when he raised his eyes to her face, he'd lowered one eyelid in an unmistakable wink.

It was so unexpected that for an awful moment, she'd thought that she was going to break out into a fit of giggles. Fortunately, she'd managed to smother the urge. At that moment, she'd known for sure that her relationship with Eduardo had definitely morphed into a non-romantic friendship, and she was really pleased about that – it felt more honest.

But much as she hadn't wanted Eduardo there with them that morning, she was surprised that Tom hadn't asked him to join them. And it was funny how when she'd mentioned Eduardo earlier on, he'd gone into a sudden frenzy of activity. What was going on in his mind? she wondered.

She stood and watched him move around the pile of discarded cardboard, lining up the corners of the flattened cartons so that they were even. Could it simply be that he thought she fancied Eduardo and felt guilty that he hadn't asked him to join them for the day so that she would have more time with him?

But how likely was that!

She was only an employee, after all. And as Tom had said in a different situation, she was meant to be thinking about *his* needs, not the other way round. But if that wasn't the reason, it was hard to see why Tom was suddenly fussing around with the leftover packaging and why he looked so uncomfortable whenever she mentioned Eduardo.

'Actually I did intend to ask you to call him,' he said abruptly, and he stopped what he was doing and straightened up, a piece of corrugated cardboard paper in his hand. 'But in the end I forgot about it in the rush to get here before the furniture arrived. And as it so happens, we didn't need him after all, did we?' He indicated around him and dropped the cardboard on to the pile. 'We managed all right, just you and me.'

More than all right, she thought happily. He hadn't mentioned Gabriela so much as once all morning.

'We certainly did. We made a great team. So what now, partner? We've unpacked the lamps, but we left them in the corner of the hall. If you want, we can go round the house and put one on each bedside table. Then we'll really be finished, or at least we'll have done all we can do for now.'

'Your enthusiasm for hard graft is commendable, Evie. However, I think we'll settle for putting a lamp in the main bedroom, and leave the rest for another time. We'll do a quick sketch of where the furniture has to go, and then we ought to set off for Montefalco.'

'Righteo.'

He glanced at his watch. 'It's a bit later than I thought. We'll have to do the plans very quickly. If I remember rightly, the art gallery closes for lunch at twelve thirty or one. By the time we've finished here and driven to Montefalco, there probably won't be sufficient time to do it justice this morning. However, it opens again at about five, and I suggest that we go to Montefalco as planned, have a leisurely lunch followed by a walk around the village, and then go to the gallery when it opens again.'

Thank you, God, for the ultra long Italian lunch hour! With luck, by the time he'd had lunch and a stroll around in the sun, he'd be far from wanting to look at any paintings.

'What a shame.' She congratulated herself on the note of regret in her voice.

He burst out laughing. 'My word, you said that as if you really meant it. Your talents are quite wasted on secretarial work. You ought to be an actress. Right, then, dissembler – the lamp first, then the furniture plan, then Montefalco, food and wine. If it turns out that we get there too late to feed our minds, we'll just have to settle for feeding our stomachs instead.'

She stood still, her mouth open, watching him go into the house. Dissembler! Didn't that mean fake and hypocrite? It had come up once in a Shakespeare play she did at school. Could that mean Tom had seen through her secretary ruse?

But no, of course it couldn't – he'd been smiling as he'd gone into the house. She closed her mouth and followed him into the hall.

He'd taken two of the bedside lamps from the cluster that stood on the hall floor and was carrying them up the wide stone stairs to the master bedroom. She hurried after him and reached him just as he was lifting the bedroom latch and pushing the door open. Hot on his heels, she followed him into the shuttered room.

A thin beam of white light shone into the dark room from a tiny window high among the rafters, falling on to the floor in a pale circle at the foot of the bed. Silvery specks of dust danced in the column of sheer light.

Tom handed her one of the lamps. 'Will you put this on the table on the other side of the bed? I'll do the one this side, and make a start on a quick sketch of the room.'

'Sure thing.' Turning round the corner of the bed a fraction too soon, her toe hit the foot of the iron bedpost. 'Shit!' she cried out in sudden pain, and dropped the lamp on to the bed.

'Why, Evie! Surely that's not another invitation for us to share a bed, an invitation that's rather more direct in nature than the last?'

'Huh, dream on! I stubbed my toe on the bed and it's absolute agony. It really hurts.' She sat on the bed, kicked off her sandal, bent over and began to rub her toe.

'Are you OK?' he asked, coming over to her side and sitting down next to her.

She heard a trace of anxiety in his voice. Her spirits lifted – could it be that her pain and suffering were going to come up trumps?

She gave a little whimper. And another.

'Just about. But I bet my toe's going to be one big bruise before the day's out. And I've chipped the varnish.' She straightened up and treated him to the Brave Little Woman look. No point in summoning the Damsel in Dire Distress effect – she'd used that one before and it had fallen on unfeeling eyes.

'Chipped varnish! Now that *is* serious. Would it help if I kissed it better?'

'Given a straight choice between that and you switching on the light to prevent any further damage to my body, I'll take the second of the two, thank you very much, tempted though I am by the thought of you on the floor at my feet.'

The smile on his face was traced by a line of silvery light. She found herself smiling back at him.

For a long moment, the only sound in the room was the loud beating of their hearts. Then he got up, went over to the bedside table and put the lamp on it. She heard a click, and light flooded the side of the bed.

'And then there was light. You see, your word is my command, Evie. Is there anything else I can do to compensate for the chipped varnish?'

She slipped into her sandal and stood up, looking anywhere but at the large bed with its deep mattress.

'You're OK. I'm all out of commands for the moment.'

'Then if your toe permits, will you be the one to draw the outline of the room?' He took a notebook and pen out of the pocket in his jeans and handed them to her. 'We'll mark on it where the chest of drawers and wardrobe should go.'

She took the book from him, did a quick sketch of the

room and then pointed to the side of the sketch. 'The wardrobe will go here, won't it? It's a no-brainer. And the chest of drawers here.'

'I agree. Mark them in, would you, please?'

She did as he'd asked, slipped the top back on the pen and glanced around the room. 'Airhead that I am, I'm wondering what colour you're going to choose for your sheets and curtains.'

'As your reward for great fortitude in the face of damage to your person, you may choose the colour.'

'White,' she replied after a moment's thought. 'White in every room. The walls are already white and there's a lot of grey stone around the house. White curtains and white bed linen would be super cool. Or do you think it'd be too much like living in a monastery?'

'That's a point.' He looked thoughtful. 'I'm not planning on living like a monk.'

'And very wise, too,' she said gravely. 'You've already shown how much you like good food and the best of wine – and both of those are forbidden to a monk. No, a life of abstinence would never do for you.'

'You're absolutely right about there not being a lot of attention paid to food and drink in a monastery, Evie. When I spoke, though, I hadn't actually been thinking about those two aspects of monastic life. But yes, having to abstain from those, too, would prove an insurmountable obstacle.'

'Nothing's insurmountable. You've just got to want it enough, that's all.'

'Aha, that all-embracing *it*. So I'll succeed if I want *it* enough, will I? It's an interesting thought. However, I fear that we ought to put it out of our mind, pleasant though I'm sure such rumination would be. We need to get off to Montefalco pretty soon – my non-monk-like desire for food is getting stronger with every passing minute.'

Wow, his comment about 'that all-embracing *it*' was pretty near the mark.

And she hadn't even intended him to take her comment the way he'd taken it. Or the way he'd pretended to take it. Could it be that Tom was nudging things forward? Urgent mental note to self – conversation along similar lines to be resumed as soon as possible. PS. Said conversation must take place in surroundings conducive to throwing off inhibitions.

She organised her features into a frown, as if a sudden thought had come into her head.

'How about this for a suggestion? There was more to do here than we realised and it's taken longer than we thought it would. As you're hungry now, why don't we cut out the idea of having lunch in Montefalco and eat in Massa Piccola instead? We could go to the restaurant just back from the main road, which we thought looked rather nice. Then we can go to Montefalco this evening when everything's open again. We can look round the gallery and maybe have a drink there. Or even dinner? What do you think?'

His reply was lost in a sudden loud banging that reverberated through the house.

'What's that?' She spun round and stared towards the staircase.

He made a move towards the door. 'I think we've got visitors. Someone's at the front door and they sound pretty insistent.' The banging came again, and they heard people moving around outside the house. Voices were talking excitedly. 'Can you hear what they're saying?'

She listened intently. 'No, not really, the sound's muffled. Someone mentioned water and someone else said something about the pool, but that's all I could make out.'

The banging was followed by the sound of a heavy vehicle being driven past the outside of the house. They heard it come to a stop, and then a second vehicle followed the first.

A moment later, there was more thumping on the door.

'Come on. Let's go and see what they want.' He tucked the plan of the room into his pocket. 'If necessary, I'll have to ring Eduardo, or rather you will. It looks as if we may end up having him with us after all today.' He gave her a wry smile and went out on to the landing.

They went quickly down the stairs and Tom opened the front door. Three men in overalls stood under the porch, three shapes dark against the bright glare of the midday sun.

'*Buon giorno!*' Evie said, stepping forward, and she asked them what they wanted.

'It's water for the pool,' she told Tom when she'd finished talking to the men and looking at the papers that they'd shown her. 'They've been filling the pool by bringing up lorry loads of water, and they were short by a couple of loads. Apparently the water is meant to come to the top of the pool and flow over the side into the white grating, but it isn't yet high enough to do that. They've got all the necessary papers. They told Eduardo that they'd be coming today and they thought he'd be here.'

'Is there anything we can do or should we call Eduardo?'

'No, we don't need him. There's something to be signed, but you can sign. They don't need us to be here at all, they just need a signature.'

'Right, then. Show me where to sign and we'll let them get on with it.'

He signed on the line that Evie indicated and handed the paper back. The men nodded their thanks, turned and went back to the lorries. Tom closed the door behind them and led the way into the sitting room.

'Your suggestion about leaving Montefalco till this

evening is a good one. All the more so because it means we can come back from lunch after the men have gone, just to check that everything's all right.' He went over to the arched glass doors and looked out at the pool. 'It's a shame we can't swim today. It would have been nice to have been able to use the pool at least once before we went back to England, but we can't – the pool man will need to do his stuff first. However, there's nothing to stop us sitting with our legs in the water, if we felt so inclined.'

Fantastic! Things were getting better by the minute. Lunch somewhere nice; a hot afternoon by the pool; wine in the evening. And just the two of them together all day. It was beyond brilliant.

'So, let's get off to Massa now, Evie – we can pick up a couple of towels on the way.'

Suppressing her inner elation, she forced a concerned expression to her face. 'What about the room plans? We've only done one room so far.'

'We can do the others when we come back. We've done more than enough for one morning. We'll leave the men to do their job and by the time we get back, they'll have long gone and we'll have the place to ourselves. So we can go if you're ready.'

She beamed at him. She certainly was!

Chapter Ten

A gal's gotta do what a gal's gotta do ...

Evie leaned back in her seat and stared up at the awning of leaves above her. The hot sun shone through tiny gaps between the leaves and sprinkled the terrace with a shower of gold. She felt blissfully relaxed.

Sighing with pleasure, she glanced across the table at Tom. He was trying to brush away a fly. He looked up and met her eyes. He sat back in his seat, abandoning his battle with the fly, and smiled at her.

God, he was absolutely fabulous.

The cornflower blue of his shirt brought out the deep blue of his eyes and brilliantly set off his light tan. He really was something.

Not that his dishy appearance and cool sense of fun would get in the way of what she had to do, she thought quickly. It wouldn't – she'd no choice but to get her story – but it was lovely to let herself imagine for a moment that she was in Italy solely as Evie Shaw, secretary and interpreter. Just that and no more – no digging into his past life; no pretending to be what she wasn't; above all, no editor behind her.

'We'll sock it to him when it hurts the most,' her editor had thundered down the phone on the night before she left for Umbria. 'The minute that stuck-up bastard stands up in court to start on some poor sucker, our readers are gonna be learning the truth about Mr Squeaky Clean. Squeaky Clean, my arse! You've got the two weeks you're back in London to flesh out the details, Evie – and believe me, I want flesh and lots of it – and then you send me the low-down on his fucking affair, and you make sure it's fucking good.'

On the Monday that her story came out – the day that his next big libel case was beginning – she'd be back in the offices of *Pure Dirt*. It was just as well that she would be. She couldn't begin to imagine what he would say about her role in the whole thing. Well, she could, but she'd no intention of going there; it would hurt too much.

She took a deep breath. She was going to have to grow a thicker skin if she wanted to keep her job at *Pure Dirt* long enough to be able to jump from it into a mainstream magazine. Perhaps it would help if she kept on telling herself that if it hadn't been for *Pure Dirt*, she wouldn't have met Tom.

'I was hungrier than I thought I was,' she said. 'That penne with vodka was yummy.'

'It's a specialty of Umbria. Eduardo introduced me to it on one of my early visits. I'm glad you liked it. How about some pudding now?'

'I really couldn't, thanks. I've had more than enough. What with the hot sun and all that food, I feel just about ready for bed as it is.'

'Tut, tut, Evie. Sexual invitations shouldn't fall upon the ears of someone at risk of developing monastic aspirations.'

Yay! He was as keen as she was to get back to the banter they'd had earlier in his bedroom. This was a very promising path, but she'd better decide quickly on where she wanted it to end – getting his confession was her goal, not getting into his bed.

She straightened up in her chair.

'I'll be more careful in future,' she said, a playful, demure lilt to her voice. 'I can assure you that I wouldn't want to put you to the blush, Tom.'

'My sentiments entirely.'

Their eyes met and they smiled at each other in amusement. Tom moved first. He picked up the bottle of wine and re-filled their glasses. 'What about a coffee, then?'

'That sounds good. Thank you.'

'I'll have one too.' He caught the waiter's eye and beckoned him over.

'*Due caffè, per piacere*,' she told the waiter.

He returned a few minutes later with their coffees and a small dish of *amoretti*. She poured some milk into her coffee and took one from the dish. She unwrapped the biscuit, and popped it into her mouth. 'Oh, they're *amoretti morbidi*.'

'How can a biscuit be morbid?'

'*Morbido* means soft. I prefer them hard, though.'

Ohmigod, did she really say that!

A wave of heat spread over her chest and up to her neck. She must have gone scarlet. What must she look like? Her frantic gaze fell on her glass of ice-cold water. Salvation! She hastily wrapped her hands hard around the cold glass, then pressed them against her flushed cheeks.

Her hands still against her face, she glanced up and met Tom's eyes. He was grinning broadly.

'I, too, feel somewhat warm,' he said. Still smiling, he looked around the restaurant. 'In fact, it's the perfect afternoon for doing nothing. That was a good idea to leave Montefalco till this evening.'

She felt the red fading and sat heavily back in her chair in relief.

'Doing nothing sounds pretty OK to me, too. Doing nothing the Mediterranean way would be to sit on the *loggia* and stare ahead. We could fold up our towels, sit on them, lean back against the wall and let the mountain breeze waft over us. We might even drop off for a bit. Or maybe we could sit on the edge of the pool, like you suggested. Then later on, when we felt more energetic, we could finish the room plans and do the Montefalco thing. What do you think?'

'I think it sounds a really good idea.'

'Which bit of it sounds a really good idea?'

'The bit you didn't mention.'

'I'm getting us some water to drink,' Tom called from inside the kitchen. 'And I'll bring out one of the bottles of wine we picked up.'

'Do you need a hand?' Evie asked, turning round as she heard Tom coming out of the kitchen. He was walking towards her, a thick piece of cardboard with two plastic glasses on it in one hand, and a bottle of wine in the other. 'You look pretty laden.'

'I'm fine, thanks. Well, perhaps you'd better take the wine – I wouldn't want to drop it.'

She jumped up and took the bottle from him. He carefully set the makeshift cardboard tray down in the space between the two towels that she'd spread out on the grass, and sat down on one of the towels. She sat down on the other, picked up one of the plastic glasses of water and stared thoughtfully down the slope at the pool.

Their conversation at the restaurant had sounded as if it might lead to great things, whatever those great things proved to be, but the drive back to the house had broken the mood, and they were back to their normal friendly relationship. She couldn't see how to get the frisson back that they'd had at the end of their lunch, but she'd have to come up with something, and before long.

She'd only got one and a half days left in which to find out about him and Zizi, and much of that time was going to be spent with two other people. This was the last afternoon that she'd be alone with him in Italy, and somehow or other, she was going to have to get him talking.

If only she'd never got into such a shitty situation.

If only she'd been offered a job on an ordinary magazine, no matter how lowly the job. If only she'd thought for a moment about what she'd have to do if she worked for *Pure Dirt*. If only she'd never put herself in the position of finding herself in the hot sun, sitting next to a really attractive, fun guy, unable to think of anything else but how to worm out of him something he'd rather not tell her, and that she'd rather not hear.

She was caught in an unholy mess.

She absolutely didn't want to do the job that she'd been sent to do in Italy, but she was going to have to do it. Her editor was the sort of man who carried out the threats he made, and he'd see her blacklisted from every magazine if she jacked in the job at that stage.

No way could she let that happen.

She had a stark choice – kissing goodbye to the dream she'd had since she was ten years old or getting Tom to talk. The Tom option was the only possible choice for her, and she had to take it, no matter how much she didn't want to. Everyone had to follow their dream, and that was that.

'A penny for them, or a euro, if you prefer. You look miles away.'

'I was just thinking how tempting the water looks.' She gave an audible sigh. 'I wished I was putting me into the water, instead of putting water into me. It's such a shame that we can't go in the pool.'

'Which reminds me, I need to ask Eduardo about the man who's going to be looking after the pool and garden. I know he's found someone – he said so the last time I was here – and the original plan was for me to meet him this week, but he hasn't said anything about it since we got here so I probably need to remind him. I'll certainly want to be able to swim when I come back in August.'

'I don't blame you. If it's this hot now, it'll be really hot then. And as you said, your parents will be here, too.'

'That's the plan. If the case finishes when it's scheduled to finish, I'll have a couple of weeks here before they join me. But these things are always unpredictable, so it's not worth counting any chickens yet. While we're on the subject, though, it might be an idea if you rang Eduardo now – perhaps he can set up a meeting for this evening, or for early tomorrow evening when we're back from Perugia. Here, take my phone.'

'With luck, he can sort it out for tomorrow,' she said, taking the phone from him. 'Then there won't be any need for him to come up to the house today.'

He looked at her in surprise. 'Why wouldn't you want to see Eduardo this afternoon? You and he seemed as thick as thieves last night. Or have I missed something?'

'Yes and no.'

'I see. No, actually I don't see. Not that this entirely surprises me, having spent some time with you this week.' He leaned back on his elbows and stared at her in amusement. 'I'm sure that your answer makes perfectly good sense, but as I can't precisely see how it does, pray do enlighten me.'

She tucked her legs underneath her and turned slightly towards him. 'It's quite simple really. Of course I like him – he's drop-dead gorgeous, easy to talk to and very romantic.'

'I take it that's the "yes" bit, then. So where does the "no" bit come in?'

'The "no" bit is that I don't want to leap on top of him, tear off his clothes and have my evil way with him,' she giggled.

'I wasn't really asking you that.'

'Yes, you were.'

He laughed. 'OK. Maybe I was, although I shouldn't

have been. But why don't you want to rip off his clothes if he's everything you've said he is? Is it because you've got a Mr Right waiting for you back at home?'

'It's because when I look at Eduardo, nothing happens. No stars, no flashing lights, no tingling, nothing. It's a shame, but there it is. And now it's my turn: you've asked me a question, so it's only fair that I ask you something. Or at least it's fair for as long as we're Tom and Evie. When you're back to being Mr Hadleigh again, you'll be the boss and fairness won't come into it.'

'What a highly gratifying way in which to view our employer/employee relationship, Evie,' he said dryly. 'Fair enough – or not so fair as the case may be – I'll answer the question that you've put, but first would you like some wine?'

'No, thanks, I'm fine. What question? I didn't know I'd asked one yet.'

'You were asking me if we were ever going to return to being Mr Hadleigh and Miss Shaw to each other again.'

'No, I wasn't, but since you think I was, I'll have it as my question. So, will I have to start calling you Mr Hadleigh again when we're back in England?'

'I don't know. Will you?'

'You've answered my question with another question. I don't think even lawyers are allowed to get away with that, are they? You have to answer properly when somebody asks you something. That's the law.'

'Ah, but you can do anything you like when you know the law.'

'You can't break the law just because you know the law. That would be wrong.'

'It's true that you shouldn't, honest Evie, but if you do break the law and you know the law, you have a better chance of getting away with it.'

The muscles in his jaw tightened imperceptibly.

What! Could he be about to spill all?

She stretched her legs out, her heart racing, and turned to him.

Chapter Eleven

So near and yet so far!

Go carefully, she told herself. Don't scare him off. He'd picked up on what she'd said about lawyers and had moved them further along that line of conversation, but getting the lowdown about him and Zizi was still a long way off.

'But there's more than one lawyer in prison,' she pursued, squashing the thought that *low* was a pretty good word for what she was trying to do. She forced a light bounce into her voice. 'That proves that knowing the law isn't everything.'

'You don't know how many lawyers have got away with breaking the law, though. Also, not everyone who breaks the law ends up being sent to prison. The naughty person might just get his knuckles rapped.'

He shifted into a different position on the grass. She surreptitiously stared at him from beneath lowered eyelashes. She could smell a story in the air. She drew her breath in, slowly, deeply.

'You seem to know a lot about the secret lives of lawyers, Tom.' Was that a bit too close to the mark? she wondered. She softened her words with a light-hearted laugh. 'What about you? Have you ever done anything you shouldn't have done and got away with it?'

Blimey, his body language! He'd gone as stiff as a board.

'You've still got a question from me to answer,' he said after a short pause. 'I wanted your take on whether we'll still be Evie and Tom when we get back to England. I think we'll return to that question.'

Her heart pounded in excitement. She thought fast. More

wine might do the trick. She gulped her water at speed and held the plastic glass out to Tom.

'I promise to answer that, but I'd like some of that wine first, please, if your offer's still open. A glass of wine and a lazy afternoon belong together like a lock and a key. Oh, dear, we're back to prisons again.' She laughed gaily as she watched him pour her some wine and then put the bottle back on the rug. 'Aren't you going to join me? It doesn't feel right to drink alone.'

'I see. It's goodbye, moral Evie, and hello, wicked Evie, is it? And wicked Evie's trying to lead me astray. But ...' He gave an exaggerated sigh, '... I can't let you drink alone, even if I *do* suspect that this is a trick to stop us from going to Montefalco to see its famous murals.' He finished his water and filled his glass with wine. 'Now,' he went on, 'I'll have an answer to my question.'

'Well,' she said slowly. 'I guess it all depends upon whether or not we're becoming friends – proper friends, that is, not just people who have to get on because they've been forced to spend time together.'

'So, are we becoming proper friends?'

She thought for a moment. 'I think so. Or put another way, I can't think of anything we've done that makes us improper friends.'

'Then that rather means we'll still be Evie and Tom in London, does it not?'

'I suppose. But it's your call.'

'Here's to Tom and Evie, no matter where they are.' He raised his glass to her and took a drink.

'Now that I've answered your question, proper-friend Tom, it's over to you to answer mine, which was, have you ever been a naughty boy and done something you shouldn't have done, but got away with it?'

'That's not very likely, is it?' he said slowly, staring

motionless at the wine in his glass. 'I'm a libel lawyer. I deal with people's reputations. The essence of libel is that one person can't destroy the good name of another if that other person has already destroyed his good name himself. My role in court is to see that any unjustifiable damage to my client's good name is punished. What kind of lawyer would I be – libel or otherwise – if I came to court with dirty hands myself?'

'So your answer is no?'

He shrugged his shoulders. 'On some level, everyone's done one or two things in their life that they shouldn't have done. I bet you nicked sweets from Woolworths when you were little. Be honest now – you did, didn't you?'

'You've done it again! It's my turn to question you, but you've turned it into a question for me to answer. You're so slippery.' She forced a laugh.

'If ever there was a case of the pretty little pot calling the kettle black, that's it. And you've cunningly avoided answering what I first asked you.'

'Huh?' She wrinkled her brow and stared at him. 'I don't think much cunning was involved. I can't even remember what the question was now.'

'I asked you if you'd found your Mr Right yet.'

'So you did. No, I haven't.'

'How come? Without the brogues and those huge glasses, you're quite easy on the eye. I would have thought you'd have been snapped up by now.'

'I don't want to be snapped up, as you put it, by any old person. It's got to be by the right person, and I haven't met that right person yet. When I do, I'll know it. And if I don't meet them, then I won't get married. And what about you? Is there a significant other in your life?'

'Yes, my work. And talking about work, we'd better make that call to Eduardo now and ask him to fix up a meeting with the man he's found. You could also suggest after breakfast tomorrow, before we set off for Perugia. That would be better than having to clock-watch at the end of the day.'

'Will do,' she said, and she picked up the phone.

A few hours later, Tom stood under the pergola outside the kitchen and watched Eduardo and Evie stroll around the outside of the pool.

So much for Montefalco, he thought. By the time that Eduardo had cleared off, it would be too late for them to go that far, and anyway, he wasn't in the mood any longer. They might as well go straight back to Il Poggio for dinner.

He stepped out from under the pergola and walked a little way across the grass so that he had a better view of what they were doing as they walked down to the grove of olive trees.

Whatever Evie may have said about not being interested in Eduardo in the way that he'd feared she was – well, not feared, that was a bit strong – not in the way that he'd *thought*, looking at them both together, it was hard to believe. They were obviously getting on brilliantly and were doing very nicely without him.

Admittedly, he could have walked round the garden with them, but he hadn't wanted to. He couldn't join in the conversation – no matter however good the interpreter, everything had to be relayed through another person and that was a distancing thing – and also he'd wanted to observe them when they were both together. Not for any particular reason, just out of interest.

He stood still and stared down the slope at them. Eduardo had stopped and was bending over, pointing to the short grass at the base of an olive tree. He heard Evie give a little squeal and saw her jump back. He smiled. Eduardo must have been telling her that they had to keep the grass cut short at the foot of the olive trees so as to avoid snakes. It was a habitat they liked.

So Evie didn't like snakes any more than she liked scorpions. Well, that was predictable. And the issue of beetles was yet to be resolved, he thought in amusement, remembering what she'd said to him on their first morning in Italy.

She turned suddenly and waved up at him. Taken by surprise, he took a step back. Then she said something to Eduardo, who also looked up and waved.

Raising a hand to acknowledge them, he realised that they'd have seen him smiling for no reason, and he quickly turned away, hoping that they'd been too far away to see him standing there, grinning at nothing. What must he have looked like!

Mildly irritated at being caught out like that, he went over to the towels and straightened them up. Then he sat down on one of them, linked his fingers in front of his knees and stared at the pool.

The shining water lay smooth and still in the late afternoon sun. Beyond the water, the grey-green tips of the olive trees stood stark against the purple contours of the distant heat-hazed hills. As he watched, the dark shape of a solitary bird swooped low over the surface, feathering the tips of the water before it rose sharply to the sky, an insect trapped in its beak. In its wake, glittering ripples widened slowly across the pool and reached out to the far corners where shadows gathered.

Every so often he heard Eduardo and Evie laugh, but they were beyond the pool and among the trees, far out of his sight. He couldn't decide if it was more relaxing not being able to see them and having to imagine what they were doing, or being able to see them and finding himself trying to decipher their body language. Perhaps relaxing was the wrong word. Neither situation had the remotest element of relaxation about it.

He glanced at his watch. Yes, time was getting on.

Admittedly his meeting with Luigi had swallowed up most of the afternoon, but it had had to be done – the man was going to look after his house, garden and pool, after all.

On the one hand, they'd been lucky that Eduardo had been able to collect Luigi immediately after Evie's phone call and bring him up to the house as it meant that they'd be able to take their time over breakfast the following morning, and then go straight from the hotel to Perugia, where they were going to meet Eduardo and Gabriela. A much better arrangement all round.

Luigi had seemed pleasant enough and the meeting had gone well. He was going to start looking after the house and garden immediately, and he even had a sister who would clean the house. Yes, Eduardo had done well there – Luigi was obviously a real find, and it was a great relief that they'd been able to finalise everything that afternoon.

On the other hand, however, he'd lost a large chunk of time that he could have spent alone with Evie.

He'd assumed that Eduardo would leave as soon as Luigi left, but not so. Apparently, Luigi had refused Eduardo's offer of a lift down to the town, saying that he wanted to look at some fields on his way back down the mountain, and he'd gone off on foot. But then, instead of getting into his noisy convertible and driving off, Eduardo had gone over to Evie and sat down next to her.

For a moment he'd thought he'd seen a look of annoyance sweep across Evie's face when she realised that Eduardo was intent on staying with them, and his spirits had soared. But the moment had swiftly passed and he wasn't entirely sure that he hadn't been mistaken.

'We're back.' Evie's words cut into his thoughts. He looked up and saw her standing next to him, a slender silhouette outlined against the sun. Eduardo was at her side.

'Good walk?'

'It was brill, thanks,' she replied. She hesitated a moment. 'About dinner tonight. I know you wanted to go to Montefalco, but Eduardo has suggested that the three of us go to a little place not far from Todi. He said they do wonderful local food there. He could book a table for eight thirty, if we wanted. Gabriela's off visiting someone she knew at school, so if he doesn't come with us he's going to be on his own tonight. What do you think? Is that OK?'

No, it bloody well wasn't OK!

He'd spent the whole of the previous day in Città di Castello with Eduardo, not to mention the whole evening, too. He'd had him up to the house that afternoon, and he was going to be spending the whole of the following day with him. Enough was bloody well enough. And now the idea of having to be Eduardo's companion for the evening, rather than him having to spend the evening alone – well, he wasn't Eduardo's keeper and it absolutely was not OK!

'I suppose we'll have to agree,' he said irritably, getting to his feet. 'I'm amazed that Eduardo doesn't mind spending so much of his time with us. Surely he's got plenty of other things he'd rather be doing. We'd certainly understand if he wanted to do them.'

He glanced at Evie's face and saw the disappointment he felt mirrored in her eyes.

A sudden rush of heat ran through him.

So she'd really meant it when she'd said that she didn't want Eduardo at the house that afternoon, and she *had* looked annoyed that he'd stayed on after Luigi had gone. And she didn't want a dinner for three any more than he did. She'd rather it was just the two of them alone. Oh,

Evie! It was worth enduring another evening with Eduardo to have found that out.

He turned away, excitement mounting within him. And then he stopped, struck hard by a sudden thought.

It might quite simply be that she wanted a break from translating, which she'd have if there was no Eduardo around. Maybe it was that and not the thought of the two of them being unable to be alone that made her regret he'd be there. He looked back at her. She was staring at the grass and biting her lip as she listened to Eduardo telling her something. It must be a strain for her always being the one at the chalk face with Eduardo. Maybe it was that and nothing more.

He mentally shook himself. What was the matter with him, wasting his time in speculating about her reasons for not wanting Eduardo with them? There could be any number of reasons, and whatever it was, it was none of his business.

He bent down and picked up the empty bottle of wine.

Chapter Twelve

The power of a peach!

'My feet are killing me,' Evie sighed. 'I can't wait to sit down – it was loopy of me to wear these heels, but I didn't figure on walking quite so far. And Gabriela and Eduardo walk so fast – they must be miles ahead of us. It's been a fantastic morning, much better than I thought it was going to be, but I think I've had enough now.'

'We do seem to have covered a lot of ground in a short amount of time, but I wouldn't have wanted to miss any of it. The huge frescoes in the palazzo opposite the cathedral are really astounding.'

'And I loved the fountain. I thought it was really beautiful. Gabriela certainly knows Perugia well. It's just that she's so intense that it's wearying. I suppose I shouldn't complain, though – her being able to say everything in English is a real break for me. There was nothing for me to do all morning but listen, which makes a change.'

'It would for most women,' he said dryly.

'Sexist pig.' She laughed, spun round towards him and made a move to dig him in the ribs. He caught her hand mid-air. A bolt of electricity shot through her. 'Well, perhaps not a pig.' Her voice came from a trillion miles away.

She coughed quickly, hoping to scale her voice back down to somewhere near normal. Fat chance of that, though – he was still holding her hand.

'Pig is probably not a recommended way of addressing your boss,' she squeaked.

'I'm sure I've been called worse things,' he remarked cheerfully. He turned them into a narrow medieval street that led to the entrance of a high-tech escalator running in sections from the old town on top of the hill down to the bottom. His hand tightened around hers. Her spine tingled. 'At least pigs are clean,' he added, 'which is more than you can say for some of the names I've been called.'

Sod the effing pigs! He was still holding her hand. What was going on inside his head?

'Aha, here's the entrance we're looking for. This *is* the escalator we came up on. I wouldn't want to end up near the wrong car park. Go carefully, Evie.'

Side by side they stepped on to the metal stair. She glanced down at the hand holding hers, then quickly looked away and stared down the moving steps. Where on earth were they going now – and she didn't mean on the escalator.

'The others must have virtually run all the way down, if you can imagine Gabriela running anywhere – I'm not sure that I can. I can't see them anywhere.' She hoped that her voice was loud enough to cover the thud of her heart. 'Come to think of it, we've not seen them for ages.'

As if she cared.

If just the touch of his hand could do what it was doing to her … Her heart thudded even more loudly.

'I'm sure we'll catch up with them eventually,' he said airily. 'They're probably in a hurry to get lunch over with. I'm sure they'll want some time to themselves between lunch and the end of the afternoon. I can identify with that. As you so rightly said, it's a stunner of a city, but like you, I feel that I've had enough sightseeing for one day.'

She glanced down at his tanned forearm, at the hand still firmly enclosing hers, at the jeans slung low on his hips. If she was totally honest with herself, there were certain sights she'd never have enough of.

'We'll get off as soon as we've had lunch.' They stepped from the first leg of the escalator and began to walk along a short stretch of street to the next section of the escalator. His hand still firmly held hers, she noticed with glee. 'I get the impression you like Gabriela a bit better now,' he said.

'I liked her when I met her the other night.'

'I'm not so sure about that, but we'll let it go. But I did think that the two of you seemed to be getting on really well over coffee this morning. You were chatting away non-stop whilst Eduardo and I were looking through the book of Perugino's paintings that he bought as we were leaving the Collegio del Cambio.'

'You're right, we were. But I know what you mean about intense – she's not exactly a laugh a minute. I'd hate to share a house with someone like that. To be honest, when I first met her, I thought she seemed a bit hard, but now that I've talked to her, I can see that she isn't hard at all. No, she's OK.'

'What did you talk about?'

She looked at him and laughed. 'I was about to say that that was something a woman might ask, but I've got an awful feeling that I'd be called a sexist sow if I did, so I'm not going to say it.'

He laughed.

They turned and went through the entrance to the next section of escalator. 'You really ought to have been a barrister, Evie. Your talent for not saying something, but getting your message across all the same, should have a wider audience than just me and a metal staircase. And why hold back now? I've already been likened to a matchmaker this week, and been seen as having similarities with your mother, so why stop short at making me a confidante?'

'OK, bezzie mate, she was asking me about living in England, if you really want to know. She wanted to know the sort of places my friends and I go to at night, our favourite clubs and the like, where I shop – but that was probably to avoid those shops. I can't see her wearing the sort of things I go for.'

He glanced down at her short, pale-blue gingham minidress with shoestring straps. 'You might well be right about that.'

'She also wanted to know how I liked sharing a house with other people. She's going to have to do that when she's in London, although I think she'll be in a separate flat in a large house that's been converted into flats. It's not the same as Rachel, Jess and me living in one house together. I think that was all we talked about. Oh, and she asked quite a lot about where you lived.'

'I'm very grateful to you. It sounds as if you've saved me some work. I told her I'd help her with what she needed to know about London, but you seem to have done that for me, and probably much better than I could have done.'

'I wouldn't say that.'

'Well, *I* would. I'm used to seeing the finished product across the dinner table. The shops and the places that they visit to get that way is outside my field of knowledge, and I'm quite content to let it stay there, thank you.'

'I'm not sure that she'll let you. She wanted to know about where you worked as well as where you lived.'

'I expect she likes the idea of knowing someone in the place she's moving to. Of knowing two people, I should say. She knows you, too, now.'

'Maybe. But at the moment, she seems to have lost the two people she knows.'

'They'll be at the bottom of the escalator, you wait and see. They can't go far without us as we don't know where the restaurant is.'

Shading her eyes with her slender hands, Gabriela stared at the exit for the escalator. Where were they? she thought impatiently. The morning had been a great success, and she wanted the rest of the day to go equally as well.

She'd booked a table at one of her favourite restaurants, and whilst everyone in Italy was fairly casual over time – more casual, she suspected, than she was going to find in England – she didn't like arriving too much after the time she'd arranged. Apart from anything else, she had managed to reserve a lovely table for the four of them, and she wouldn't want the restaurant to despair and give their table to someone else.

However, they were late for a good reason, she realised, and she should not be too impatient with them. Both Tom and Evie had clearly enjoyed seeing the sights of such a beautiful city, and their responses showed that they had appreciated everything she'd shown them. As a result, at times they had lingered longer than was wise, given that they had a lunch reservation. But they couldn't be blamed for this; it was understandable.

She looked across at Eduardo. He, too, was watching the exit, although trying not to be as obvious about it as she was. She smiled inwardly. He certainly had a bad case of infatuation over Evie, and this somewhat surprised her – the women friends of his that she'd met in the past were generally of a cultured nature.

Which Evie wasn't.

Although Evie *had* seemed to enjoy the morning very much – far more than Gabrielle had expected, in fact. And she'd been somewhat amazed at how well Evie and Tom seemed to get on. They had clearly become friends. Obviously it was no more than that, and it was unlikely that their friendship would survive their return to Italy – they were just too different as people – but it was a surprise to her, nevertheless, how much they seemed to enjoy each other's company.

She glanced at her watch, and sighed. Hopefully, they wouldn't be much longer.

'Remind me, will you, to swap details with Gabriela before we leave?' said Tom. 'She'll need my contact numbers in London, although I suppose she could always get them from Eduardo. Ah, here we are. And, look, there they are across the road. What did I tell you?'

'What a burden it must be to always be right,' she said with a smile as they stepped off the escalator.

'No one's that, Evie.'

She shot a quizzical look at him, then turned back to Gabriela and Eduardo, who'd just caught sight of them. Eduardo had been leaning against a wall, but he promptly straightened up and started waving across the road to them. Gabriela's face broke into a wide smile.

How the hell did she do it? Evie wondered as they started across the road. Gabriela looked as cool and elegant in her cream linen trouser suit as she had when they'd first met up that morning – not a crease; nothing – whereas she was sure that her favourite Kate Moss dress had been reduced to a limp rag in the heat.

What's more, she could tell that numerous strands of hair had escaped from the two barrettes she'd put in that morning because they were hanging damply around her heat-flushed face. She must look a total wreck.

As they reached the other side of the road and stepped on to the pavement, she saw Gabriela's gaze slip to their linked hands. A look of surprise fleetingly crossed her face, and of something else she couldn't quite put her finger on, but the expression swiftly passed and was lost in the welcoming crimson-lipped smile that Gabriela gave them.

'*Ci dispiace*,' Evie began.

'There's no need to apologise, Evie. It's difficult to walk

past so much beauty and not stop and examine it closely. Eduardo and I were happy to have time to catch up with each other. But come, Tom, let me quickly show you this before we go to the restaurant.'

Turning slightly from Evie, she put one hand lightly under Tom's elbow, and with the other, pointed to the intricate engravings on the stone arch around a heavy wooden door near where they were standing. As she moved closer to the doorway, she took Tom with her, and Evie's fingers gradually slipped through his.

Her hand felt empty.

Damn! Gabriela's timing couldn't have been worse – by the time that the lesson in architecture was over, the togetherness with Tom would also be over, and there was no certainty that they'd get back to where they'd been. Thank God there was only lunch to get through before they could go off on their own.

She turned to Eduardo in desperation and asked how far the restaurant was.

'That's the one!' Evie cried, standing in the middle of the sitting room, staring up through the glass roof to the now-illuminated stone tower above them. Caught in the beam of the spotlight, the column pierced the night.

'And this is the last one.' Tom flicked the switch as he spoke.

She turned to look through the windows as light flooded the pool.

'Wow!'

'That's a pretty good word for it. Eduardo certainly knew what he was doing, I'll say that for him.' He came and stood alongside her, staring with her at the spotlit gardens. 'His Mediterranean gallantry may be a bit much at times, but he's bang on when it comes to restoration.' He pushed the glass doors open and walked out on to the *loggia*. 'It's a beautiful night. Shall we have a short stroll, if you've any energy left after Perugia, that is?'

Did he really need an answer?

'I think I can just about summon up enough oomph to take a few steps,' she said, and all but ran out after him. 'Look at the sky! You can hardly see it for stars. That means it'll be good weather for the flight home tomorrow, doesn't it?'

'Something like that. Come on, let's walk.' He took her hand and led them down the path, along the edge of the shimmering blue-green pool and down the slope beyond the pool to the rows of spectral olive trees.

At the edge of the dark groves, she stopped suddenly and glanced down at her feet. Tom gripped her hand more tightly. 'There are no snakes here now, Evie, if that's what you're thinking. They like the sun, and that's in short supply when it's almost midnight.'

She started walking again. 'I hope you're right. I've got open-toed sandals on.'

'I'm confident that the colour of your toenails would scare them away, if nothing else. Trust me.'

She looked at him in amusement. 'Oh, I do, Tom,' she murmured. 'I wouldn't be here alone with you in the dark, with you clutching my hand so hard that I couldn't escape if I wanted to, if I didn't thoroughly trust you.'

'Don't say that!' he cried out, looking at her in feigned alarm. 'You're laying a moral responsibility on me to live up to your trust by doing the right thing, and I'm not entirely sure I want that.'

Huh! What did he mean by that? He didn't want the moral responsibility or he didn't want to do the right thing? Jeez, please let it be the latter! With difficulty, she switched her focus back to what he was saying.

'There's something in human nature that makes one keen to do the very opposite of what one ought to do, and I think I'm about to find out that I'm no exception to that rule.' He stopped walking, turned to face her, and took a step closer.

Ohmigod, she knew what was coming! And it wasn't more talk. Her heart started to race.

'Is that so?' She tried to infuse a touch of – more accurately, a huge dollop of – bouncy provocation into her words.

She'd obviously hit the right note; he took another step towards her. He was only inches from her face.

She tilted her head slightly upward, positioned her lips at an inviting angle and slowly ran her tongue along her lower lip. Moist, glistening lips, *Glamour Puss* had advised, were unmissable and sure-fire kissable. She'd often wondered if two sets of lips, one of them over-moistened, ever skidded off each other. With luck, she'd soon find out. Motionless, she stood with her eyes half closed, waiting.

'Unfortunately, it *is* so.' God, was he *still* talking? There was a limit to how long she could hold the position. 'I feel I have to finish something I started a few days ago, but didn't complete. And if I don't do it now, I'm afraid I never will.'

Darn! Her eye muscles were about to go on strike – she'd have to change her pose. She opened her eyes to their full size and assumed an air of wide-eyed innocence. 'What do you mean?'

He smiled into her face.

'I think you know very well what I mean, Evie.'

Behind him, moonlight filtered through the trees, defining every angle, every plane of his features. She stared up at him. Her breath caught in her throat and her mind went blank.

'I do?' she croaked.

'Yes, you do. From the moment I saw you standing on

that bed, I've wanted to do this, and you know it.' He slid his hands up her bare arms and pulled her to him. 'Somehow I've held off till now, but I'm not going to hold off a minute longer. I think you want this, too.'

She looked deep into his eyes. A thunderbolt struck her, and she gasped from the shock of it.

She did; she really did. And it was nothing to do with any story.

She moved imperceptibly closer. He gently cupped her face in his hands, lowered his head and brushed his lips against hers.

'Tom,' she whispered, and he brought his mouth down hard on hers.

She sank into his arms, his raw scent surrounding her, his heart pounding against hers. Oblivious to everything but her need for him, her arms wound behind his head and she pressed closer still, his body hard against hers.

He pulled back sharply.

'I shouldn't be doing this,' he said, his voice thick. 'You work for me; it's taking advantage; it's all wrong.' He took a step back.

She put her hands out to him, but he moved out of her reach, and her hands fell helplessly to her sides.

She stared at him in panic. She had to come up with something, and quickly. They couldn't stop now, not now that she knew how much she wanted him.

An idea came to her. She felt a burst of hope.

She wrinkled her brow and cocked her head to one side. 'But I don't work for you, Tom. I work for the agency, don't I?'

A slow smile crossed his face. 'Why, so you do.'

Opening her eyes wide, she gestured with the upturned palms of her hands. 'And as for what you were doing that you thought you shouldn't be doing, I don't know what you mean. I think I must have blinked and missed whatever it was.'

His eyes crinkled in amusement as he gazed down at her. 'And what do you think I might have been up to, temptress Evie?'

'Oh, I don't know – something to add to my list of favourites, maybe?' Her voice was playfully teasing.

'Now that's a challenge if ever I heard one, and as you know, I can never resist a challenge. Right, so I've got to replace the peaches and *prosciutto*, have I? Well, here goes.'

He moved closer to her. His eyes staring into hers, he ran his thumb very slowly along first her upper lip, then her lower lip, then he leaned over and gently kissed her on the forehead.

She felt his breath hot on her face, and a shiver ran down her spine.

Lowering his head, he kissed the tip of her nose, then lightly grazed her lips. Pressing his mouth harder against hers, his tongue prised her lips apart and slid into the moist warmth of her mouth. His arms tightened around her, and her toes curled in delight.

He pulled away.

She gasped in shock and disappointment.

He stared down at her, his chest rising and falling with his heavy breathing. 'And what was the verdict that time?'

She nibbled her lower lip and made a massive effort to look as if she was weighing up his efforts.

'I'd say that you've knocked the *prosciutto* off the list,' she said finally. 'But I'm afraid those peaches are still right up there at the top.'

'Coming second to a peach! That will never do.' His voice shook with mock horror. 'I'll just have to see if I can do better. If you're up to it, that is.'

'I think I'll risk it.'

Their eyes met.

He stepped forward, ran his fingers through her hair and crushed his lips on hers. The heat from his body spread through her. She put her hand against his chest to steady herself, and felt the solid muscle beneath his shirt. A streak of electricity shot through her. Her every nerve was on fire.

He pulled away.

Drawing their breath in ragged gasps, they stared at each other.

'That's gone to the top of the list,' she said at last. 'Peaches? What are they?'

He shook his head. 'No, Evie, we're not at number one yet.' He held out his hand to her. 'Let's go back to the house and work at hitting that top spot.'

She stared at his hand. Then she raised her eyes to his face and took the hand that he offered. Without speaking, they turned and began to walk back through the olive groves.

By the time that they reached the house, they were laughing and running.

Chapter Thirteen

As for the nitty-gritty

They lay on the large bed, staring up at the rafters, which had been cast in dense shadow by the shaft of silver moonlight that fell through the small skylight into the centre of the room.

'Seeing those wooden beams reminds me how much I owe that scorpion,' Tom said. He tightened his arm around Evie's shoulders and pulled her closer to him. 'Thank God it found its way into your room that first night. If it hadn't, you might still be wearing thick specs, mannish suits and sensible shoes, and I'd have missed out on one of the best weeks of my life. It doesn't bear thinking about.'

'Agreed.' She stretched her arm across his bare chest and nestled into the crook of his shoulder. 'You're absolutely right. We wouldn't have had nearly as much fun as we've had, and we certainly wouldn't be here like this now. So thank you, Mr Scorpion, wherever you are.'

Tom leaned over and kissed the top of her head. 'Talking of suits and sensible shoes, the real world is coming horribly close. Starting on Monday, I've got two weeks of relentless preparation before my next case opens. My only comfort will be knowing that you're beavering away back at the house, a sight for sore eyes if I'm able to get home early enough to see you.' He turned on his side and smiled at her. 'But not a sight to make my eyes sore. I want the new Evie at home – not the old.'

Oh, hell! Panic shot through her.

For several scrummy hours, she'd totally blanked out why she was there. Not why she was in his bed – she was in his bed because she wanted to be in his bed and for no other reason at all – but why she was with him in Italy.

She'd let herself get so carried away, almost literally, by a bloke who was sex on two legs, that she'd completely forgotten that she was there on a job. The fact that she fancied Tom like mad mustn't be allowed to get in the way.

They'd had fun in Italy, but it would come to an end back in England – he'd go back to doing his job and to dating the sort of women he usually dated, and she'd go back to her career. And if her career was going to be that of a journalist, she ought to be focusing on what she was meant to be doing, not on how luscious he was.

Yes, that was what she ought to be doing. She glanced up at him, and her heart gave a lurch. But she couldn't do it. She couldn't use what they had between them to wheedle out of him something he'd never want the world to know.

Swallowing the lump that threatened to block her throat as she realised that she was putting an end to her life's dream, she moved closer to him, needing to feel his warmth next to her.

He inched back his head and glanced down at her. 'Are you all right, Evie? You're suddenly very quiet.'

She attempted a laugh. 'You're not the only person who's not in a hurry to go back to work,' she murmured into his chest. 'I'm not looking forward to returning to the agency.'

He glanced down at her in surprise. 'How come? I thought you were quite happy there for the time being.'

'I am, or rather I was. The agency boss is a bit of a pig and I'm not that keen on having to start taking orders from him again.'

With a sudden movement, he raised himself on his elbow and stared intently at her, his face serious. 'Wait a minute. Your agency boss – that's not boss as in would-be stud, is it?'

'God, no! He wouldn't be able to find the necessary part for a start. No, it's nothing like that.'

An overwhelming temptation to tell him the truth sprang up, and to say how sorry she was for lying to him. She swiftly pushed it away. He might hate her for what she'd thought about doing. She'd tell him on another occasion, when she'd had more time to think about the best way to approach it.

Snuggling closer to him, she blanked all thoughts of confession out of her mind.

'It's not just the idiot boss, it's the thought of the other clients they'll send me out to. I bet no one else brings me to Umbria. After this week, everything else will seem boring, and that's made me decide to start thinking about my future.'

He settled back down again and slid his arm around her. 'That's all right then. In fact, it's better than all right if you're serious about finding a career that's more suited to your talents than working for an agency.'

'What talents did you have in mind?' she asked with a giggle, and she ran her fingers lightly across his chest.

'Nothing like that,' he said with a laugh. 'You're very good with people, Evie, and whatever you do, you should make sure that it doesn't confine you to an office.' He paused. 'In fact, I've had an idea. I think I know someone who might be able to help you. If she can't actually offer you anything, at the very least she'll be able to give you some advice. I'm thinking of Zizi Westenhall.'

She started in surprise. 'The one you just defended?'

'That's the one. But I didn't defend her, as such – I acted for her against that filthy rag, *Pure Dirt*. We sued them for Libel after they accused her of having had an affair. It was one of their so-called exposés. As you can imagine, it was an allegation that didn't exactly delight her husband.'

'I saw her picture in the paper the other day. She's beautiful.'

'Yes, she is. And with a high profile marriage to protect, she couldn't afford to ignore such a malicious slur on her reputation, so we took *Pure Dirt* to court. Happily, the paper lost and was forced to eat its grubby words. I'm glad to say that they had to pay her costs as well as theirs, and also pay a substantial sum in damages. They're the lowest form of scum, that bunch.'

Her eyes filled up. She struggled to take control of herself. Thank goodness she hadn't told Tom she was a *Pure Dirt* reporter. If they never saw each other again after her contract was up, he might never need know and he'd always think well of her.

'I'll get in touch with Zizi as soon as my next case is over,' he added.

'How would she be able to help me, though?'

'Her husband gives a lot of his money away – not just in England, but in other countries, too. Zizi runs some of Howard's charities. It's just possible that they might be able to use you in one of their foundations.'

'That would be fantastic. Did you ever get to meet Howard?'

'When he came to court with her, but not apart from that.'

'Was she nice, Zizi, or was it a case of beauty being only skin deep?'

'Not at all. She's lovely to look at and lovely as a person.'

A shard of jealousy cut into her. Had he slept with Zizi? she wondered. Curiosity joined hands with the green-eyed monster and got the better of her. 'Then you must be a saint to have been able to resist her.' She put her hand up to the side of his face, gently pulled his face to hers and kissed him on the lips. 'It's the first time I've kissed a saint. I just might have to revise my opinion of your suitability for a monastery.'

'I hate to disappoint you, faithful Evie, but I'm not as saintly as you might think.'

'Don't tell me you and Zizi W got your act together?' A pang of misery shot through her, and she held her breath.

He rolled over so that he was half lying on top of her. 'No, we didn't.' He started to run his fingers slowly through her hair. 'We got on really well, went out for dinner a few times, but it ended there. In other circumstances – had she not been married, for example, and had I not just argued her case claiming that she'd done nothing to diminish her reputation – then maybe it would have ended differently. I think it's fair to say that we liked each other. But when it came to it, neither of us wanted more than that, and we've come out of it as friends.'

She let her breath out.

'So you do deserve your saintly status.' She smiled broadly up at him. 'Admittedly, you've done some things I don't exactly associate with a monk or a saint – quite recently, in fact – and I wouldn't have it any other way, but I'd second you for sainthood.'

He shook his head. 'I don't know about that. I reckon we've all done something wrong at some point in our lives, and I'm no exception.'

'But you didn't sleep with Zizi.'

'I wasn't thinking of her. I was thinking of something that happened some years ago. It involved a fax.'

'A fax! What on earth could you do that you shouldn't with a fax? No, don't tell me,' she laughed. 'I think I'd rather not know.'

'Right, I won't.' He rolled back and stared at the ceiling. She glanced across at him and saw amusement flickering on his lips.

'OK, I give in. You've got me curious now. So what did you do with the fax, then?'

He turned towards her, his face suddenly serious. She felt a throb of alarm. 'Don't tell me if you don't want to.'

'I do want to. I've never told anyone before and it'll actually be a relief to tell someone.' He gave her a wry smile. 'Call it my confession, if you like.'

Biting her lip, she nodded.

'As you can imagine, a person can mistakenly be faxed information meant for someone else. If that happens to a barrister, he must instantly send it back without reading it. Information like that's called privileged information, and it's a great offence to read privileged information. If you were caught, you'd be hauled up before a disciplinary committee and you'd certainly be punished. As it happens, I wasn't caught, and I've felt guilty about it ever since. But I've done my best to make amends – I do a lot of *pro bono* cases for people who can't afford to pay.'

'But reading what you shouldn't read happens all the time in offices. It's no big deal.'

'Maybe so in offices, but not at the Bar. I knew I'd be breaking the barristers' code of conduct if I went ahead and read the fax – it was something that the prosecuting barrister had sent to me by mistake – nevertheless, read it I did.'

'Maybe you shouldn't have read it, but as you said just now, we've all done things we shouldn't have done at some time or another.'

'The Bar Standards Board might not agree. They're hot on the rules governing privileged information. I'd been mistakenly sent a list of the strengths and weaknesses of the prosecution's case. I was the defence lawyer, on my first solo libel case, and because of what I'd read, I knew the weak points of the prosecution's argument even before I went into court. Not surprisingly, I made a huge success of the case, and that gave me a terrific start to my career. But in my heart, knowing what I'd done took the gloss off my win.'

'I imagine you've helped a lot of people through your work, Tom. Doesn't that go some way towards making you feel better about what happened?'

'You've a good heart, Evie, and you want to think well of people. In my defence, I was very young at the time. When the document fell into my lap, I couldn't resist the chance it gave me. Also, I might add, the correct person won – my client's reputation had been maliciously damaged and he deserved to win. But I still wish I'd won the case more honestly.'

'As you say, though, it was ever so many years ago, and you were very young.'

'Hey, I'm not that old!' he laughed. 'But it's nice of you to want to defend me.'

She buried her face in his chest and nestled closer. 'So maybe you don't qualify for sainthood. I'm not sure that being in bed with a saint would be high on my wish list, anyway.'

He looked down at her and gave her a lazy smile. 'Thanks, Evie,' he said quietly.

She stared out of her bedroom window in Il Poggio, watching the early morning sun inch its way above distant Todi. Trailing in its wake were long streaks of white-gold light, which slowly drifted across the sky, widening into each other, merging into giant sheets of pale light which swept away the dark of night.

Had she still been on her mission, it would have been accomplished, she told herself. There was nothing incriminating about the Zizi affair – or rather the non-affair – but the fax story, along with the photograph her editor already had, would be enough for him to publish the salacious article he was after.

The paper could say whatever it liked about Tom and Zizi. Since he'd been shown to have done something dishonest in the past, people could easily be persuaded to think he'd crossed the line with his married client whilst at the same time telling the court that she hadn't done anything to damage her reputation.

She could hand in the story. Her editor would be pleased with her and her job would be secure. But as she'd realised in a flash as she lay beside Tom, that wasn't going to happen, not now, not ever.

How ironic, she thought drily, getting something she'd so badly wanted when she no longer wanted it.

She turned away from the cold glass and looked slowly around the room. Her gaze fell on the bedroom door and lingered there. She remembered the look on Tom's face when he'd burst into her bedroom on hearing her scream that first night. She smiled at the spot where he'd stood.

That was the moment when she'd fallen in love with him – she just hadn't allowed herself to recognise it. Not until last night.

Her eyes now wide open, she realised what Eduardo had seen in them when he'd watched her gaze at Tom. It was amazing that she'd managed to fool herself for one whole week that while Tom was fun to be with, he was no more to her than a boss who happened to be a brilliant companion. She'd been so blind.

And not just about Tom. She could see herself clearly for the first time in ages.

Even if she hadn't fallen in love with Tom, she would never have been able to do what *Pure Dirt* had asked her to do; not in any circumstances – she just wasn't wired like that. Yes, she desperately wanted to be a journalist, but not so badly that she'd bring herself to do something absolutely vile to someone else in order to achieve her goal. No way!

She cringed as she remembered telling Rachel and Jess that she was going to focus on the *Pure*, not on the *Dirt*. How naïve of her. The minute you pried into someone's private life and made it public, you were up to your neck in crap. There was nothing pure about printing something about someone that they'd rather other people didn't know, whatever that something was.

God, she'd been so stupid. If only she'd faced the truth about herself and the job earlier in the week, she could have mentally ditched *Pure Dirt* and concentrated on having a bloody good time in Italy. Instead she'd wasted precious time worrying about how to get a story.

No matter how much she dreaded the thought of him knowing why she'd gone to Italy with him, and no matter how much she wanted to think that he might never need to know, she owed it to him to tell him the truth. The way she'd met him was a lie, but there weren't going to be any more lies between them and she wasn't going to live in fear of him learning the truth at some point in the future. She was going to tell him up front about *Pure Dirt*.

But she had to be super cool about the way in which she did it. Blurting it out on their first date in London would be a sure fire way of killing their relationship before it had hardly got off the ground. No, she'd have to do it carefully and at the right time. Which meant she'd have to keep her job at Pure Dirt, and therefore the agency, a little while longer.

Once they'd re-established their relationship, she could tell him about *Pure Dirt* and how she'd turned her back on what had been one ginormous mistake from the start.

She loved Tom and she was convinced that he loved her. With luck, her past wouldn't come between them.

One thing was for certain, though – whatever happened or didn't happen between her and Tom in the future, no one would ever know what he'd told her that night.

Chapter Fourteen

When is a proposal not a proposal?

Tom threw back his cover, walked across the hotel bedroom to the window and pushed open the shutters. Leaning forward against the wooden window sill, he watched as the night began to break up into wide swathes of pale grey and blue that reached out across the sky, each of them outlined by the white sun that rose up behind them, heralding the dawn of the new day.

Their last day together in Italy.

It was true that Evie would be working for him for two more weeks, so in a way they would still be together when they were in England, but it might not be the same. And anyway, his work schedule meant that they wouldn't be physically together, and that's what he wanted. She'd brought a breath of fresh air into his life and he wasn't ready to return to life as it had been before he'd met her.

And he might not have to. Who knew how things would turn out in the future?

But that was for the future.

Their time together in Italy had been a dream. Holding Evie in his arms the night before, having her in his bed, that had been a dream come true – it had been something that was very, very special. For him, anyway. And for Evie, too, he was sure. She wasn't the sort of girl to pretend to feel something that she didn't feel. It was why he always felt so comfortable with her. Or one of the reasons. She was lovely to look at, and she was great fun. There were so many reasons why he enjoyed being with her.

And he fervently hoped that she felt the same about him.

One of the sprinklers came on in front of his window. The scent of damp grass reached him. He leaned further forward and inhaled the morning air. He'd miss that aroma when he was back in London. His small paved garden was lovely, but not as lovely as the Umbrian garden that was waiting for him whenever he drove through the wrought-iron gates and on to his drive.

And Evie liked the house and garden, too.

He could tell that she genuinely did. The longer the week had gone, the more she'd glowed with happiness and relaxation. There wasn't any place that they'd been to, any sight that they'd seen, that she hadn't responded to in a positive, lively sort of way. She had a natural charm, a lovely way with her. And while he'd always appreciated the skill and professionalism of his regular interpreter, he was absolutely delighted that the man had been unable to come with him. Otherwise, he would never have met Evie. And that would be a loss.

He straightened up. He'd have a shower, make a start on packing, and then go for his last breakfast with Evie on the terrace. As he turned away from the window, he suddenly felt very forlorn.

Evie stood beside her packed bags on the terrace and glanced at her watch. In just over four hours they'd be on the plane going home, and that was a depressing thought. It had been a brilliant week and she didn't want it to end.

But come to an end, it had. They were about to go back to the real world, a world full of tests they'd both have to face, and there was no way of knowing what the future would bring. The end of their week in Italy might just herald the end of her relationship with Tom.

'Ah, Evie!' The husky tones of Gabriela sounded from behind her. She spun round and saw Gabriela coming quickly across the terrace towards her. 'I'm very glad that I'm not too late to see you. I was so worried that you would already have left.'

'Gabriela!' She smothered her dismay. Gabriela, cool in a body-hugging, scoop-necked grey silk dress, was the very last person she wanted to see. 'Tom's on the phone. I didn't expect to see you here – I thought you would have had more than enough of us after yesterday. It was a lovely day, by the way. Thank you again.'

'Eduardo and I couldn't let our friends go back to England without saying goodbye, could we?'

For God's sake, why not? And surely they weren't going to get Eduardo, too! She could just imagine his leave-taking rituals before they flew off to England, if his goodbyes earlier in the week were anything to go by. Her heart sank.

'My poor Evie, you look so sad. I know that this is because you and Tom are going home, but I'm sure you'll be back in Italy before too long. And we will be meeting many times before that. Indeed, sooner than you think. You and Tom are not the only ones who are flying to London very soon – I shall be going on Tuesday.' Scarlet lips beamed at Evie.

Ohhhh, shit!

She'd have enough to do in London in the following couple of weeks, what with Tom and *Pure Dirt* to deal with, without having to think about Gabriela, too. Gabriela was OK, but she was quite intense. She'd have to find a way of politely keeping her at a distance if she and Tom were going to have a chance to see how they got on in London.

'How come you're going so soon? I thought you weren't going for at least another week.'

'I start my work in a week's time. By flying out on Tuesday, I will have some days to settle in before that time. I'm hoping that we will meet next week in London.'

'Who's going to be meeting who next week in London?' Tom asked, coming up to them. 'Sorry to keep you waiting, Evie. I had a call from Chambers and I couldn't not take it.'

'I'm hoping that I will be meeting Evie.' Gabriela's smile all but reached from ear to ear. 'I am flying to London on Tuesday, and I have just a few days before I must start work. I'm hoping that Evie will come with me in those days to help me to get some things I need.'

'I really wish I could, Gabriela, but I'm working for Tom for the next two weeks so I'm afraid it won't be possible.' Evie's smile was almost as wide as Gabriela's.

'Oh, that is such a shame. I think you have taste and could help me. She does have such good taste, does she not, Tom?'

Tom's gaze ran down Evie's purple and lime green striped sundress, then back up to the dark blue barrette on top of her head. 'Pass,' he said with a wry smile.

'Perhaps, if you are not too tired, we could meet at the end of one of the days to shop a little, Evie.'

Which bit of 'no' didn't Gabriela get? Although come to think of it, she hadn't actually said the word 'no'. She opened her mouth.

'Oh, I think we can do better than that, Gabriela. You can work at the house on Monday and Tuesday, Evie, but for the rest of the week, your job will be to help Gabriela to find what she needs and to settle in. Perhaps you'd come back to the house on Friday afternoon, though, in case there are any loose ends that need tying up before the weekend, but Wednesday and Thursday are yours to spend with Gabriela. There now, you've got your helper, Gabriela.'

'That is very kind of you, Tom.' Gabriela was positively purring. Evie struggled to hide her annoyance.

'Not at all, Gabriela,' Tom said cheerfully. 'It's the least I can do after everything Eduardo has done to help to me.

He's gone way beyond the requirements of the job, and the result is one stunning home. No, you and Evie go off and have some fun – perhaps take in some places of interest between the shopping, maybe even see a show.' He glanced across the terrace towards the car park. 'Speaking of Eduardo ...'

Evie and Gabriela turned at the same moment and saw Eduardo hurrying towards them from the parking area on the far side of the terrace.

'*Buon giorno!*' he cried as he reached them, his hands outstretched, his face wreathed in smiles.

'I must settle the bill,' Tom said quickly, turning to leave. 'Then we'll go. I'm off to Reception. I won't be long.'

There was a rustle of silk as Gabriela moved swiftly to Tom's side and started walking alongside him towards the hotel entrance. 'I'll come with you, Tom,' Evie heard her say. 'I have written down my London address for you, but I'd like to give you my mobile number.'

'I bet you would,' Evie thought, as she turned back to Eduardo. He put his hands on her shoulders, looked into her face for a long moment, then leaned forward and lightly kissed her on both cheeks. The musky scent of his cologne embraced her. She stepped back and smiled brightly. It was very kind of him and Gabriela to come and see them off, she told him, especially as it was still very early in the day.

Oh, no, he exclaimed. After such a wonderful week, he couldn't let them go without saying goodbye in person, and Gabriela felt the same. She was happy to know that she already had friends in London, and he was happy to feel that Tom had become a good friend. He looked forward to seeing him frequently in Italy. And, he added happily, Tom would need an interpreter until he was able to speak Italian or until he, Eduardo, was able to speak English.

Tom would probably use his regular interpreter in the

future, Evie cut in, but Eduardo waved aside her comment with a flourish of his hand. Evie was so much better in the role and so much more beautiful to look at. Tom would never go back to using that other man. His grimace of distaste was accompanied by a gesture of dismissal.

She glanced across to the reception area, but Tom and Gabriela were hidden behind the other people there, so she turned back to Eduardo and began to thank him for everything he'd done for them during the week. In a graceful gesture, he raised his hand to interrupt her. Profusely apologising for doing so, he said that time was short and there was something he wanted to ask her; he would rather ask her it while she was by herself.

God, he wasn't going to propose, was he? She stared to him in horror. That would be so, so embarrassing.

He gave a little cough. He'd sensed that she and Tom were close, he began hesitantly, but if this closeness did not last – he knew that he was being bold to suggest such a thing, but he was sure that she would understand why he'd said it when he finished what he had to say, and that she would forgive him for speaking in such a way – but if she and Tom drew apart when they were back in England, he would like her to consider returning to Umbria to work for him.

Her mouth fell open in amazement.

With his business expanding, he quickly explained, and with many people coming from England and America to buy properties in Italy, he needed to take on someone who was fluent in both English and Italian, who got on well with people, who had an eye for design – he paused for a moment and she thought she saw him wince as he glanced at the purple and lime green stripes in front of him – and who knew something about the property world.

He would like Evie to be that person.

He realised that she didn't know much about the property business, but he could teach her what she needed to know, and he was confident that if they put their talents together, they would be able to make his enterprise one of the most dynamic in the region.

She stared at him, momentarily stunned by what he was saying. It was a proposal all right – but very different from the one she'd feared.

'*Grazie mille*,' she began. She was very flattered by what he was offering, but although she'd loved her year in Lake Garda and her stay in Umbria, and hoped to come back again as often as she could, she couldn't possibly imagine permanently leaving England and her friends.

He shrugged his shoulders – England and Italy were not so far away that she couldn't often visit her friends in England. What was it – just over two hours in the air? That was nothing. He asked of her only to think about it, and to know that even if she turned his proposal down, the offer would always be there in case one day she might want to take it up.

It was very kind of him, she repeated, but she couldn't imagine anything happening that could ever make her want to leave London. However, she assured him, she would think about it.

'*Prometti*,' he insisted with a smile.

'*Prometto*,' she laughed.

And she need not worry, he added with a sad smile, whatever he felt deep in his heart, he would ask no more of her than that they be friends; very good friends, but no more.

Then he glanced at the watch on his slender wrist and threw up his hands in horror. He had a property to look at in Deruta and he had to be off. Regretfully, he would have to leave without saying a proper goodbye to Tom. Asking her to give him his best wishes, he took his business card from his pocket and gave it to her. Then he gave her a little bow, turned and went back to his car.

Life's a bitch, she thought as she watched his convertible glide out of the parking area and turn down the steep hill. If only she could have fallen in love with Eduardo, everything would have been so much easier.

She turned to look back at the hotel. The crowd of people had moved away and she caught a glimpse of Tom and Gabriela standing in front of the reception desk, talking and laughing together. They were getting on like a bloody house on fire, she thought irritably. Fair enough, Gabriela had turned out to be OK, but she would be even more OK if she stayed put in Italy.

Tom looked up and caught her eye across the terrace. He nodded to her, said something to Gabriela and they made their way out of the hotel and across to her.

'Where's Eduardo?' Tom asked, looking around.

'He couldn't wait any longer. Something about a property in Deruta that he had to visit.'

'I must have been longer than I realised. I'm sorry about that. We'll be able to get off in a moment. I see that your bags are already here. They'll be bringing mine out any minute now.'

'That's them, isn't it?' She pointed to a couple of black leather bags being carried on to the terrace.

'You're right. You wait here and I'll go and get the car.' He turned to Gabriela. 'There's not much point in saying goodbye now, Gabriela. I'm sure we'll meet up in the next couple of weeks. And if we don't, which I regret is possible – I've got a mass of work to do for the case that's starting shortly – if we don't, I'll make sure that we get together as soon as the case is finished. You can count on that. So *arrividerci* for now!' He kissed her on both cheeks and started to go across to the parking area.

'My car is in the *parcheggio*, too. I'll walk with you,' Gabriela said quickly. 'I have your telephone number, Evie, and I shall ring you when I am in London. *Ciao per il momento!*' With a little wave at the air beside Evie, she joined Tom.

A few minutes later, Evie saw Gabriela's car drive out of the car park, and soon after that, Tom appeared in the four-by-four. He pulled up on the terrace in front of her, jumped out and loaded their bags into the car. Then he went round to the passenger side and opened the door for her. Bowing low, he indicated with a sweeping gesture that she should get in. She giggled.

'You see, I'm catching on to the Italian way of doing things.' Grinning, he swung the door shut behind her, walked round the back of the car, climbed into the driver's seat and switched on the engine. Then he threw the car into gear and began to drive slowly out of the hotel precinct.

'It's a pity that Eduardo had to dash off. I wanted to thank him again for his help this week,' he remarked as they reached the foot of the slope and turned in the direction of Todi. 'It's been a superb week.' He glanced at Evie. 'And its success has been down to you, Evie. You've been great fun and a bloody good translator.'

She laughed. 'OK. What's the punch line?'

He sent her a quick smile. 'For once, there's no punch line.'

'Well, then, I'll say that I, too, think it's been a brilliant week. And, what's more, I'm returning to England with the offer of a job.'

'A job? What job?'

'Eduardo's asked me to work for him.'

'The hell he has!' He looked quickly at her, then his eyes returned to the road and he headed the car for the Rome motorway. 'Doing what exactly?'

'Doing a bit of this and that, I think. Although he said he'd teach me what I needed to know about the property business, I think the main thing would be to translate for prospective American and English buyers, and he's just tarted it up a bit.'

'He's got a nerve, trying to poach someone who's working for me, don't you think?'

'But I'm not exactly working for you, am I? I work for the agency. I've only got two more weeks with you – Eduardo knows I'm a temp.'

There was a short pause. 'Well, what answer did you give him?'

'That I wanted to stay in England, of course. Why would I want to leave my mates?'

'Good answer, Evie.' He smiled broadly at the road ahead. 'Very good answer indeed.'

Chapter Fifteen

Yes, it's only just begun ...

Reaching Fiumicino Airport in excellent time, they checked in their luggage and found a sofa in the executive lounge. Tom ordered them each a cappuccino.

'Right,' he said when their coffees had arrived, 'tell me about these mates of yours that you don't want to leave. You share a place with them, I think you said earlier in the week.'

'That's right. Rachel, Jess and I go back a long way – we were at school together. I certainly wouldn't want to live in a different country from them. No way.'

'Where did you say you lived?'

'In Camden Town. Not that far from you, in fact – we're at the bottom of the hill and you're at the top. It's a fun place to live. It's got a great mixture of people and a real buzz to it. And you can't beat the Camden Lock market, which is very near us. Most weekends we have a trawl around it. You can get some fab things there, like amazing vintage clothes.'

'And are Rachel and Jess also temps?'

'Temps?'

'Yes, temps like you. Do they work for an agency like you do?'

'No. Rachel is a PA for a production designer. Come to think of it, she and Eduardo might get on well together. Perhaps not – she doesn't know a word of Italian and I can't see her lasting long in a silent relationship.'

'Most men would describe that as the dream relationship. I can see that it might be viewed differently by a woman, though.'

She smiled at him across the low coffee table. 'I'm not going to rise to that. As for Jess, she's an events' planner.'

'The three of you sound quite a mix, with Rachel sort of in the world of production design, Jess planning extravaganzas and you the sharpest agency temp that I've ever met.'

'Don't say that word! I inwardly groan every time you say agency. I think we should ban the use of that word for the whole of the next two weeks. More and more I'm hoping that Zizi Westenhall can come up with something.'

'I'll have a word with her as soon as I'm able. I promise. In the meantime, are you going to let me see you next week?'

'That's a strange question, unless of course you're planning to walk in, out and around your house with your eyes shut. If you're not, you can count on seeing me next week, and hopefully the week after.'

'Not so strange, literal Evie. Much as my eyes might wish to, my work schedule is unlikely to allow me to see you by day, so we must focus on the night, and in fact, only on Saturday night as I'll be working the other nights.'

Thank you, thank you, God! He *did* still want to date her when they were back in London. Bloody brilliant! And since in her head she'd already quit *Pure Dirt* – as they'd soon find out – she could let rip and have an amazing, guilt-free time with Tom. It didn't get much better than that. She felt the tension that she hadn't known she'd felt drain away from her. It was all coming together.

The sound of Tom's mobile phone cut into her thoughts.

He pulled his grey jacket towards him, took his phone from his pocket and flicked it open. 'Why, Gabriela, this is a surprise. We only spoke a couple of hours ago.' He leaned back against the sofa, stretched his legs out in front of him and pushed his jacket away from him.

In the sweeping movement of his arm, she glimpsed his lightly tanned chest through his open-necked shirt. God, he was gorgeous, and he was hers – well, for the time being anyway. Her gaze travelled from button to button, moving slowly down his crisp white shirt to the belt of his charcoal grey trousers, skimming his hips and settling on his thighs, and on the hint of hard muscle beneath the light material. Absolutely gorgeous.

'Fine, Gabriela. Thanks for passing that on. Tell Eduardo to do what he thinks is best. I trust him.' He was silent for a moment as he listened to the voice at the other end of the line, then he laughed, said goodbye and flicked shut the phone.

'Some problem with the poplar we wanted for the chests of drawers. The co-operative phoned Eduardo about it, and Gabriela was anxious to catch me before we left. You heard me say that Eduardo can sort it out. I suspect she's a bit of a worrier, Gabriela. I suppose it'll be quite pleasant to see her in London, though. In a way it'll be like having a part of Umbria with us in England, don't you think?'

No, she didn't think. And even if it was, she'd much rather that the whole of Umbria stayed in Umbria.

Before she could come up with a tactful yet honest reply – she was done being a fake – Tom suddenly sat up and stared intently at the information board above her head.

'What's up?'

'We've been asked to go to the boarding gate, that's what's up. What perfect timing. They've waited for us to finish our coffee and now they're asking us to board the plane. So, Evie, let's go home.'

Slipping on his jacket as he stood up, he held out his hand to her. She took it, and they joined the stream of travellers who were making their way towards the airport train that would take them to the area of their boarding gate. After a short wait to board the plane, they found their seats and settled down. He clicked his seat belt shut, leaned back against the headrest and turned to look at Evie.

'You know that song "We've only just begun"? Well, that's exactly how I feel – we've only just begun, you and I. It's been a marvellous week, and I know we're going to have a lot more weeks just like it in the future.' He paused. 'Well, haven't you anything to add, then?'

She laughed. 'Are you fishing for an ego-massage?'

'If that's the only massage on offer,' he said with a grin, 'bring it on.'

She glanced across at Tom. His eyes were shut, and she turned back to look out of the window at the world in miniature beneath them.

They'd only been gone a week, but it felt a zillion times longer. What a week it had been.

When she'd left London, she hadn't been in love, and now she was.

A week ago, she'd thought she'd make an awesome investigative journalist, and now she knew she wouldn't.

Seven days ago, she hadn't known that she was going to defy her editor, and now she did.

Her editor. She felt a stab of cold fear. Knowing how best to tell him was going to be a problem.

It was essential that she and Tom had some quality time together before she told him the truth, which meant that she mustn't quit her job till after that. If she did, her pig of an editor might go berserk, pick up the phone and tell Tom why she'd really gone to Italy with him. And if she hadn't already told him the truth by then, it would certainly be the end of their relationship. So somehow or other, she was going to have to string the editor along for at least the first week she was back.

She glanced out of the window again and saw that the plane was losing height. They must be very close to Heathrow.

She couldn't wait to get back to Camden Town to tell Rachel and Jess that she was turning her back on *Pure Dirt*. The minute they heard her news, they'd go back to being the way they used to be. Obviously, she wouldn't tell them what Tom had told her – she'd never pass his secrets on to anyone – but she'd make sure they knew she could have given a story to *Pure Dirt*, but had chosen to quit instead. They needed to know that faced with a choice, she'd made the right one.

She gave a deep sigh. It would be a tricky couple of weeks ahead, but she'd make sure she got it right – there was too much at stake to make a mistake. She and Tom were meant to be, and that was the way it was going to stay.

The landing gear ground noisily into position. Tom opened his eyes.

She turned to him and smiled. 'You were right earlier on, Tom. You said it had been a marvellous week, and it has, and I've got a feeling that the next few weeks are going to be even better still.'

Chapter Sixteen

From one friend to another ...

'That's day one of minding Gabriela gone. Only one and a half more days to go. She's turning out to be OK, though,' Evie told Rachel and Jess as they reclined on dark brown leather sofas around a low table in their favourite wine bar. She leaned across and helped herself to the last of the nachos from the plate. 'To be honest, I wasn't that keen on her at first as she looks quite hard, but the more you get to know her, the nicer she is. Also, I was a bit put off when I met her in Italy as I thought she might have set her sights on Tom, but now I'm sure I was wrong about that.'

'What makes you think you were wrong?' Jess asked. 'You've hardly met her. A person's first instinct is often spot on.'

'Well, I'm certain mine wasn't. Call it a gut feeling, if you like. And what makes me even more sure is that at lunch today, she told me that she's really keen on someone in Florence. They've been an item for several months, but Eduardo doesn't know about him yet.'

'And that's why she's come to England for a year, is it? Because she's so keen on him,' Jess said, glancing at Rachel in amusement. 'Yeah, that makes good sense.'

'Very funny. It's not that simple. Gabriela's high-powered, and I bet she's also high-maintenance. Her guy's changed his job a few times and that's a worry for her. Just because she loves him, it doesn't mean she's brain-dead. She's put a bit of distance between them so they can find out what they really feel about each other.'

'Quite a big bit of distance, if you ask me.' Rachel picked

up the bottle of red wine from the centre of the table and topped up their glasses.

'Duh! Italy's not that far away. She'll go back to Florence, and he'll come over here. They'll see each other – just not as often. And if they're still together at the end of the year, they'll know that it's obviously meant to be. That's the plan, anyway.'

Jess gave a derisory laugh. 'It sounds a bit of an iffy plan, if you ask me. If you want to find out whether you can live with someone, you spend time with them – you don't leave them for months on end. Also, absence makes the heart grow fonder – everyone knows that – so how will she know at the end of the year what's real and what's not?'

'To go back to something you said before we got on to the love life of Gabriela, Evie,' Rachel cut in, 'you said she was nicer than you'd thought she'd be. Nice in what way? Nice as in a saintly sort of person, i.e. mega dull and to be avoided at all costs, or nice as in cool and fun to hang out with?'

'I wouldn't exactly say she was cool – cool's a bit funky and she's super sophisticated, not funky at all. She's so together, always dressed to the nines and not a hair out of place – at least, she has been every time I've seen her so far. That's what makes her come across as hard. She doesn't come across as saintly and boring, either. She's pleasant, that's all.'

'Where did you go with her today, you jammy individual?' Jess asked. 'What wouldn't I give to be paid to wander around the shops all day?'

Evie laughed. 'It's a tough life, but someone's got to do it. We wandered down New Bond Street, hung around that area, had lunch in the Carluccio's in Fenwick's, then we got a cab to Knightsbridge and walked around there for a bit.'

'Did you go into Harrods?' Rachel asked.

'Yes, but not for long. We wandered around the departments and had a quick look at the Diana memorial downstairs, but today was more about getting to know each other. She obviously wants to be friends. Why, I don't know, but she does. Anyway, we finished up with a glass of wine at the top of Harvey Nicks. The only things we bought were some magazines for Gabriela and some food and drink.'

Rachel held up her hands in mock disbelief. 'What, no shoes? That's got to be a first for you. But to move on to something even more interesting than la bella Gabriela – I can't wait to meet her, by the way – what's the latest on Tom? When's he taking you out? And very important, when are we going to meet him?'

'Give me a chance! I haven't seen him since we got back from Italy, he's got so much work to do. He's got a big case starting in two weeks' time. And being away for a week didn't help.'

'But surely you can find a moment to be together,' Rachel said in disbelief.

'It's not that easy. On Monday and Tuesday, he was gone before I got to the house and he didn't get back till after I'd left. He wrote me a note each day, though, saying how much he was longing to see me again and how frustrated he was at having to go into Chambers so early and stay on so late. But now that I'm babysitting Gabriela, I don't go to the house at all, and I won't till Friday afternoon, and he'll still be at work then, anyway.'

Jess looked at her curiously. 'Why don't you visit at night, once he's home? Don't you want to see him?'

'Of course I do. I can't wait to see him and I think about him all day. Despite the fact that I feel soooo bad about the *Pure Dirt* thing, and am dreading what he'll say when I tell him the truth, I want to spend every single minute I can with him. But he said at the start that he'd be working long days and in the evenings, and even on Sundays, and we'd probably only be able to see each other on Saturdays.'

'So no prizes for guessing you're seeing him on Saturday then,' Rachel said. 'Where are you going?'

'He's taking me out to dinner.'

'What are you going to wear?' Rachel and Jess asked at the same time.

'God knows! Gabriela wants to buy some new clothes tomorrow so I'll probably look for something for myself while I'm out with her, though I'm not convinced that Gabriela's sort of shop will be mine. In fact, I'm sure it won't be.'

'Rachel and I thought that the three of us could go to Wagamama on Friday evening and then perhaps on to a club. Why don't you ask Gabriela to come with us? I bet she likes noodles – they're not that different from spaghetti – and then we can show her some London nightlife. I'm curious to meet her. We both are. If we get on well with her, she might be willing to see if the company she's with can throw some work my way. They must have events that need planning.'

'Why not? I reckon I could put up with her for an evening. But only for the Wagamama part of the evening. I don't think she'd be into clubbing, and I'm certainly not going to get wasted on the night before my first date in England with Tom. My first date with him, period – in Italy we weren't dating. No, I'll definitely give clubbing a miss. I'll ask Gabriela when I see her tomorrow.'

Rachel leaned forward in her chair. 'So, Evie,' she said firmly. 'We want the lowdown on *Pure Dirt* now. You've told us about Tom and you've told us about Gabriela. You've said that you're jacking in *Pure Dirt,* but that's all that you've said. We know you've come to your senses at last, but we want the gory details about why.'

136

'Rachel's right. We want to know what happened to your Pure intention of digging up Dirt on Tom, so spill the beans before we explode.'

'It's dead simple: both of you were right and I was wrong. I thought I could do it, but I found I couldn't. I must have been completely delusional ever to think I could do such a nasty thing to anyone. That means that soon I'll be out of a job. And whatever I finally manage to get, it won't be to do with magazines. I can't even bear to think about that.'

Jess leaned forward. 'Wait a minute – when you say you found you couldn't do it, does that mean that you found a story, but came to your senses and decided that it was a shit-awful thing to do to anyone? Or is it that you couldn't discover anything nasty about Tom?'

'The first. Sort of. I did find out something, but it was something Tom volunteered after I'd realised I could never go through with it. I don't think it's that much, but my frigging editor could easily make it into more than it is. He rang yesterday and asked – and that's a nice way to describe his tone of voice – asked me where my copy was.'

'What did you tell him?'

'That he originally said I didn't have to send it in till my last day of working for Tom – he'd thought I might need the two weeks in London to get more details. I told him that I needed that time if I was going to make it as good as it could be. He bought it. I could hear him drooling and dribbling at the other end of the line, the pig.'

'But why didn't …?' Rachel began.

Evie hunched her shoulders and held up her hands in front of her. 'OK. You don't need to say it. You're going to ask why I didn't tell him straight out where to stick his effing job.'

'Hole in one.'

'I haven't quit yet because before I do, I must tell Tom the real reason why I went to Italy with him. If we've got any future together, even if it's only a short term future, I don't want it to be built on top of a whopping great lie.'

Jess beamed at her. 'At least you're thinking like a human being now, not like a muckraker. Isn't she, Rach?'

Rachel nodded.

'If I told the editor that I hadn't been able to find out anything, or if I just quit the magazine, he'd be so bloody mad at me for wasting a once in a lifetime chance to wreck the life of someone he really hates, that he might be vindictive enough to tell Tom the truth about me. I'd never put it past him. You can't predict how a scumbag like that will react.'

'Would it really matter that much if he told him?' Rachel asked.

'It would if he told Tom before I told him. He'd put me in the worst possible light, and it would instantly kill off any chance of there being a Tom and me – Tom would never believe that I'd intended to confess all to him. I don't know for sure if the pig would do that, but I'm not taking any chances.'

'I suppose that makes sense, when you think about it,' Jess said.

'It really does. By stalling him like I did, I've got him off my back for a bit, and I've given myself time to see if Tom and I click in England like we did in Italy. I'll have some idea of that when we've been out on Saturday. Saturday evening is mega important to me.'

'Suppose you don't click?' Jess asked. 'What then?'

'Then nothing. I'll never tell anyone what Tom told me – that stays with me whatever happens or doesn't happen. There wouldn't be any need to tell Tom about *Pure Dirt*, though, as it wouldn't matter. Tom would go his way and I'd go mine. I'd temp until I get another job.'

'And if you do click?'

'I'll tell Tom at the end of next week, probably on the Friday or Saturday. Instead of giving the editor a story on the Friday, I'll tell him to get stuffed. If I don't see Tom that night, I'll tell him on the Saturday. The editor wouldn't be able to contact him till the following week, and by then he'd be too late.'

'It's brill that you've seen the light, Evie. Rachel and I knew you would.'

'You could have fooled me! You were really shitty to me before I went away.'

Jess shrugged dismissively. 'That's water under the proverbial. So how about we celebrate the return of the Evie we know and love with another bottle of wine? Yeah, I know – any excuse. And we'll get some more nachos. This time we'll go the whole hog and have the works – nachos, sour cream, guacamole, salsa and jalapeno peppers. Not to mention lashings of melted cheese on top.'

Chapter Seventeen

Come into my parlour ...

It had been a highly satisfactory first full day in London, Gabriela purred inwardly. Her coffee cup in her hand, she strolled over to the large front window of her first floor apartment in the Holland Park house leased by the Italian design company she worked for, and gazed out. Highly satisfactory.

It had been just the sort of day that she'd had in mind when she'd brought forward the date of her flight to London, thereby giving herself the chance of having two or three days alone with Evie before she started on the project that she'd been sent to England to oversee. These were days in which they would begin to get to know each other, to bond closely and to see each other as friends. And this was what was happening.

She gave a thin smile of satisfaction.

The invention of Alessandro had been inspired. And how easily she'd been able to make Evie believe that she, Gabriela di Montefiore, had fallen in love with a man of no status. As if she, with her superior background and education, would find herself enamoured of a man the English would term a loser. She gave a short laugh of derision, raised the small white china espresso cup to her lips and moved over to the window.

Sipping her coffee as she stared out at the leafy garden in the centre of the square, her dark eyes gradually narrowed their focus to a man and woman who were lying in the middle of the grass, clearly hoping to catch the last rays of the late afternoon sun. The man had undone his shirt and opened it wide in order to let the sun hit the bare skin of his grotesque belly, and the woman had rolled her denim skirt up to the top of her wide thighs and lay with them splayed apart.

An expression of distaste flickered across Gabriela's face and she turned away from the window.

She'd never understand the obsession of the English with getting their skin as brown and leathery as possible. They had no sense of what was beautiful, and they seemed completely unable to appreciate the elegance and the refinement of pale skin. Instead of rejoicing in the natural pallor of the English skin, they removed their clothes at the first hint of sunshine and put themselves where everyone could see their ugliness and watch the sweat pouring off their obscene bodies.

Shuddering at the image that filled her mind, she went out of the sitting room, across the hall and into the narrow kitchen. There she carefully put her cup and saucer into the dishwasher, straightened the brushed stainless steel toaster that stood on the granite worktop so that it was in line with the rim of the white cupboard, returned the coffee beans to the wall cupboard and went back to the sitting room again.

Pausing in the middle of the room, she stood for a few moments looking around her, thinking about possible ways of dressing the room so as to give it the appropriate aesthetic appeal for somewhere that was to be her home for several months, somewhere that would, in effect, be an extension of herself and a reflection of her values. Then she moved to the long glass coffee table in front of the black leather sofa and bent over the table to the large pile of magazines that she'd bought when she was out with Evie.

Early in the day, she'd mentioned to Evie that she'd like to buy a magazine or two. To her surprise, Evie had stiffened. She didn't even know if Evie was aware of it, but there was a definite charge in the air, and it was noticeable that she'd had to remind her several times in the day about the magazines.

In the end, Evie had selected some magazines about fashion, design and houses, but she'd pressed her to include the most popular of the celebrity magazines. These were not really seen in Italy where people's privacy was something to be respected, she'd added, and she was curious to discover if they were as unpleasant as she'd heard.

After a quick flick through the heap of magazines on the table, she selected three and sank gracefully to the sofa. She smoothed her trousers over her knees, pulled the first of the magazines to her and opened it. Her mobile phone sounded. She dropped the magazines on to the floor, hurriedly took the phone from her bag, glanced at the contact name and gave a slight exclamation of disappointment.

'*Pronto, Eduardo*,' she said into the phone, and leaned back, waiting for him to draw a breath between the questions he was excitedly plying her with, one after the other.

Her apartment seemed to be well-located, she was eventually able to tell him. It was in a lovely large house, which had rooms with very high ceilings. He would adore the ornate carvings on the cornices and ceiling roses. Yes, she was quite certain that both the apartment and its location would suit her well.

And yes, she had seen Evie. In fact, they had just spent a very pleasant day together and were fast becoming good friends; she would be seeing her again the following day. And no, she hadn't forgotten that he wanted her to try to encourage Evie to think seriously about his offer of a job. She obviously hadn't had time to bring up the subject yet, and nor would it have been appropriate, but she would definitely approach it when the time was right.

Poor Eduardo, she thought, as she ended the call with an assurance that she'd speak to him again before the weekend. She could hear the emotion in his voice at the mere mention of Evie.

She slipped her phone back into her bag. What a relief it had been that Evie hadn't been interested in Eduardo. For Eduardo, with his breeding, talent and good looks, to have allied himself with someone as paltry as Evie would have been completely out of the question, and the whole situation, had Evie felt differently about Eduardo, could have led to unpleasant dissension within the family.

Evie most assuredly did not have the style, education and background that were the prerequisites for anyone being admitted into the Montefiori family. Admittedly a sense of style could possibly have been taught to her – she was reasonably attractive and could have been shown how to carry off the right sort of clothes – but breeding was something that you either had or did not have, and Evie most definitely did not have it.

But it was, of course, too soon for Eduardo to be thinking about the realities and practicalities of the situation. He still imagined himself to be in love and was languishing in the knowledge that her interest lay elsewhere, but when his misery had passed – and pass it would – he, too, would see that such a union would never have been suitable and he would find a girl from among the best families in Tuscany and Umbria.

Now that Evie was back in England out of his sight, Eduardo would more swiftly come to his senses. She, Gabriela, would ensure that Eduardo's healing process continued uninterrupted. Evie was never to be encouraged to consider for so much as one moment taking up the offer of a job made to her by her besotted brother.

She leaned back against the sofa and stared at the wall on the other side of the room. But it was more than just the Evie and Eduardo abomination that had brought her prematurely to England: it was also the situation between Evie and Tom.

After the night the four of them had had dinner together in Casigliano, high on the hillside, she had gone back with Eduardo to his house in Todi and he had told her that he feared that Evie had eyes only for Tom.

A shiver ran through her as she remembered how she'd felt at that moment.

To remove Evie from his thoughts, she'd encouraged him to keep on thinking this way, telling him that it was more than likely that someone like Evie would try her luck with such a rich, successful man in the week that they'd been thrown together. She had honestly believed that this might be so. She didn't tell Eduardo, however, that she was confident that it would never be any more than a passing fling on Tom's side, if, indeed, he had succumbed to Evie's advances.

Evie was no more suitable to be the wife of a rich, successful lawyer like Tom, an intelligent, educated man, who had two homes, possibly more, with his main home being in one of the most desirable and exclusive parts of London, than she was for Eduardo. A man in Tom's position could do so much better for himself, and he would be well aware of that.

Tom would be looking for an educated woman, well bred, with a natural elegance and flair, who knew how to dress and to move in the best of social circles; a woman capable of being a skilled hostess in his home and of presiding over elegant dinner parties thrown for friends and colleagues; a woman who was of the same intellectual level as he was. She knew exactly the sort of person that Tom needed.

The thought of him and Evie together on a permanent basis was ludicrous, and she was ninety-nine percent certain that this would never happen.

But there was one percent of uncertainty, and it was that one percent that accounted for her being in London sooner than she'd planned.

She impatiently kicked aside the magazines on the floor with a foot shod in a neat, black crocodile pump, stood up and went to the large, silver-framed mirror that hung above the mantelpiece.

Her reflection stared back at her. Her cap-sleeved designer black top was tucked into tailored black trousers that skimmed her slim hips, and a narrow, black leather belt encircled her waist, defining its slenderness. Her dark hair curved sleekly down the sides of her face, emphasizing her high cheekbones as it wound into a sleek black chignon that was coiled at the nape of her neck. She didn't need to see the back of her head to know that not a single hair was out of place. Her mouth widened into a thin smile of satisfaction.

Yes, just as she knew exactly the sort of person that Eduardo needed to marry, she knew exactly the sort of person that Tom needed to marry. She'd known it from the moment that Eduardo had told her about his English client, and had shown her the photograph of Tom standing next to the Umbrian house he'd just bought.

So convinced had she been that Tom was the man for her that she had promptly set in motion a transfer to London for a year, confident that all she needed to do was put herself in Tom's path in order to achieve the desired outcome.

Seeing Evie and Tom through Eduardo's eyes had given her a jolt. It had shown her that she must not be complacent. If she was going to be sure of securing Tom for herself, she would have to remove Evie from his life. The only way she could do this was by getting to know the girl, finding the weak spot in her relationship with Tom, and exploiting it. It would be a kindness to Tom to do so.

Her eyes narrowed as she turned away from the mirror and looked around her. Nothing, and no one, was going to thwart the desires of a Montefiori.

Chapter Eighteen

If it's Friday ...

Evie sat back in her seat and watched in amusement as Gabriela looked around the restaurant, her eyes coming to settle on her paper place mat and the series of squiggles that the waiter had written on it.

'It certainly is very different from any restaurant I've been to before,' Gabriela remarked. 'I like it very much. I don't think we have such places in Italy, but we should. I like the way we sit at one long table and are given our food as soon as it's cooked – it's very clever the way they send the order to the kitchen. And the food was *molto buono*, as we say in Italy. It was very good.'

Rachel nodded. 'We like it. I always have thin noodles, but Jess goes for the thick. And the white chocolate and ginger cheesecake is to die for. I swear I ate most of your half as well as mine, Gabriela. No wonder I'm larding it on and you're dead slim.'

'Larding it on?' Gabriela repeated. Her forehead wrinkled. 'What does that mean? I don't know these words, I'm afraid.'

Jess laughed. 'Rachel just means that she's gaining weight. Don't bother to learn it – it's slang. You know, you speak brilliant English, Gabriela. Did you learn it at school?'

'Yes, I did. I was very lucky – I was sent to an excellent school by my parents, who thought it as important to educate their daughter as their son. Not everyone with our social standing feels that way, but my parents did, and Eduardo and I had an equally good education. I enjoyed school, but he did not, and he was quite a naughty boy.' Her voice softened and she smiled indulgently. 'He was made to learn English, too, but he learnt very little and forgot it all as soon as he left the school. He is not a linguist, shall we say.'

'It sounds as if I've got a lot in common with Eduardo,' Jess said with a grin. 'I hated school, too. And like Eduardo, I do a creative sort of job. Fingers crossed that he visits you soon and I get to meet him.'

'Huh! You'll have to join the queue,' Rachel cut in. 'I'm ahead of you. I work for a production designer, which is more creative than being an events' planner, and it's closer to what Eduardo does. Being PA to a production designer trumps events' planning. So there.'

All three girls laughed.

Evie noticed that Gabriela's smile narrowed imperceptibly. She was protective of her brother, she thought.

'What about clubs in Italy? Do you go clubbing a lot?' Rachel asked, turning her attention back to Gabriela. The red-lipped smile widened again.

'There are clubs in Florence, as well as in other towns, of course. Many people go to them, although I think that the young Italians do not drink as much as the young English. As for me, though, I don't really like clubs. They are very noisy and you cannot hear what people are saying when they speak to you.'

'So what do you when you're not working?' Jess asked.

'I go to the theatre and to concerts. But I've been engaged in building up my career so there isn't very much free time for me, and in the last year, I have spent any free time that I had with Alessandro.'

Rachel threw a surreptitious glance at Jess. 'Evie told us about you and him. It must be minging to be away from him for a whole year. You know, unpleasant.'

Gabriela gave a slight shrug. 'It is better to spend a year

apart now than make a mistake that could last a lifetime, much better. And it will not be a year without seeing him – we will visit each other.'

'Don't you hang around with your friends like we do?' Jess asked in surprise.

'And talk clothes and share secrets with them?' Rachel added.

'No, not really. I don't have friends like the three of you are friends. It is a big regret. My school was far from my house and I boarded there, and the other students also travelled a distance. We talked and played with each other and were friends during the school term, but in the long holidays we didn't see each other, so I never made very close friends in my school years.'

'That sounds dead sad,' Jess said.

'It *is* sad. I have always felt that I've missed an important part of life, and when I met Evie …' she paused and turned to look at Evie, '… and when I met Evie, I knew that I'd met someone I could be a close friend with. I would have liked a sister very much. Eduardo is a good brother, but you can share so much more with a sister, and a really close friend would have been like having a sister. At least I've always felt it would.'

Evie felt a lump come to her throat. She reached across and hugged Gabriela. 'You're right about that, and that's such a fab thing to say. I haven't got any brothers or sisters, but I've never missed having any because I've known Rachel and Jess since school – they're like sisters to me.'

'This is where someone comes round with a violin, and we throw our arms around each other's necks and burst into tears,' Jess giggled.

Evie and Rachel joined in with her laughter, and the three of them did a high five. Gabriela glanced at them, bemused; then she, too, started laughing.

'Let's have a peach iced tea,' Jess suggested when they'd settled down again. 'You'll love it, Gabriela, I promise you.' She turned to Evie. 'So, have you decided what you're going to wear tomorrow night for your first date with Tom on home territory? You said you might get something new.'

'I'm not sure that I can be bothered now. I kept my eyes open this week every time Gabriela and I went into a shop, but nothing really struck me as a must-have. You got a couple of dresses and a trouser suit, didn't you, Gabriela, but I didn't try on so much as one thing. I'll find something in my wardrobe, and if not in mine, in one of yours, so beware.'

'But you must get something new for this important first date with Tom,' Gabriela insisted, her voice registering her astonishment that Evie could consider doing otherwise. 'A woman feels special when she's wearing a new dress. This is your chance to impress Tom, and you must take it. He'll want to know that there's more to you than what he saw in Italy. I know that from the way my brother speaks about the women he meets.'

Evie gave a deep sigh. 'You may well be right. In fact, I'm certain you are. But I can't face going into Central London again this week, unless that's where Tom takes me tomorrow night,' she added, laughing. 'I wouldn't exactly leap out of his car if I saw us following signs pointing in that direction. And going up to Hampstead is totally out of the question as everything's mega expensive there.'

'What about Camden Lock?' Jess volunteered. 'You've got loads of good things there in the past. That vintage shop is right up your street.'

'Now, that's a thought. Yes, I think I'll do that, even though it means getting up horribly early for a Saturday – if I don't get there soon after ten, all the best things will have gone. That's a good idea, though. I don't know why I didn't think of it.'

'If you are going to Camden Lock tomorrow, perhaps I could come, too.' Gabriela's face shone with eagerness. 'I should love to see it. You mentioned it in Italy. It sounds a very interesting place, with shops that are much different from the shops we've visited so far. But you must say no if I would be in the way.'

'Of course you wouldn't be in the way. But do you really want to get up that early when you don't have to?'

'I always rise early. I don't like to stay late in bed. If I'm awake, I get up. I would love to come with you. We've had such fun this week, and I know that this market will also be fun. And very English.'

'And very a few other countries as well. OK, then. If you're sure you really want to come, I suggest we meet up near the market at about ten. How about in front of Camden Town tube station? We can't miss each other there and it's very close to the Lock.'

'I'm very much looking forward to that. Thank you, Evie.' Gabriela sent a bright smile around the table.

'Be warned, it gets crowded,' Evie added. 'Wear something comfortable. For a start, I'd leave those killer heels at home if I were you. What about you two – are you coming tomorrow as well?'

Rachel looked questioningly at Jess, then back at Evie. 'I don't think we will, if it's all the same with you. Jess and I are going on to a club when we leave here, and getting up at the crack of dawn after a night out on the town doesn't exactly appeal. What say you, Jessica?'

'Ditto.'

Evie started to stand up. 'I suggest we skip the peach teas and hightail it to our various destinations. We've not ordered them yet and I want an early night. What about you, Gabriela? Do you want to go clubbing with Rachel and Jess or have you had enough for one evening?'

'If you want to come with us, you're very welcome,' Rachel told her.

'I don't think so, thank you, but it's very kind of you to ask me. I wonder if I could go back with you, Evie. I can take a cab from your house to my apartment. I'd like to see where you live, but not to visit as we both now have an early morning tomorrow.'

'If you really want to. I won't ask you in, though – it's a bit of a pigsty at the moment and you might get a culture shock.'

They all laughed.

Gabriela looked round at the three of them, and smiled warmly. 'How lucky I was to meet Tom, and through him to meet the three of you. I know that I'm going to enjoy being in England very much. Very much indeed.'

'It's only a few minutes from here,' Evie said, as they turned off Camden Road. 'It's very convenient for everywhere.'

'I can see this,' Gabriela said with a smile. 'You are fortunate to be living in such a place.'

'It was Rachel who found it.' Evie's mobile phone sounded. 'Sorry, it's my phone,' she said, taking it out. 'It'll be Rachel or Jess. We'll have left something behind, you watch. Hi!' she said into the handset.

Her editor's voice was loud at the other end of the line. She abruptly stopped walking and listened, stunned horror on her face. 'Of course. I understand,' she gasped into the phone as the line fell silent. She clicked to end the call, stared at the handset, the blood draining from her face, then slid it into her pocket.

'Oh, God,' she whispered, and she cupped her hands in front of her mouth.

'Evie, what is it? You have gone so pale.' Gabriela's voice came through the drumming in her ears.

Oh, no! She'd forgotten about Gabriela in the panic of the moment. She must get rid of her fast so she could think clearly, decide what to do. If there was anything she *could* do. Her eyes filled with tears, and she pressed her knuckles to her eyes to stem the flow, but the tears fell over her fingers and trickled down her arm.

'Evie? Evie, what is it?' Gabriela's voice rose a notch in alarm. She put her hand on Evie's arm. 'Has something happened to Tom?'

'No, really, he's fine.' She tried to steady her voice. 'At least as far as I know. It's just that I've had a bit of a shock – well, a huge shock really.' She pushed back the strands of hair that were sticking to her damp face and tried to smile reassuringly.

Gabriela opened her bag, took out a tissue and gave it to her.

'I just need to clear my head and think what to do,' Evie told her. She blew her nose. 'I feel awful about this, Gabriela, but I may have to sort out some things in the morning. I don't think I'll be able to look for clothes tomorrow. Would you mind if we gave the Lock a miss? We can always go another time.'

'Of course I don't mind. You are obviously very distressed. You will find something beautiful in your wardrobe to wear tomorrow night, I'm sure. Tom will love you in whatever you wear.'

Evie broke out again into loud sobs.

Gabriela went closer to her and put her arm around her shoulders. 'Do tell me what is wrong, Evie,' she said gently. 'We are like sisters, remember? You say you need to think what to do. Well, two heads are better than one, are they not? Let us put our two heads together and sort out whatever it is. It cannot be anything so bad that together we cannot put it right. You don't want to be awake all night and too tired to enjoy your date with Tom, do you?'

'I doubt I'll be going anywhere with Tom,' she wept. Gabriela tightened her grip on Evie's shoulders.

'Are you crying because Tom has just told you that he is unable to see you tomorrow? If you are, it will only be because he is too busy, there could be no other reason. Or has he said that there is some other reason, and is that why you are crying?'

'No, it's nothing to do with Tom. Well, it is, but not like that.' She turned to Gabriela, her face bleak. 'Oh, Gabriela, I've been really, really stupid and I don't know how to get out of the mess I've got myself into. I just don't know what to do.'

'Well, I do. For this minute, anyway. You say we are close to where you live, so we shall go there, sit down and have a coffee, and you will tell me what has happened. Then I shall tell you what you should do, and you will soon be full of smiles again. Come now, Evie. You have been a good friend to me all week. It's my turn now to be a good friend to you. Let me help you with your problem. Now, where is your house?'

With Gabriela's arm still around Evie's shoulders, they started walking again.

Chapter Nineteen

Run, Evie, run!

'You make yourself comfortable while I get you a drink,' Gabriela ordered. 'Have you any wine? I think that maybe you need something stronger than coffee. You have obviously had a terrible shock and wine will be the best thing for it.'

'A glass of wine sounds good. Thanks, Gabriela. You'll find some bottles over there in the corner.' She indicated a small wine rack under the window. Gabriela went and took two bottles from it.

A few minutes later, she returned from the kitchen with the bottles and two glasses. 'This will help you feel better,' she said as she sat down opposite Evie and poured them each a glass.

Her tears slowing down, Evie wiped her eyes again.

Gabriela pushed one of the wine glasses towards Evie and picked up her glass. 'I believe it is right to say Cheers,' she said, 'when it is the first time you are in a place. Cheers!' She waited for Evie to raise her glass, and together they began to drink their wine. After a couple of sips, Gabriela put her glass back on the table.

'You're right,' Evie said. 'The wine's hitting the spot. Good thinking, Gabriela. With this, plus what I've already had at Wagamama, I'll sleep like a log tonight and I'll see things more clearly in the morning. Cheers, indeed!' She took another drink, and sat back, clutching the glass in her hands.

Gabriela raised herself slightly, leaned across the coffee table and re-filled Evie's nearly empty glass.

Evie raised her glass to her lips again, had another drink, then put the glass down on the table and looked across at Gabriela. 'You know, you're being really nice, and all I've done is made you have a later night than you wanted, and change our plans for tomorrow.'

Gabriela gave her a warm smile 'I'm here for a year, Evie,' she said. 'There will be other Saturday mornings at Camden Lock. *You* are what is important now. Nothing else matters.' She picked up her glass and took a small sip. 'Cheers!' she said, raising it again with a little laugh. 'This time it is because I see your face looking better now. I think you are now feeling that things are not so bad as you first thought.'

'Wrong. Things aren't bad – they're bloody awful. I've screwed up big time. Oops.' Evie pushed herself upright and stared at Gabriela. 'Naughty me. That was rude of me. I shouldn't talk like that in front of you. 'Snot polite. Cheers anyway.' She clanked her glass against Gabriela's before cradling it against her chest once again. Some of the wine spilled on to her top. 'And that's not polite either,' she muttered looking down at the wet patch. 'Naughty wine.' She wiped the damp spot with her hand. More wine spilled. 'Only one thing to do,' she said with a giggle, and she drank the rest of the wine in the glass and put the glass back on the table.

Gabriela filled it again.

'Now that you feel a little better, this is perhaps the time to tell me what has happened to upset you so much.'

Evie sat back against the sofa and sighed deeply. 'There's not much to tell. I've got myself into a pickle – that means into a mess, you know – and I can't see how to get myself out of it. It's a nasty mess, mess, mess. But you mustn't worry, good friend Gabriela.' She waved her finger vaguely in Gabriela's direction. 'I'll sort it out, one way or another. I know I will.'

She felt her cheeks begin to redden and she started to cry again.

'This is all your fault.' Her words ended in a hiccup. 'You being so nice has started me off again. Don't be nice to me. Be mean and nasty. I order you.'

'Please tell me what's wrong, Evie,' Gabriela said gently. She went round the table and sat on the sofa next to Evie. 'Seeing you so unhappy is making me unhappy, too. Please let me help you. In this next year, I may need help from you. But how can I ask you for help if you will not let me help you now?'

'It's just such a silly thing really.' Evie shook her head from side to side, dismissively. 'I'm probably fussing about it and I shouldn't be. I can fuss for England. Rachel and Jess will tell you.'

'You said it's something to do with Tom. What did he do?' Gabriela's voice was warm and sympathetic.

'He didn't do anything. It's what I did to him. Or was supposed to do to him. But I won't.'

'I don't understand.'

'Oh, if you really, really want to know, a magazine sent me to work for Tom, not an agency. I wish it had been an agency. The magazine – well, it's a filthy rag, really - wanted me to find out if something they suspected about him was true.' She cocked her head to one side and stared at Gabriela. 'Does that make sense? Maybe it does, I don't know.' She looked back at her knees. 'Anyway, I'd only just joined them, but I was given the job because I could speak Italian. Not many people speak Italian as it's not taught in schools, you know? Don't know why 'cos lots of English people go there.'

'I'm guessing that Tom was about to go to Italy and needed an interpreter.'

'Brownie point! You're a good guesser, Gabriela. There

was I, on the staff, able to speak the lingo. The editor couldn't believe his luck.'

'And Tom didn't know anything about the magazine?'

'Good God, no! He thought I was an agency temp.'

'I take it this magazine – this filthy rag, as you call it – is one of those celebrity magazines that are so popular here?'

'Celebrity gossip, muckraking, whatever. Yup, one of those. I'd only taken the bloody job because I was desperate to work for a magazine and that was all I could get. I'd been trying for over a year. It's amazing how you can kid yourself that working for a rag like that will help you to get a job on a top magazine. It's amazing, but I did just that. Even more amazing, I thought I'd be able to do the job without writing anything nasty about anyone. I must have been mad. Mad and stupid.'

'But you now know that this is not for you, so you can leave … what did you say the magazine's name was?'

'*Pure Dirt*.'

'… so you can leave *Pure Dirt* and keep on trying to find work on a better magazine. I don't understand why you are crying.'

Evie leaned forward, put her elbows on her knees and covered her face with her hands. Tears fell down her cheeks. 'It's not that simple,' she said at last, her voice wobbling. 'I want to be the person who tells Tom why I really went to Italy with him. It must be me …' Her voice trailed off and she paused.

'Which is the right thing to do,' Gabriela prompted.

'So when I spoke to the shitty editor last Tuesday, I told him I'd send in the story at the end of next week, on Friday. Friday's the day we originally agreed. But really I was going to pack in the job on Friday, and tell Tom the truth on Friday evening or on Saturday. Not tomorrow night. I absolutely don't want to tell Tom tomorrow. I mustn't.

But now I must.' She looked at Gabriela. 'Does that make sense? It doesn't, does it?'

'I think something has happened to alter your plan. Something to do with the phone call. Am I right?'

'Spot on. It was the editor on the phone. He wants – no, he insists on having the story on Wednesday morning at the very latest. They need to plan the layout with the text, he said, putting in photos and all that. At least that's what he says. He's going to publish the story a week on Monday. That's the day that Tom starts his next big libel case, you know. He said anything I find out after Tuesday can go into a follow-up article in the next edition. It means I'm stuffed, Gabriela.'

Gabriela picked up Evie's glass of wine and handed it to her. Evie took a sip. 'Really stuffed,' she repeated into the glass.

'But it is only Friday today. There are still four more days before you must send a story. Is it necessary to speak to Tom tomorrow night? Can you not leave it in case you have an idea?'

She shook her head. 'Tomorrow, it must be. He's so busy that I won't be able to see him again before next weekend.'

'But anyway, you haven't anything to give the editor, have you? Whatever they suspected about Tom will have been wrong, will it not? There cannot be anything in Tom's life that is worth publishing. He's an upright man. And as there is nothing to publish, there will be no need to say anything to Tom tomorrow. Is that not so?'

Evie turned away and looked down at the table. Out of the corner of her eye she saw Gabriela open the second bottle of wine, lean across and refill her glass. She must have spilled more of her wine than she'd thought.

Gabriela sat back and delicately sipped from her glass. 'This is a pleasant wine,' she said. 'Quite pleasant.'

'Good or bad, it's helping. It's just what the doctor ordered. Here's to you, Dr Gabriela.' She raised her glass. 'You knew exactly what I needed tonight. Down the hatch. D'you know that English expression? It means down the hatch.'

'Tom's life will have been blameless, I'm sure. You will have found nothing that could be of interest to your editor.'

Evie gave a dismissive shrug. "Smazing what rags like *Pure Dirt* can do with teensy weensy innocent little things. So he and Zizi went out to dinner a few times. That's all it was. No affair, just dinner with a friend. But that slob of an editor would say they'd been sleeping together during the trial. Think how it would look, Tom telling the court that Zizi had a stainless reputation and hadn't been having an affair outside her marriage, while all the time sleeping with her. *Pure Dirt* would love the irony in that! It would all be lies, but he couldn't prove it. Not good.'

'Firstly, what Tom does is no one's business. And secondly, Tom could bring a case against the editor for lying, could he not?'

'It would be very difficult to prove. I've seen enough TV shows about lawyers to know that a barrister would ask him in court if he'd ever had a candlelight dinner alone with Zizi, and he'd have to say yes. Even if they didn't have the photo proof, he wouldn't lie – not Tom. The man would then point out Tom's history of dishonest behaviour as a young barrister and everyone would believe that he had slept with Zizi during the trial. Tom would look bad and Zizi would probably have to return the money she'd won from *Pure Dirt*. After all, they'd shown she wasn't such an angel after all.'

'What do you mean, dishonest behaviour? Did Tom do something he shouldn't have done when he was young?'

'Something that would only seem important to other lawyers, but that wouldn't stop my scumbag of an editor from making it sound like the crime of the century.' Evie put her glass heavily on the table, and filled it again. 'I must go to bed after this. Thanks to you, Gabriela, I shall sleep tonight like a baby.' She leaned back, clutching her glass.

'What did Tom do?'

'Something about when he was getting ready for his first solo libel case, and he read something he shouldn't have read. It was a fax sent to him by mistake. He should have sent it back without reading it, but he was so keen to do well that he broke the Bar rules.'

'And what happened?'

'Nothing happened. No one found out. He won his case and his career got off to a brilliant start.'

'What Tom did with Zizi is not so serious. He has behaved as many men behave. Nor is the fax so very bad. This is so awful what these papers do.'

'There's a hidden agenda. Do you know what that means?

'Yes, I do.'

'The editor wants to wreck Tom's career. He hates him as Tom's got the better of him in court on several occasions. That's the truth. Believe me, he'd go to town on the Tom and Zizi story. Yes, he would. And he'd make the fax thingy sound horrible.' She waved her glass in the air. 'The two together could be dynamite in his slimy hands.'

'These things Tom has done are such unimportant things. We all do silly things in our life. But I know what you mean about these celebrity magazines. I've glanced at the ones we bought – everything in them is written in big letters and made to sound very naughty and very sensational.'

'Naturally I'm not going to tell the editor anything at all about Tom. I was just trying to play for time so that we can go out together at least once – just once – without risking anything coming between us. But now, when I come clean to the editor on Tuesday, there's a real risk that he'll explode and go straight to Tom and paint me in the worst possible light. I can't let that happen so I'm going to have to tell Tom the truth tomorrow, even though I know it'll ruin everything.' A tear rolled down her cheek.

'Oh, Evie.'

'I can't let the editor tell him first.' Gabriela handed her another tissue and she wiped her eyes.

'You poor, poor thing. I can see that this is a difficult situation.' Gabriela squeezed her hand in sympathy.

'Don't I know it?'

'I don't think you *should* tell him tomorrow, not if you want to make sure that you and Tom stay together.'

Evie stared at her. 'What do you mean? What else can I do?'

Gabriela leaned forward. 'You hold the cards, Evie. They are all in your hand – I think that that is the English expression – not in the editor's hand. He wants the story that you have, or that he thinks you have, and this gives you the power.'

Evie stared at Gabriela thoughtfully, biting her lower lip. 'I suppose it does. So what do you suggest I do?' There was a flicker of hope in her eyes.

'You should stay with your first instinct. You feel that you and Tom need an evening in which to get to know each other again, and you are right. This is very important and you do not want anything to spoil it for you.'

'But the editor ...'

'You will tell your editor on Wednesday morning, or better still, on Tuesday evening, that you will not give him the story until Friday morning, which is what you first agreed with him. You will say that if he pushes you any more, you will take the story to a rival magazine. What can the editor do but wait until Friday?'

'You think he'll agree to wait?' She put her thumb to her mouth and bit her nail.

'I think he will. He will not want the story to go to another magazine, especially as you will be making it sound very meaty. And you are back to your original plan. You can relax and enjoy tomorrow night, knowing you don't have to tell Tom the truth until next weekend.'

'That's bloody brilliant!' she exclaimed, her eyes shining. 'Absolutely brilliant!' Her wine glass shook in her excitement. Gabriela reached across, took it from her and put it on the table.

'No, it is not,' Gabriela laughed. 'It's easy to see what to do when one's head is not in a turmoil.'

'I can't believe how different I feel! I feel happy. And a bit drunk, if I'm honest,' she added with a giggle. 'I owe you, Gabriela. Thank you, thank you.'

'I'm very happy to help you. Now you must put all of this worry behind you. All you will have to do is make two telephone calls in the next week: one to the editor on Tuesday evening, telling him that he will have the story on Friday, and the other to the editor on Friday morning, telling him that there is no story and that you resign from the job. After that, you can tell Tom the truth. Tomorrow night, you can just enjoy being with him. As for tonight, I think it's time you went to bed,' she said with a laugh. She stood up.

Evie gazed up at her. 'I'm so pleased you walked back with me this evening. I don't know what I'd have done if you hadn't.'

Gabriela smiled down at her. 'Go to bed now, Evie. Sleep very well, and when you wake up, take yourself into Camden Lock. I'm sure you can find the perfect dress for what will be a perfect evening.'

Alone in her apartment later, Gabriela stood up from the sofa, the magazine she'd bought at the 24 hour shop on the way home still in her hand. She moved towards the door of the sitting room, leaving her empty coffee cup sitting on the table. She reached the door, went out of the room and crossed to the small office that led off the hall.

Her laptop was on the light oak desk and she placed the magazine next to it, ready for tomorrow. She paused a moment and glanced at the cover of the magazine. A smile of quiet triumph flickered across her lips and she let herself give way to a fleeting sense of excitement.

Never in her wildest dreams had she expected the day to turn out as it had.

What had promised to be no more than a rather uninteresting evening in a restaurant with Evie's probably dull friends, a further stage in the tedious process of bonding with the girl, had ended up as an evening to remember: it was the evening upon which she had begun the process of erasing Evie from Tom's life forever.

She, Gabriela di Montefiori, was about to take a giant step towards the goal that she increasingly craved. Let Evie Shaw have her moment with Tom for the present – his future belonged to her.

She straightened up and took control of her emotions. She needed a good night's rest. Tomorrow would be here soon enough.

Chapter Twenty

The calm before the storm

Evie opened her eyes. They felt heavy and sore. Her head hurt and her mouth felt dry. She ran her tongue around her lips. Why on earth had she drunk as much as she had last night? She gave a low groan, reached across for the plastic bottle of water that she dimly remembered putting on her bedside table, and pulled it to her.

Tipping the bottle up, she drank to the last drop and let it fall to the floor. Then she curled up on her side. She'd never in her life felt so awful, so seedy. Why, oh why, had she and Gabriela put it away like they had last night?

At the thought of Gabriela, a wave of guilt swept through her – she'd said a lot more about Tom last night than she'd meant to, a lot more than she should have done. For someone who'd resolved never to tell a soul what he'd told her in Italy, she'd fallen badly at the first hurdle.

If only she hadn't been so panicked about her editor.

Thank goodness it was only Gabriela she'd told, she thought with relief. Gabriela wasn't likely to tell anyone else – she didn't know anyone in England to tell, for a start. But it was a lesson on how easy it was to let things slip out when you didn't intend them to, and she'd be on her guard at all times in the future to make sure that she never did such a thing again. She never again wanted to wake up feeling as guilty as she felt now. Guilt and a hangover did not make a good start to the day. Especially not to the day on which she was going on the long-anticipated date with Tom.

She turned over on to her other side, relishing the cool of the pillow and the sheet, and she closed her eyes. She'd feel better after more sleep, she was sure. She had to. She must look her very best for Tom. Her eyes closed and her breathing got heavier.

I shall see Tom soon, she thought, and she smiled as she drifted into sleep.

'You look stunning, Evie.' Tom gazed at her over the slender-stemmed pink rose in the centre of the table. 'Absolutely lovely.'

'Wow, I think you'd better change the subject, Tom. I'm not used to getting compliments from you, and they're making me suspicious. Either you want me to feed your hungry male ego so you're making me have to compliment you in return, or your body's been taken over by an alien force. I kind of hope it's not the alien takeover – that would be a real waste of a pretty good body.'

He grinned. 'You see, I got my compliment in the end – my male ego is satisfied. Unfortunately, though, my hunger isn't. I was too busy to stop and eat today, and I'm starving.' He picked up his menu and ran his eyes down it. 'I think I'll have the goat's cheese salad, followed by the grilled fillet of beef with celeriac. And what about you? Have you decided yet?'

She closed her menu and put it back on the table. 'I'll have the same as you, please.'

He smiled at her. 'I see that we still want the same things. That's good, very good.' He placed his menu on hers, leaned across the table and moved the vase to one side. 'And that's even better. I've missed you, Evie,' he said, his face suddenly serious. 'I've missed you every single day.'

'And I've missed you, too. I've had masses of things to do since we got back, but it's still felt as if there's been a huge hole in my life. Things aren't as much fun when you're not around.'

A wave of anxiety swept over her. Did she sound too keen?

Tom had started the ball rolling with what he'd said to her, but perhaps she should have been more laid-back. *Glamour Puss* always said to play it cool if you wanted to keep them interested, which she did, yet she'd sounded as if she was gagging to leap on top of him. True, she wouldn't need much persuading, if any – he looked dead sexy in that pale grey shirt – but maybe she shouldn't have been quite so obvious. She bit her lip nervously.

Tom took her hand. A shiver of pleasure ran down her spine. 'I feel exactly the same,' he said quietly.

Relief.

So much for *Glamour Puss* – they obviously hadn't a clue what they were talking about. Being honest about her feelings was clearly the way to go. Memo to self: bin all of her copies of *Glamour Puss*. Well, perhaps not bin them – that was a bit drastic – but not take everything they said for gospel.

'Would you care for bread?'

They glanced up and saw a waiter standing by the table, holding a basket of bread. Tom released her hand and the waiter served, then Tom gave him their orders and chose a bottle of red wine from the wine list. The waiter left and he sat back and looked across the table at her, a warm smile on his face.

'So tell me, what have you been doing this week? I'm curious to hear how you and Gabriela got on. And did it go all right, working for me part of the week and being with Gabriela the rest of the time? You certainly seem to have coped with everything I left you to do. Or to put it another way, I didn't find any anguished messages of despair when I got home, and I took this to be a good sign.'

'It was fine, thanks. Leaving a recording each day of what I had to do was a cool idea.'

He laughed. 'A second compliment, no less. I can see that I'm on a roll here. But whilst I hate to put the brakes on it, I think I'd better own up – after all, honesty's always the best policy, is it not?'

She picked up the piece of bread closest to her and bit into it. A lump of the bread stuck in her throat. Struggling to swallow it, she nodded furiously.

'It was the temps who suggested I use the digital dictation that you find in most offices these days. I took their advice and it's worked really well.' He reached across the table and took her hand again. Blue eyes looked deep into hers, and her toes curled. 'But telling you what to do in person would have been so much nicer than talking into a machine.'

She swallowed again and the bread finally slid down. 'And I would have liked you being there in person, telling me what to do.' Her voice cracked and she coughed to clear her throat.

He leaned closer. 'You see, Evie, that's another thing we feel the same way about. Although to be honest, I'm not sure how much telling there'd have been. I suspect that showing you the way I felt about you might have jumped to the top of the agenda.'

A wave of emotion welled up inside her and she could have burst into tears. She tried to laugh. 'I see we're back to lists again. We never seem to get far from them, do we?'

'It seems that we don't,' he said. Their eyes met, and he gave her a lazy smile.

The waiter returned to the table with their starters, and Tom straightened up as the waiter poured a little wine into his glass, stood back and waited while he tasted it.

'That's fine, Pierre.'

'Will there be anything else, Mr Hadleigh?' the waiter asked as he filled their glasses with wine.

'I don't think so. Thank you.'

The waiter moved away.

'Do you come here often? They all seem to know you.'

'Yes, quite a bit. I like the place very much. The food and service are excellent, and it has a friendly atmosphere – at least, I think it has; I hope you agree – and it's a bonus that I can walk here so I don't have to worry about parking. Or about drinking, for that matter. Obviously tonight's different – I've got the car because I collected you.'

'You're right, it's really nice here,' she said, picking up her fork and starting on the salad. 'It's certainly a whole lot different from Wagamama, which is where we took Gabriela last night. I'm afraid we had a bit too much too drink, so I'll be going carefully tonight. Well, *I* had a bit too much to drink. From what I can remember, Gabriela held her drink better.'

Her heart gave a sudden thump of guilt. She'd had more than just a bit too much to drink the night before – she'd had way too much. If only she'd had the same degree of self-control as Gabriela. For a start, she would never have opened up to her about Tom in the way that she had. It was something private about Tom that should have stayed private. Damn the drink.

The sound of Tom's laughter brought her back to the present with a jolt.

'You took her to Wagamama! That's priceless. I must confess I can't see Gabriela in such a place. Nor having more than an elegant glass of wine. What on earth did she make of it?'

'She said all the right things, like it was great fun and different, that they ought to have Wagamamas in Italy, and so on, but what she really thought of it, I wouldn't like to say. She's much too polite and self-controlled to say if she didn't like it, but I'd be very surprised if it heads her list of things to do again. Oops, another list.'

'Who's the 'we' who took her there?'

'Rachel and Jess came, too. Gabriela seemed to get on really well with them, and they're both dying to meet Eduardo. I'm not sure how keen she is on that idea, though. I saw the expression on her face when they were joking about it.'

'I presume that Rachel and Jess own the heads that were hanging out of the window when I got to your house earlier on.'

She giggled. 'Bang on. They were desperate to get a glimpse of you, which is why I dashed out of the house before you'd even switched the engine off. I was saving *you* from their scrutiny, and *them* from falling out of the window.'

'Admirable, indeed! But back to Gabriela, how did it go this week? Did you get on all right?'

'To my amazement, we got on really well.' She swept her hair back from her face. 'We did lots of different things, far more than I thought we'd do.'

'Such as?'

'Well, for example, we went round London on one of those open-topped buses. I've never done that before – you don't when you live in a place – but it was really interesting. The weather was fantastic, which helped. And we hit the shops – that goes without saying. Gabriela bought a few things, mainly clothes as she's not yet decided what she wants to do to her flat. I didn't get anything, but it was fun watching her shop. She certainly knows what she wants and she's determined to get it.'

'Did you go to her flat? It's in Holland Park, isn't it? I've got her address somewhere.'

'I think it is. I haven't got her actual address, though. No, I didn't go there. There just wasn't time and we weren't really in that part of London. The closest we got to her flat was probably when we were in Harrods.'

'I see what you mean. That's still quite a hike from Holland Park.'

'From what she's said, it sounds very nice. I expect I'll see it before too long. The more you get to know her, the more you realise that she's quite lonely, which explains why she's going out of her way to make friends with Rachel, Jess and me, even though we don't really have anything much in common with her. Apparently, she doesn't have any close friends in Italy. She sort of explained it away, but we all think it's a bit strange. There's probably something she's not told us, but that's up to her.'

'Everyone needs good friends so she was lucky to meet the three of you. I'm glad you've been able to take her under your wing this week. If you speak to her again before I do, you can remind her that I'll call her once the case is over. I'll take her to dinner or something.'

A vision of Gabriela, clad in something stunning, smiling across a candlelit table at Tom, sprang to her mind, and a wave of emotion rose up in her. She struggled to push it back. Of course he had to see Gabriela in England. He'd said he'd take her to dinner and he'd obviously honour that promise. She wasn't jealous. Not really.

'Don't worry, I'll tell her.' She forced herself to smile.

'And you must come along, too. Your presence will help to lighten the conversation,' he added with a teasing smile.

She beamed at him. 'I'll let that pass, but only because the salad was so good. And also because it's your turn to go under the spotlight now. Has your week gone well? Your working days have certainly been long enough.'

'That's par for the course with these big cases, I'm afraid. And if you think that I work long hours, you should see the length of the day that the junior barristers sometimes have to work. They often don't pick up a brief until the evening before they have to argue the case. It's not unknown for barristers to work through the night and then go straight into court.'

'God, how gruesome!' She moved back a little to let the waiter remove her plate. 'What about the libel case you're working on now – is it going well?'

'I think so. All one can do at this stage is prepare as well as is humanly possible, and that's what I've been doing. I'm trying to cover every conceivable angle – I don't like surprises in court.'

'Not surprises in court, maybe, but some surprises can be fun – like surprise presents. My parents used to ask me every year what I wanted for Christmas and my birthday, and I had to come up with something or they'd get me a boring, sensible present, such as something for school or gloves. I always hated knowing what I was going to get before I got it. I'd have loved them to have chosen something for me that they thought I'd like.'

'Even if you didn't like it?'

'Yup, even if I didn't like it. It's the thought that counts, after all.'

Oh, no! She shouldn't have said that – she didn't want to think like that.

Suppose Tom was in the same mindset and focused on her original intention, not on the fact that she'd changed her mind. She'd been so walking on air since Gabriela's reassurance that she hadn't for a minute considered that possibility. Oh, if only her throwaway comment hadn't put that thought into her mind!

The waiter approached with two plates of food.

'I think that's our beef's coming,' she heard Tom say, his voice coming from far away.

She stared down at the plate that the waiter had put in front of her, and all she could see were the words *Pure Dirt*, written large in lurid red. Her stomach lurched.

Get a grip, she told herself. Bloody well, get a grip. If she couldn't control her thoughts, she'd end up blurting out the truth just to feel better. She absolutely didn't want to do that, but she could see it happening so easily. She was going to watch what she drank and she was going to make sure that she kept to herself all the things she wasn't ready to say.

For a start, she must stop second-guessing what Tom would say when he knew the truth. It was pointless – she hadn't really got a clue how he'd respond. Secondly, she must dig deep into her psyche and find the enterprising Evie of Italy – the Evie who'd jumped on top of her bed in a nightdress and begged her boss to get into that bed. That Evie would be able to cope brilliantly with the present situation and with everything that the coming week was going to throw at her.

She took a deep breath, and picked up her knife and fork. 'So where were we?' she asked with a bright smile.

'We were just about to return to the agency, I believe, or rather you were. In a week's time, I think you said.'

'Don't remind me.' She wagged her finger at him admonishingly.

'All right, I won't. But they're lucky to have you, and I bet they know it. You're the sharpest temp I've ever had. I just hope that Zizi can find something you'd like better.'

'By "ever had" …?'

He laughed. 'That I've ever had working for me, pedantic Evie.'

She beamed at him and took a bite of her food. 'Wow! On a different subject, this mousse is yummy.'

Tom paused in the midde of cutting a piece of meat and glanced across at her plate. 'You mean the celeriac? Yes, it's delicious. Celeriac's lovely in soup, too.'

'To be honest, I don't think I've ever had it before. I was

thinking it was celery, but it's obviously not. That's me being an airhead again.' She shook her head, and cut into her beef.

'I'm not so sure about that airhead thing. Not at all. I suspect that there's more to you than meets the eye.' Her heart switched into treble speed. Where was he going with this? She started to eat more quickly.

'I think you're a very bright cookie,' he went on when he'd finished what he was eating, 'although for some reason you don't like to show it. But whatever the reason, you're a cookie that I'll miss having around the house. And don't ask me if I'm talking about ginger nuts,' he added with a laugh.

Relief flooded through her. Thank you, guardian angel! They'd moved away from a potential minefield and were back on safe ground.

'But we haven't been at the house at the same time at all this week, have we?' she said lightly. 'So me not being there in the future won't be that different for you, will it?'

'Oh, yes, it will. In a way, you were there when I got home Monday and Tuesday night, with your presence all around me: your scent was in the air; the cushion you leaned against was crumpled into your shape; the sheet of paper you doodled on was lying on top of the desk; the little heart you drew at the end of your every message spoke to me. Yes, you were there with me, Evie, even though I had to close my eyes to see you.'

'Oh, Tom,' she said softly.

'And it was a bloody marvellous feeling to come home to you, even if it wasn't the physical you. It was so good that it made me wonder what it would be like to come home to the actual you.'

Their eyes met, and held.

'Would you like me to remove your plates, Mr Hadleigh?'

'What!' he exclaimed with a start. He stared down at their empty plates. 'Oh, I see. Yes, I think so, we both seem to have finished. Thank you.'

When the plates had been cleared away, the waiter returned to their table. 'Would either of you care to see the dessert menu?'

'Would you like some dessert? They do a wonderful chocolate pudding that would be right up your street.'

She shook her head. 'I don't want another thing, thank you,' she replied. Her eyes ran lightly across Tom's face. 'I might think of something later, though.'

As they made their way from the restaurant back to the car, strolling up a narrow cobbled lane lined on either side with black bollards, Tom slid his arm around Evie's shoulders. He heard her sigh happily, and he smiled to himself as he felt her nestle more deeply into the crook of his arm.

He'd been longing to see her again from the moment he'd left her, and he'd been intensely frustrated that his work was so all-consuming that he'd had to wait until Saturday to see her. On a couple of occasions in the week when he'd got home late in the evening, he'd been tempted to call her and ask her round, but he'd held off. He hadn't wanted her to think that he took her for granted. No, their first time together in England had to be a proper date.

As he'd left his house earlier to go and collect her, he'd felt a momentary twinge of fear that the night might not live up to his expectations, which had been growing daily. But the evening had been everything that he'd hoped it would be, and more.

He glanced down at Evie and tightened his hold on her. She was even more beautiful than he remembered, and every bit as much fun. It had been as easy to talk to her as it had been in Italy, and he could truthfully say that he'd never had a dinner conversation that was as pleasant and relaxed as their conversation had been that evening. And nor had the time passed as quickly.

And the night wasn't over yet.

He felt a stab of anticipation in his groin. She'd hadn't hesitated to say yes when he'd suggested a nightcap back at his place, and unless he was very much mistaken, she was longing for what he hoped would take place as much as he was.

Glancing up at the sky as he walked along, he saw that it was full of stars. They would be the same stars that had shone down upon them on their last night in Italy, he thought – that unbelievable last night in Umbria.

He felt her eyes on him, and he looked back down at her.

'You're thinking about the stars in Italy, aren't you?' she said.

He laughed. 'You must be psychic.'

'No.' She smiled up into his face and moved even closer to him. 'As I've said before, just on the same wave length.'

He leaned down and kissed her hard on the lips.

The same stars that shone on Umbria and Hampstead shone also upon Holland Park.

Night had long since fallen by the time that Gabriela shut the lid of her laptop, got up from her computer chair and closed the magazine that had been lying on the desk next to her. She pressed it flat with her hand and carefully aligned it with the computer.

She took a small step back and stared at the magazine.

Then on a sudden impulse, she leaned over and ran her fingers slowly across the garish red letters that screamed out from its cover. With a thin smile of pleasure, she straightened up, switched off the desk light, and went out of the office and across the hall into the sitting room.

The moment she entered the sitting-room, she saw the empty coffee cup on the top of the glass table where she'd left it the night before. Next to it, the magazines were still in an untidy heap.

Through no fault of her own this had not been a normal day, she excused herself.

From the moment she'd returned home the night before, her routine had been disrupted. On a normal day, she would never have allowed anything to be out of place in her apartment, but this day had been different. On this day she'd had something to do that was more important than a momentary disarray. But she had now finished the writing she was doing, and had checked several times that it was to her satisfaction, and she would restore order the following day.

Yes, it was finished. A sense of anticipation stirred within her. She slid the fingers of her right hand between the fingers of her left hand, curled her fingers over the backs of her hands and pressed her palms together, squeezing hard until her knuckles were white.

She couldn't wait for the next few days to arrive, and for the weekend, and for the Monday after that. The thought of seeing her plan in action, watching it bear fruit, filled her with ice-cold excitement, and she was impatient for the week to begin.

Restlessly, she dropped her hands, went over to the window and stared up at the sky, straining hard to see into the dark void beyond the stars. As she watched, the blackness of night gave way to the faces of the principle players in the events that were going to be acted out in the course of the following two weeks.

But hers was the starring role!

She almost laughed out loud. Yes, she had the starring role, but no one would ever know it. And that didn't matter;

not at all. It was more than enough for her that she would be the only person to know that she'd been the author of her own good fortune.

She sighed as she turned away from the window. It had been a long day, a day in which she'd had much to do, and she was now tired. But there was one more thing to be done before she could reward herself with sleep, and that was to note down what she must do in the coming week, as she did every Saturday.

Taking her slimline diary and a gold-topped pen from her bag, she perched on the edge of the sofa and started to list what she must do on each of the following seven days.

Top of the list was to ring Evie on the Monday or Tuesday evening without fail. That wouldn't be a problem, though – she would be starting at the design firm on the Monday morning and there was bound to be something that she'd need to know that evening, and that would give her a plausible reason to telephone Evie, or maybe even to visit her.

And she must telephone Eduardo. He'd called her twice that day, but she hadn't taken the calls; she'd been much too busy to stop what she was doing to talk about Evie, which was all he would want to do, she was sure. The sooner he got over that silly crush, the better. However, she must ring him in the morning. When she did so, she'd be sure to tell him how close Evie and Tom had become. She would leave it until quite late in the morning, though – Eduardo did not get up early on Sundays.

Evie and Tom. She paused. They'd probably ended up in bed that evening. Her lip curled in disgust – she didn't want to think about it. She didn't like to think about that side of any relationship. She'd had to let Evie have her evening with Tom – there'd been no choice – and there may even be one more such evening, but that would be the last; of that there was no doubt.

She slipped the top back on to her pen, and returned the pen and diary to her bag. Then she got up, walked out of the sitting room and went into her empty bedroom.

Curled up in Tom's arms, her eyes wide open, Evie listened to the sound of his steady breathing, helpless against the cold dread that was creeping over her and wrapping its icy tentacles around her heart.

Full of regret and apology, Tom had told her that he had to work all through the next day, and that he had conferences every night in the coming week and wouldn't be able to see her. But he wanted to take her out again on the following Friday evening, and on the Saturday, and she'd said yes to both nights. Friday could be the last occasion, though, on which she'd see his eyes crinkle with warmth as they gazed down at her; on which she'd sink into his arms and feel them tightening around her, sending a surge of electricity through her; on which she'd feel his bare skin next to hers.

Anguish tightened its hold on her and the night ticked slowly away.

Chapter Twenty-One

Those storm clouds gather...

'That Gabriela's bloody brilliant, Jess,' Evie shouted in the direction of the kitchen as she threw herself on to the sofa in the communal area of the Camden Town house.

'Does that mean you rang the editor and it was all OK?' Jess asked, coming out of the kitchen, a cup in each hand. She gave one of the cups to Evie and went round to the deep armchair on the opposite side of the teak coffee table. Clearing a space on the table, she put her cup down and sat in the armchair.

'Spot on. Gabriela phoned last night about something she was unsure about after her first day at work, or so she said — really I think she just wanted to talk — and she said I should definitely ring the magazine tonight, rather than leave it till tomorrow morning. That way I'd avoid having yet another sleepless night. She'd picked up on the fact that I was tired from my voice, and she was dead right. I've been so worried about what the wanker would say that I haven't slept properly for ages. She thought I ought to have as clear a head as possible when I phoned him.'

'So how did you start the conversation?'

'I said exactly what Gabriela suggested; that is, that he wouldn't get the story till Friday morning.'

'And what did he say?'

'Everything you would have expected. The shitbag's got a limited vocabulary — virtually every word began with an *f*. I had to "effing well get the effing thing into his effing hands by tomorrow effing morning". You know the sort of thing. I just let him rant, and when he'd more or less finished shouting down the line, I put the phone back to my ear and told him that if he wasn't prepared to stick to our original agreement, I'd take my story to someone else. I was sure that there'd be any number of takers for the juicy little number I'd got.'

Jess giggled. 'You've got some nerve, Evie, I'll say that for you. Perhaps you should have stuck to muckraking as a career.'

Evie laughed happily. 'You should have heard the change in his voice. It was like chalk and cheese. By the time I hung up, he was more than happy to wait till Friday morning – they'd find a way to work round my schedule, no problem. I shouldn't worry my pretty little head about anything.' She hugged her knees to her chest and grinned ecstatically. 'Fantastic or what?'

'Fanfuckingtastic, I'd say. You've done so well. That Gabriela is obviously pretty smart. Fancy her zeroing in right away on the fact that you were the one with the power.'

'Or else she thinks like the sleazy element thinks. But whatever the reason, I'm soooo grateful to her. It feels as if a huge weight's been lifted off me.'

'So what happens next?'

'Nothing till Friday. I'll phone the editor on Friday, leaving it as late in the day as I possibly can to make it hard for him to talk to Tom before I do. I'll tell him where to stick his job, and then I'll tell Tom the truth when I see him that evening. Tom suggested that I stay on at the house on Friday until he gets home, which I shall do. We're going out for a meal in the evening and there's no point in my coming all the way back here first.'

'It's all coming together, isn't it? I'm so pleased for you, Evie.'

'You've no idea how much better I feel about everything now. I really can't believe that me having been on the staff of *Pure Dirt* for a few minutes will mean the end of Tom and me – it's not as if I ever gave them a story about anyone. No, that's not going to happen. I think it's going to turn out alright. All the same, though, I'll be glad when Friday night is over.'

'I can't see Tom holding it against you, either. He must know you well enough by now to know that you're not the sort of person who'd ever dish up dirt about anyone.'

'I certainly hope he does.' She gave a deep sigh, stretched her legs out in front of her and stared at her fluffy pink slippers. 'It's a shame it's Tuesday, or I'd suggest that we go out and celebrate when Rachel gets home, but I don't fancy having a head like whatever tomorrow morning. I want to have my wits about me this week.'

'You ought to ring Gabriela and tell her what happened, if you haven't done so.'

Evie pulled a face. 'I seem to have had rather a lot of Gabriela lately. But you're right, I should. After all, it's thanks to her that I'm still with Tom and not a distraught wreck by now. I'll make sure I don't get into a conversation, though. I wonder what time she gets home. I don't like to ring when she's at work – it might be awkward for her.'

'If it's awkward, she won't pick up.' Jess stood up, picked up the empty cups and took them into the kitchen. There was a clatter as she put the crockery next to the sink.

'Hey, talk of the devil,' she shouted a moment later. 'Get the door, Evie. It's Gabriela – she's getting out of a taxi. Wow! That gold jacket's to die for. And my God, her fuck-me heels could be Miu Miu sandals!'

'Shit, shit, shit,' Evie muttered under her breath. A quick phone call would have been so much easier. She absolutely was not in the mood for another girlie evening with Gabriela, not in the middle of the week, not when all she wanted was a quiet evening with her housemates. Yes, she was very grateful to Gabriela, but enough was enough, and enough was fast becoming too much.

Reluctantly hauling herself up off the sofa, she shuffled to the door in her slippers. As she raised her hand to unlock the door, the bell sounded.

'Hi, Gabriela!' she said, opening the door wide and standing back to let her in. 'I almost beat you to the door. Jess saw you getting out of a cab.'

Gabriela beamed at her. 'Hello, Evie.' As she stepped into the house, her expression changed to one of apology. 'I hope you don't mind me visiting you without an invitation. I had to call on a design company in Highgate to introduce myself, and the taxi driver said that we must pass fairly close to where you live, so I asked him to drop me here. But if it is difficult, I can leave.' She half turned back to the door.

'No, you're OK. You must have a cup of something or a glass of wine. I won't suggest a meal, though, if you don't mind, as we're eating scraps tonight. We're clearing the fridge of everything left over from the last year – anything that isn't too mouldy or green will be eaten. Also I'm pretty tired and want an early night. But come on in.'

She closed the door behind Gabriela and led the way into the communal area.

'You can be sure that I will not stay for long,' Gabriela began apologetically. 'I know you are tired and that's one of the reasons I am here. You sounded so tired last night that I was quite worried about you. Another reason is that I wanted to know how things were with the editor. These two things are obviously connected.'

'That's very kind of you, but you needn't worry. I'm fine, or I will be when I've had a good night's sleep. Here.' She indicated the armchair. 'Take a seat. What can I get you to drink?'

'Just a coffee, please.'

Jess appeared in the kitchen doorway. 'Hi, Gabriela! It's nice to see you again. You sit down, Evie. I'll get the coffee. D'you want another one?'

'OK, thanks.'

'Right. I won't be two ticks.'

Evie sat down on the sofa and curled her legs under her. 'You were absolutely right about the editor. I was going to phone you and tell you so. I've got a stay of execution until Friday, and that's when I'll quit the job. I'm really grateful to you for your advice – I would never have thought of that myself.'

'Not at all. It was a pleasure.'

Jess came into the room carrying a tray with three coffees.

'Thank you, Jess,' Gabriela said, taking one.

'I didn't know if you took milk so I've put some in a jug. And there's sugar, too. Just help yourself.'

'You're very kind.'

Jess put the tray down on the table and went and sat next to Evie. She took the last two mugs from the tray, gave one of them to Evie, leaned back and took a sip of her drink. 'So, how's the new job coming, Gabriela, or is it too soon to tell?'

'No, I don't think it is. I think I'm going to enjoy it. It certainly will be a challenge, but I like challenges. They bring the adrenalin and add excitement to life.'

Jess laughed. 'I'm afraid I like my excitement to be outside my work. What exactly are you going to be doing? It's a design company, isn't it?'

'Oh, it will be too boring for you if I explain. And it will take too long. I am overseeing a rather complicated design project for an Italian company. The company that I work for in Italy has transferred me here for a year to do this. But Evie is tired and I want her to have some rest so I will tell you about the project some other day, if you wish. Besides, I have something quite interesting to tell Evie.'

'You do?' Evie asked, surprise in her voice. 'What sort of interesting?'

'Our family has found a wife for Eduardo, and Eduardo is very happy about it.'

'No kidding!' Evie exclaimed. 'That's a bit sudden. Or isn't it?'

A stab of mixed emotion shot through her. She was pleased for Eduardo – of course she was – but she was also a touch put out that he could transfer his affections from her to someone else with such speed. Mentally she kicked herself – how petty was that? She pushed back her grievance and focused on being pleased that a very kind man had found someone who wanted to share his life.

'Not really. They've known each other for many years. Eduardo was very attracted to her, but her family could not resist an offer made to her by a very wealthy man with businesses that would have been compatible with her family's businesses. They accepted his offer, and the two became engaged. Eduardo was heartbroken. But now, some months later, there is a problem about the engagement, and the girl's family has approached my family this week, indicating very subtly that Eduardo would now be welcomed as a suitor.'

'I'm so pleased, Gabriela,' Evie said. 'That's wonderful news. He's such a nice person, and he deserves to be very happy.'

'I'm glad that one of us is pleased,' Jess muttered. 'I'm not. And Rachel won't be.'

Gabriela laughed. 'You'll get over this great disappointment, I think, Jess. Rachel, too.'

'I must ring Eduardo and tell him how happy I am for him.' Evie looked at her watch. 'In fact, despite the hour's difference, it's still quite early in Italy – I could ring him this evening.'

'No, you must not,' Gabriela cut in quickly. She leaned forward in her chair. 'These are delicate matters, Evie, and family honour is involved. The discussions could still break down, although we hope very much that they will not. It would be humiliating for Eduardo if they broke down and people outside the family knew about this. Please, do not ring him, not until I tell you that it is a formal engagement. Then he will be very pleased to hear from you.'

'I can see what you mean. OK, I won't ring him until you give me the all clear. I'd hate to hurt him. I do like him very much. Now, Gabriela, to change the subject. Jess and I want to know your secret.' Gabriela seemed to stiffen slightly. How strange, Evie thought. She shrugged inwardly and carried on, 'How do you manage to look as immaculate at the end of the day as you do at the start of the day?'

Gabriela gave a tinkling little laugh, slipped off her gold jacket, sat back in the armchair and crossed one cream-trousered leg over the other.

How easy it all had been, Gabriela thought with an inward sneer as she walked away from the Camden Town house. It was like taking candy from a baby, as the Americans would say.

A few well chosen words, and there was no longer any risk of Evie contacting Eduardo when Tom threw her out of his life. As he would. Very soon.

There would never again be any risk of an alliance between Evie and Eduardo, and the Evie and Tom abomination would not survive beyond the start of the following week. And it had all been so easy.

With a spring of euphoria in her step, she raised her arm and hailed a taxi.

Chapter Twenty-Two

... and the sky darkens.

For the second time in five minutes, Evie stared at the clock on the corner of the large mahogany desk. It now said a quarter past two.

As soon as she'd arrived at Tom's house that morning, she'd turned the clock to face her and she'd glanced at it at regular intervals ever since. She hadn't been able to concentrate on her work at all, she'd been in such a state of anxiety. And her anxiety had got worse with every silent passing minute.

She was absolutely certain that her editor was going to call. He would give her a verbal lashing, followed by an ultimatum that reversed everything he'd said the evening before, and it was all going to go pear-shaped.

How different everything had looked that morning when she'd got up, compared with the way it had looked the night before.

The night before, she'd been on a super high.

On cloud nine that the editor had caved in so quickly, she'd been able to relax for the first time in ages, and when Gabriela had finally left and Rachel had got back home, the three of them had had a real fun evening. They'd binned the contents of the fridge, sent out for pizzas, drunk a couple of glasses of red wine, and then a couple more, and when she'd finally gone to bed, she'd slept amazingly well, considering the day she was about to face.

But that was last night.

Things looked very different in the cold light of the new day, and by the time that she'd got to Tom's house that morning, every ounce of confidence had vanished and she'd convinced herself that the editor would come back fighting.

He'd have had time to think things through and he'd have found some way of backtracking on what he'd said about waiting for Friday. She could see herself being forced into a spot where the only way out was to quit the job there and then, and if that happened, she might as well accept that she and Tom were history. Even if she returned that evening to see Tom, he was hardly likely to give a positive reception to a confession made at the end of his overlong work day.

Her mobile phone rang and she gasped aloud.

She pulled it to her and glanced at the contact name – it was Gabriela. For God's sake, what did she want now? She seemed to have either seen Gabriela or spoken to her every other minute since the woman had arrived in England. She was beginning to feel as if she had a sodding stalker in her life.

'Hi, Gabriela,' she said into the phone. 'This must be quick as I'm snowed under with things to do.' She glanced at her almost empty desk and felt a twinge of guilt. She owed a lot to Gabriela, and it wasn't really her fault that she was so damn needy. 'Well, I suppose I could take five as I haven't yet had a break. So, how are things with you?'

'I'm fine, thank you,' she heard Gabriela say. 'More important, how are you? I was wondering if everything was all right with you, or if maybe you had heard from your editor today.'

'Great minds think alike. I've been panicking all day that the shithead would ring at any minute. I've been dreading him regretting what he said yesterday and coming out with all guns blazing this morning, but so far not a dicky bird from him. I guess I'm not going to hear from him after all. It's pretty late in the day for him to ring now. I can probably let myself relax again.'

She heard Gabriela give an audible sigh of relief.

'That is very good to hear. And now, Evie, now that I am reassured about you, I must go. I have someone I must see. I just wanted to check that my friend was feeling cheerful today. I shall speak to you very soon. Yes?'

'Yes, of course.' Evie heard the line go dead. She flipped shut her phone and sat back heavily against her cushion.

Gabriela was a good friend – she'd certainly proved that – and she'd sounded genuinely anxious about her just now and really relieved that their plan was still on track. If her relationship with Tom survived the huge hurdle it was facing, it would be thanks to Gabriela. She knew that, and she'd always be grateful to her, but she could really do with having a break from hearing her at the other end of the phone or from seeing her in person. At least for a while.

All she wanted now was a bit of time in which to settle down to normal life again, and to have some space in which to move on with Tom. If only Gabriela could be sent on a course to a place that was miles away and didn't have phone coverage, or if only Alessandro would collect her from England and whisk her off to a desert island.

Every cloud may well have a silver lining, but she was fast learning that behind the silver lining, there could be one enormous black cloud.

Tom walked into his house Thursday evening, disabled the alarm, dumped his black leather hold-all at the foot of the stairs and threw his suit jacket over the banister. Unbuttoning his waistcoat, he went into the drawing room, and stopped abruptly in the middle of the room.

Silence hung heavily in the air. He could almost hear it, almost touch it. He looked around him for a minute or two, then he started to walk slowly towards the kitchen. Silence walked with him at his side; it was there with every step that he took.

His brow furrowed; he'd never been aware of such a sensation before. At some point – he didn't know when – the peace and solitude that he'd always valued so highly seemed to have changed into a sterile emptiness. An oppressive sterile emptiness. And he couldn't really put his finger on the reason why this should have happened.

Shaking his head, he went down the three steps that led into the kitchen.

It must be the Italian effect, he decided as he went over to his granite worktop. That week in Italy, in the land of art and music, must have brought out a fanciful streak in him that he'd never known he had. It would gradually fade, of that he was confident, and he'd go back to being the way he used to be, but for the moment it was all very unsettling.

He switched on the kettle. He'd have a cup of tea – the English answer to everything, even if there wasn't anything that needed an answer – and then he'd go up to his study and read through the draft of his opening statement to the court.

He made his tea, put a couple of ginger nuts on his saucer with a wry smile, and then, carrying the cup in one hand and his leather hold-all in the other, he went upstairs and sat down behind his desk.

Leaning against the back of his chair, he picked up one of the ginger nuts and dunked it in his tea. His gaze slid along the desk to the place where Evie worked and to her chair on the opposite side. He noticed that the cushion was crumpled up and he quickly finished the biscuit, stood up and went around the desk to her chair. He gave the cushion a good shake and propped it against the back of the chair, ready for the following day. Ready for the last day she would be working for him.

He slowly returned to his seat, sat down again and picked up his cup. His eyes on Evie's chair, he sipped his tea. His tea finished, he mentally shook himself. He must get on; he had work to do. He pulled the hold-all towards him, took out a bundle of papers, put them on to the desk in front of him and began to skim through the top sheet. Minutes later, he realised that his eyes had returned to Evie's section of the desk, and to the piece of paper on which she'd been doodling that day. She'd left it at the back of the desk, weighted down with the heavy stapler. He'd almost missed it.

Pushing his papers aside, he reached across the desk to the sheet and pulled it to him. The usual squiggles covered the page, and yes, it was there – the heart she always left him. She'd drawn it very clearly in the space at the bottom right-hand corner. She'd remembered what he'd said about liking the notes she left him, especially the little heart that she drew at the end of each message. There was no message this time, but there was a heart.

He smiled to himself, sat back in his chair and looked around him, the sheet of paper still in his hand.

The following day, he wouldn't be coming home to an empty silence, to a discarded doodling sheet with a small heart on it; the following day he would be coming home to Evie. He was amazed at how much he was looking forward to that, he who had always dreaded the thought of someone invading his space. He would never have believed that he could ever have welcomed such an invasion, but there was no doubt that he was very much looking forward to her being there when he got home the next evening.

It just showed that nothing was written on tablets of stone, he mused, and that even someone like him, who'd been confident that everything in his life was filed in the correct slot and was going to stay that way, could mellow somewhat in the face of a person who was a really pleasant companion. How long his life was going to be out of kilter like this, he didn't know, but he'd do well to make the most of it while it lasted.

Reluctantly, he put Evie's piece of paper back on the desk, picked up the draft of his statement for the court and glanced at it. He gave a deep sigh – it obviously still needed work. He couldn't leave it all for the weekend, not if he wanted some time with Evie, so he must get his head together fast and read it properly. Which wasn't going to be easy. His concentration was all shot to pieces because, if he was really and truly honest with himself, he wasn't just looking forward to the following day – he bloody well couldn't wait for it to come.

Chapter Twenty-Three

The best laid plans ...

The clock on Tom's desk said twelve thirty.

She'd woken up at four that morning and had tossed and turned for the rest of the night, wondering how the day would end.

She'd already decided that she was going to ignore all of the editor's phone calls until she'd reached the point that she couldn't ignore him any longer; anything to reduce the risk of Tom hearing about it before she could tell him. But it was a delicate balance – leaving it as late in the day as she dared, but not leaving it too late to reach him – and she was nervous about getting it wrong. Whatever happened, she had to quit before she saw Tom. That was a must.

On the way to Tom's house, she'd rehearsed her speech for the editor. One part of her was dreading the conversation; the other part was longing to get on with it, longing for the moment when she'd be free of *Pure Dirt* forever. By the time that she'd reached Tom's house at nine o'clock, she'd completely lost count of the number of times she'd gone through her words.

As she'd expected, he had already left for his Chambers. She'd switched off the house alarm and hung the clothes that she'd brought to wear that evening in the cupboard beneath the stairs; then she'd made herself a cup of strong coffee and taken it upstairs, just as she'd done every morning. Sitting down at her desk, she'd taken out her mobile phone, put it next to her, and then switched on the computer to see what Tom had left for her to do that day.

Time had passed slowly, and she'd felt every minute go

by. Although it was her last day working for Tom, he hadn't left her much work, and she'd resorted to looking for things to do to make the time pass more quickly. Finally, she'd given up the search, switched off the computer and sat there doodling, impatient to get the conversation over with, but still determined that it was going to take place later rather than earlier.

In her mental planning, she'd assumed that they'd expect her to email the story early in the morning – perhaps at about eight o'clock – and that they might start to think about phoning her when they hadn't received it by mid-morning. She wouldn't answer the first calls, though. When it got to the afternoon, she'd use her judgement about when to respond.

By the time that the hands on the clock had said ten thirty and there'd been no word from the editor, her growing amazement at not hearing from him, or from anyone else at *Pure Dirt*, began to be tinged with fear, although she didn't quite know what there was to be afraid of.

The editor must be frantically busy, she'd told herself. He would have been at his desk since God knows when, and there was bound to be chaos everywhere, given that it was so close to Monday's publication day. His feet probably hadn't touched the ground since he'd got to the office that morning. And a further possible reason was that he might be trying to give her as long as he could – she held all the power, after all, as Gabriela had said. It was just a matter of being patient.

She'd watched the hands of the clock crawl slowly around the face until they reached twelve thirty.

Every instinct told her that something was wrong, and she'd waited long enough – she was going to ring him.

She picked up her mobile and clicked on the editor's number.

'What?' she heard him bark down the line.

She cleared her throat. 'It's Evie Shaw.'

'What d'you want, Evie? D'you wanna add something? It was fucking good stuff as it was, but now that the boys have gone to town on it – it's dynamite. So what d'you wanna add? Better still, send it in. It can go in the follow-up. That's best. I'm up to my fucking eyes in it; we all are.'

'What are you talking about? What's good stuff?'

'You fucking losing it or what? Your story, of course. The one your mate dropped off at reception a couple of days ago. The gen on Hadleigh. What else would I fucking mean? Glad you didn't wait till today – the raw material hit the spot, but it needed work to get it up to the standard our readers expect. The boys would have been pushed to do it in a day. But well done, anyway. Not bad for a first story. It'll certainly run for a couple of editions, and if what else you've got ticks the right boxes, it might even stretch to a third. That fucking Hadleigh's gonna find himself up to his neck in shit. Now, if there's nothing else …'

She heard someone in the background shout out to him.

'Gotta go. Use email – it's what it's fucking for.'

The phone went dead at the other end of the line.

The clock ticked loudly in the silence of the room.

She'd stood up, she realised. At some point in the short conversation, she must have got to her feet, but she didn't remember doing so. Numb, she flipped her mobile shut. Her arm fell limply to her side and the phone slipped from her fingers and landed on the parquet floor with a dull thud. She stared down at the place where it lay.

They had a story, a story about Tom, a story that she hadn't given them – a story that someone else must have given them. But how? And who? She needed to think clearly about what the editor had said, about what it could possibly mean, but she couldn't. Her mind was frozen in fear as an ice-cold shroud wound tighter and tighter around her.

Only her instinct was working, and her instinct was telling her to get as far away as she could from Tom and his house, and as quickly as possible. There would be time for thinking later, much later. But not yet.

Her heart thumping fast, she pulled a piece of paper to her, wrote a hurried few lines, put the paper in front of Tom's place at the desk, then she picked up her bag and her phone, spun round and ran to the door.

Full of anticipation for the evening ahead, Tom left his Chambers as early as he could. He had to make a short detour on the way home to collect the present he'd had made for Evie, but fortunately, given his state of impatience, it didn't take long and he was soon back on the road.

His excitement growing with every passing minute, he drew up at the kerb in front of his house, switched off the engine, got out and crossed the pavement to his front door in long strides, pressing the car's central locking device as he went. He couldn't wait to see Evie's face when he gave her the present. He couldn't wait to see Evie, period.

He turned the key in the lock and went into the entrance hall.

'Evie!' he called as he kicked the door shut behind him. 'I'm back.'

He slung his jacket over the banister, felt in his inner pocket to make sure that the small package was safely there, and then went into the drawing room, loosening his tie as he walked. It wasn't just seeing her and giving her the present that he was excited about, he couldn't wait to see the expression on her face when he told her the plans that he'd made for that evening.

He knew the name of the show that she was really keen on seeing, and he'd called a friend in the theatre world and managed to get good tickets, which would be waiting at the door when they got to the theatre. After that, he was going to take her to The Ivy for dinner. With luck, they'd spot some celebrities – she'd like that, he thought. The evening would be a good way of celebrating the month that she'd worked for him and a pointer towards the fun that they were going to have together in the future.

The gift he'd bought her was for later, when they returned to his house at the end of the evening.

He'd called her a couple of times on his way home, not to tell her what they were doing that evening, but just to hear her voice. Frustratingly, however, her mobile had been switched off each time, and when he'd tried the land line, he'd got the answerphone. But he was home now and could speak to her in person, which was better all round. He went back out into the hall.

'Evie!' he shouted up the stairs.

He stood and listened. Silence. She'd probably fallen asleep at the desk, he thought in amusement. She was certainly somewhere in the house – there was no way she'd have gone out without switching on the alarm – and she obviously wasn't in the kitchen or she would have heard him the first time he'd called out, so she must be upstairs. Right, he'd go up to Sleeping Beauty and surprise her.

Taking the stairs two at a time, he quickly reached the first landing, and he paused. On a sudden impulse, he pushed open the door to the bathroom she used – it was empty. She must definitely be in the study then, or possibly even in his den on the top floor.

A few more steps and he was in front of the study door.

The door was slightly ajar. Moving quietly forward so as not to disturb her, he pushed the door further open and peered round the door. He stopped short in surprise. Her chair was empty. His gaze fell to the floor, and he saw that her cushion was on the floor next to the chair.

He let go of the door handle, went slowly into the room and looked around him. Her used cup was still on the desk. That was unusual, he thought – she always put any dirty cutlery and crockery into the dishwasher before she went home. How strange. He glanced under the desk by her chair to see if her bag was there. No, there was no sign of any bag. So where was she? He ran out of the study and bounded up the stairs to his den, shouting out her name.

His den was silent, empty.

She wasn't in the house; and whatever the reason she'd left, she'd left in a great hurry. Perhaps she'd been taken ill – a sudden chill came over him – or maybe someone she knew had been taken ill. A serious illness would explain her leaving the house as quickly as she could and forgetting to activate the alarm.

Deep in thought, he went slowly back down to his study and walked over to her place on the desk. The area in front of her chair was empty and the computer was switched off. He turned and looked towards his swivel chair and saw a small piece of paper on the desk where he usually sat. He felt almost weak with relief – whatever it was, she'd had time to leave him a message. He leaned across the desk, picked up the paper and read it.

I'm sorry, Tom. I didn't do it. You must believe me, but I know you won't. I'm really sorry. Love, Evie

No doodling. No heart.

Breaking out in a cold sweat, he pulled his phone from his pocket and clicked on her number again. Her phone was still switched off.

He pulled out her chair and sat down heavily. Didn't do what? What on earth could she be talking about? And why wouldn't he believe her? What could she have done – or what could people say she'd done – that was so awful that she'd have to walk out on him just like that. She was an agency temp, for God's sake!

The agency! How stupid of him! He should have thought of the agency at once – they were certain to know what was going on. He'd wasted valuable minutes.

He glanced at his watch and saw that it was almost seven o'clock. His heart sank: it was highly unlikely that anyone would be at the agency that late on a Friday night. The most he could do would be to leave them a message, asking them to call him the following day.

And the following day was hours away.

He pulled his large desk diary over to him and looked up the agency's number. He might just strike lucky, he thought as he listened to the dialling tone, there could be an eager beaver working later than the rest.

The answerphone cut in after the ringing tone had sounded five times, and he heard a mechanical voice welcoming him to the agency and asking him to leave his name, contact number and a short message.

Stressing the need to speak to someone as soon as possible about their temp, Evie Shaw, he left his number, reminded them that he was an excellent client and said that he expected to be contacted by someone the moment they picked up his message; then he put the phone down and sat back. At least he'd made a start towards finding her, pathetic though it was, but there must be something else he could do.

He picked up her note and read it again.

Think clearly, he told himself. If she, or someone she knew, was ill, she would have said so in the note, no matter how briefly. But she didn't say anything along those lines – so illness must be ruled out. The facts that the note was rushed, that she'd denied doing anything wrong but was obviously afraid that he wouldn't believe her, and that she'd left the house at speed, all pointed towards her being in trouble.

So where would she go if she was in trouble? Of course! There was only one place she'd go – she'd go back to Camden Town, to Jess and Rachel. He was being amazingly dense that evening. If there was any sort of crisis in her life, she was bound to want to be with her friends. That should have been the first thing he'd thought of. He stood up. He didn't have a phone number for the house – in fact, he didn't even know if they had a land line – but he did know where the house was.

Please God, he prayed as he ran down the stairs two at a time, please God, let Evie be there.

Chapter Twenty-Four

O Evie, Evie! Wherever art thou, Evie?

Twenty minutes later, Tom had parked the BMW and was standing in front of the Camden Town house. His heart beating fast, he rang the doorbell and stood back. Muffled chimes reverberated throughout the interior of the house. There was no other sound from within.

He tried the bell again. Still no answer. Damn, there was clearly no one in the house, which was a bit surprising. He wouldn't have thought they'd all still be at work at that time. Although, come to think of it, Evie had said that one of them was an events' planner, which meant that she was bound to work some evenings.

Of course, it might simply be that they'd stopped for a drink on their way home, in which case there was a strong possibility that Evie had joined them. He stared at the closed door and wondered whether or not they were with her, and if so, where they might be.

He took a step back from the house and looked towards the upstairs windows. It was a warm evening, but the windows were all closed. No, there was definitely no one at home. He glanced in both directions along the street, but there was no sign of Evie, nor of anyone likely to be one of her two friends.

Dejected, he turned away from the door, went back to his car and got into it. Drumming his fingers against the wheel, he stared ahead through the windscreen. He'd just have to be patient and stay there a while longer – one or all of the girls might have only gone for a short walk and be back at any minute. And even if they were out for longer than that, possibly at a restaurant, he'd still stay on – they'd have to come home at some point and he was going to be there when they did.

He positioned the windscreen mirror so that he could see the pavement behind him, and settled back into his seat, alternating keeping his eyes on the pavement in front of him or on the reflection in the mirror.

An hour passed with no movement at all. He didn't really know what to do, whether to carry on sitting there or whether to drive around for a bit on the off chance that he might see her. She'd told him that she and her friends sometimes ate at Wagamama, so he could make a start there and come back to the house later on if he didn't have any luck.

He groaned out loud. What bloody use would it be to do that!

He put his hands to his head in despair. Even if he went to every restaurant, bar and club in Camden Town, if Evie wasn't with Rachel and Jess, he'd be totally wasting his time – he hadn't a clue what her housemates looked like. He could hardly walk into the middle of a place and shout out, 'Anyone here called Rachel and Jess?' Well, he could, but he'd soon find himself facing a charge of disturbing the peace.

A movement in the windscreen mirror caught his eye and he swiftly slid up in his seat, twisted round and stared through the car window. A blonde girl carrying a large bag in each hand was coming along the pavement behind him, walking towards him. She passed his car, went up to the front door of the house and put her bags down on the ground.

He jumped out of the car and dashed up to her.

'Are you Rachel or Jess?' he asked in a rush. 'Do you know where Evie is? I can't get hold of her.'

The girl stopped looking for her key and stared curiously at him. 'Tom, I presume. Or an escaped nutter.' She glanced pointedly at his flapping waistcoat and shirt sleeves.

'You're right, I'm Tom. And you've just confirmed that you do, indeed, own one of the two heads I saw hanging out of the window last Saturday night.'

'Spot on. I'm Jess.' She held out her hand to him. 'Pleased to meet you, Tom.'

He shook her hand. 'I know that I've dispensed with the social niceties, Jess, and I do apologise, but I badly need to see Evie. I don't know if you know what's happened, but one minute she was working in my house, and the next she was gone. She's just disappeared and I don't know where she is.'

'Have you rung her?'

'Over and over again, but her phone's switched off. I rather hoped she was here. She left the briefest of messages and I don't know what to make of it all. Here, look at this.' He pulled out the piece of paper that Evie had left him and held it out to her. She took it and glanced at it. 'We were meant to be going out this evening. I don't know what to do.' He shrugged his shoulders helplessly.

Jess stared at him for a moment. 'Come on in, Tom. Have a coffee with me. You look like you need one, or even something stronger.'

'Coffee's fine,' he said, and he followed her into the house.

He sat down in the armchair and forced himself to sit patiently while she put her bags in the kitchen and then went and rummaged in one of the upstairs rooms. At last she came back downstairs, made them each a coffee and sank down on to the sofa opposite him.

'I seem to have bought enough food to feed a whole army,' she said. 'As always.'

'Look, if it's not rude, Jess, can we cut to the chase? Have you heard from Evie? Do you know what's going on? Because I haven't a clue and I'm worried about her.'

'Has it occurred to you that if she wanted to speak to you, her phone wouldn't be switched off and she'd be where you could find her?' Jess asked bluntly, watching Tom over the rim of the mug as she sipped her coffee.

'But why wouldn't she want to speak to me? What can have happened to make her take off like that?' He stared at her, bewildered.

'Who knows what goes on in other people's heads?'

'You do know where she is, don't you? She must have called you.'

'Nope, I've no idea where she is, but she did phone earlier – you're right about that.'

'And?'

'And nothing. It wasn't exactly a conversation – she just said that someone had done the dirty on her, but she didn't expect me to believe her, and she ended the call. That's all I can tell you. It's more or less the same as she said to you.'

'Do you have any idea what she means?'

'I'm not sure. Nor is Rachel – she phoned Rachel, too, and Rachel called me after she'd spoken to Evie. We can make a guess, but it's such a far-fetched idea that we could be wrong and we're not going to say anything. Not this side of the weekend, anyway.'

'Do you mind if I stay here for a bit until she comes back? Presumably she'll have to come back at some point tonight. If it's not convenient, though, I can always sit in the car.'

Jess hesitated a moment. 'I'm afraid you might have a long wait. When I got in, I checked Evie's room – she's been back here since leaving your house and she's taken some clothes. Also, her make up and stuff have gone. I don't think she plans on coming back for at least a few days.'

'Gone? Gone where?'

'I'm sorry but I've absolutely no idea.' She stood up. 'I hate to say it, Tom, but I've got to get changed – I must get off shortly to meet some friends. And no, Evie isn't one of them. I'd tell you if she was. I promise you that if she rings again, I'll try to persuade her to call you, but that's the best I can do, I'm afraid.'

He stood up, pulled his wallet out of his pocket, took out a couple of business cards and handed them to Jess. 'There's a card for you and one for Rachel; you'll find my number on it. I'd be grateful if you asked Rachel to call me if she has any news.'

'Right you are.' She started to lead the way to the front door. 'I'm sorry for what Evie's doing to you, Tom. I can see that you're really upset. I promise I'll contact you if there's anything at all to tell you.'

'What about her parents?' He stopped abruptly, a note of hope lifting his voice. 'Girls always go back to their mothers, don't they?'

'Not if their parents are in Australia, they don't. Or at least, certainly not on the spur of the moment. I think you need papers and visas and whatnots. Anyway, I can't see her turning to her parents. Even though she loves them, she's not seen them for yonks. I can't imagine her running off to them just because she's done something wrong and everything's in a mess.'

'So you *do* think she's done something wrong?' He stared intently at her. 'Yes, you do. I can see it in your face.'

'I don't know what to think, Tom, I really don't.' She hesitated. 'I can make a guess at what it might be, but it's so unlikely, and such a long shot, that I'm not going to say any more than that. All I know for certain is that if she did do something she shouldn't have done, it'll have only been because she was put in a position where she couldn't avoid doing it. I'm not saying any more now – I think I've probably said more than I should as it is.' She walked to the front door, opened it and stepped back to let Tom pass through.

Nodding to her, he went out of the house, got into his car and drove off.

Evie stared at the last two messages she'd just received on her mobile: one from Rachel and one from Jess, both of them urging her to get in touch with Tom. He was worried. He deserved an explanation of what was going on. They all did.

That was today. Things would change on Monday, once everyone knew the truth. Or thought they knew the truth. She hated herself for what had happened, and if *she* hated herself for what she'd done, then she could just imagine the way that Tom was going to feel about her.

She scrolled back and looked at all of the missed calls and messages from Tom. She'd read the first two texts he'd sent her, and then no more – their warmth and anxiety hurt too much. She looked again at the last messages from Rachel and Jess, then she turned the phone off and tucked it back into her pocket. On Monday, the messages would change their tune and there was no way she was going to read them. The phone would stay off.

Tom went slowly up the stairs to his study and sat down behind his desk.

If she'd left Camden Town and wasn't with Jess and Rachel – and he was pretty sure that Jess wasn't lying – and she wasn't with her parents, where could she be? It hit home hard to him that he didn't really know her that well. Apart from Rachel and Jess, he'd never heard her mention any friends, except Gabriela, of course.

Gabriela! He sat bolt upright. Now that was a possibility.

Gabriela might well know where Evie had gone. There was a real chance that Evie might have taken refuge with her from whatever it was. She and Gabriela had spent quite a bit of time together recently and had obviously been hitting it off brilliantly. If they hadn't, Evie and her friends would never have taken Gabriela out with them in the evening. Doing that was way beyond the field of duty, so to speak.

His shoulders slumped in relief. Sometimes, if you got yourself into a mess, which was clearly what Jess and Rachel thought had happened, you needed someone who could stand back from it all and give you good advice, rather than a really close friend who might be too emotionally involved to think clearly. What could be more likely than that she'd turned to Gabriela in time of need? How stupid of him not to have thought of that sooner. He pulled his wallet out of his back pocket and rifled through an assortment of business cards. Ah, there it was: Gabriela's card with her details.

The telephone rang only twice before someone picked it up, but the wait felt like an eternity.

'Hello?' a female voice said at the other end of the line.

'Hello, is that you, Gabriela?'

'Tom? It is Tom, isn't it?' She sounded surprised to hear his voice, but pleased. Maybe a little nervous, too, he thought.

'Yes, it is. Look, Gabriela, can I skip everything else and come straight to the point? I'm trying to get hold of Evie as I'm desperate to speak to her. She's not at her house and she won't take my phone calls. Is she by any chance with you?'

'I can't help you, Tom, I'm afraid. She's not here.'

His momentary hope sank into despair. 'I knew it was a long shot, but I just thought she might be with you. I don't suppose she's called you or given you any idea where she is?'

'I'm afraid that I really don't know where she is.' Her voice was full of regret. 'If I did know, I would tell you at once. She seemed so mixed up when I spoke to her.'

'Mixed up? What do you mean?'

The other end of the phone fell silent.

'Gabriela, if you know anything, please tell me. What do you mean, "mixed up"?'

'I don't like to say.' Her voice was hesitant with obvious reluctance. 'Evie is my friend.'

'And I'm sure you know what I think of her. You and I, we're both her friends. If she's done anything she shouldn't, or anything at all has happened to upset her, please tell me where she is so that I can go and help her.'

'I don't know where she is.' Her voice broke into a little sob. 'But I *am* worried about her, Tom. She said that she had done something she really regretted, and that you'd hate her when you found out. I think that that might be why she has gone.'

'But what could she have possibly done that I could ever hate her for doing? I don't understand.'

'I don't, either. That's why I don't like saying this to you. I'm only repeating her words to you because I can hear how worried you are.'

'Of course you are, and I'm most grateful to you for telling me what she said. I'm afraid that I'm going to have to accept defeat for the moment. I can't think of anywhere else to look, or anyone else to ask. I shall have to try to put the whole thing out of my mind for the next few days and focus on the work I've got to do over the weekend. I'll contact you when the case is over and we'll get together – we may have a better idea of what Evie was talking about by then.'

They said goodbye and Tom put the phone down.

He stared at his desk. There was nothing more he could

do about finding her until he'd spoken to the agency, and that may not be until Monday evening – his phone would be switched off when he was in court. Of course there was still a chance that Evie might make contact with him, either directly or by sending him a message through someone else, but that chance seemed like a slim one. For the moment, he'd have to force himself to be patient and to focus on his work, and that was just about the hardest thing he'd ever asked himself to do. On the plus side, it would keep his mind off Evie. Or he fervently hoped it would.

He glanced at the phone on his desk. Thank God, Evie had friends like her two housemates and Gabriela, he thought; friends who really cared about her and who would do their best to help her if she finally turned to them.

Chapter Twenty-Five

Black Monday!

Tom stepped out on to the top step in front of the Royal Courts of Justice, pulling his black leather wheelie bag full of files behind him. He'd not had a single moment in which to check his messages all day, but his long wait to see the agency's reply was almost over, and he felt a sense of mounting excitement.

A sudden movement in front of him caught his eye, and he glanced down as a large crowd of people surged forward. A barrage of flashbulbs went off in front of his face.

He stopped abruptly and stared in amazement at the mass of photographers gathered on the pavement behind the railings. Pushing forward in one heaving body, they were jostling each other to get as close as possible to the black iron gate that held them back from the foot of the shallow stone steps.

Involuntarily, he took a step backwards and turned to his junior in surprise. 'I knew it would be a fascinating case, but I rather thought the fascination would be for the lawyers, not for the public. However, this is manic. We'll try to get out of here as fast as we can. We're making no statements, not at this stage of the proceedings. Come on. Let's go.'

He took a step forward and the cameras burst into action again.

Forced to stop, he blinked furiously at the fresh explosion of bright lights that confronted him. His vision gradually clearing, he saw some reporters that he recognised trying to elbow their way through the jumble of photographers to get to the front.

'This way, Mr Hadleigh,' a voice called from the body of the photographers. 'Look this way.'

'Have you got any comment to make?' one of the reporters shouted.

'What *is* this?' he said under his breath, as much to himself as to his junior.

'They can't expect you to make a statement today – we've only just chosen the jury,' the junior replied.

'And what the hell do they want my photo for?' He stared in bewilderment at the crowd, and the flashbulbs sparked off again. 'This is abnormal. You'd expect this for big celebrity names, but not for a man libelled in business, no matter how important he is, nor how legally significant the case. What on earth can be going on! We may well have to go back and leave through one of the rear exits.'

'Mr Hadleigh, sir.' The voice came from behind him, from the inside of the court building. 'A word, if you please, Mr Hadleigh,' the voice said. It came closer.

He turned and saw one of the court officials coming towards him across the tiled foyer. He was waving his hand to attract Tom's attention. Tom indicated that he'd seen him, and the official stopped where he was and beckoned him back into the building.

'You get off home,' he told the junior. 'I'm going to see what the official wants. Hopefully, he'll be able to shed some light on what's going on. I've never seen such a madhouse as that lot outside. You know the points I want you to research this evening – I'll ring later if there's anything else I need to tell you. Otherwise, I'll see you in court tomorrow.'

'Good luck with whatever it is, sir,' the junior said as he started to make his way down the steps.

Tom watched him skirt the iron barrier and move away from the crowd with difficulty, then Tom turned back, went into the vast entrance hall and walked over to the waiting official. Together they went across to one of the benches running along the wall at the side of the hall and sat down.

'We won't be troubled here, Mr Hadleigh,' the official said quietly. 'I think that there's something you should see before you make another attempt at leaving the building. I take it you haven't had your phone on at all today, sir.'

'That's correct. I switched it off when I arrived at court, just as I always do. Anything you can show me that will make sense of the pandemonium outside will be more than welcome, I assure you. I've never before seen anything like it for this sort of case.'

'I think that this may be of some help.' The official pulled a rolled-up magazine out of his pocket, put it on the bench between them and unfurled it. 'I think you'll find that it's not your case, sir, that has drawn the press hounds.'

'It's not?' Tom started in surprise. 'So what has?'

The official looked down at the magazine cover. Tom followed his gaze. His eyes flew to large red letters written across the photo of a bewigged barrister who was hurrying into the High Court: 'BONKING BARRISTER!! HORNY HADLEIGH – EXPOSÉ!' The barrister had put his hand up in an attempt to shield his face from the camera, but it was unmistakably a photo of him.

'My God, that was taken a month or so ago!' he exclaimed. 'A photographer shoved a camera in front of my face as I was going into court. I remember it happening quite clearly. But looking at this, it's made me appear quite furtive, as if I had something to hide. What's this all about?'

As he asked the question, he realised that he knew the answer.

Unable to move, he watched the official flick through the pages until he came to the place he was looking for. He flattened the magazine on the bench and Tom saw a huge blow-up of his face splashed across the centre of a double page. A line of bright red words printed across his photograph swam before his eyes. All he was able to register was, '... exposé by Evie Shaw, *Pure Dirt*'s crack new reporter.'

Fifteen minutes later, the magazine in his pocket and the official's hushed words of sympathy ringing in his ears, he made his way out of the court building through a rear door and returned at speed to his car.

He needed to get home, to get back to peace and quiet and somewhere to think. He lifted his bag into the boot of the car, climbed into the driver's seat, left his mobile switched off – he couldn't deal with anything nor speak to anyone; not yet – and drove back to Hampstead, his mind in a turmoil.

As soon as he reached his house, he disabled the alarm, left the wheelie bag of files at the foot of the stairs and went into the drawing room and over to the cocktail cabinet. He took out a glass and a bottle of single malt whisky, carried them upstairs to his study, sat down at his desk and poured himself a stiff drink.

As the whisky hit the back of his throat, he leaned back in his chair and shut his eyes for a few minutes. Then he poured another shot of whisky, took the magazine out of his jacket pocket, opened it and started to read slowly through the article.

When he'd read every single word of the report for a second time, he sat back and stared ahead of him. In his mind's eye, he and Evie were lying in bed, laughing and chatting together. He saw himself telling her about his friendship with Zizi and about breaching the Bar Code when he was very young. Some time after that, she must have told someone what he'd said.

He pushed back a rising sense of hurt and betrayal as he pictured Evie passing on to another person the words he'd spoken to her in a moment of intimacy. He glanced again at the magazine.

So this was what Evie had been talking about when she'd said in her note to him that she didn't do it, also when she'd told Jess that somebody had done the dirty on her. On the phone, Gabriela said that Evie had told her that she'd done something she very much regretted doing, and that he would hate her for doing it. It was a slightly different take on things, and Gabriela may have misunderstood what Evie was saying, but whatever she said or didn't say, it was clear that she hadn't expected him to believe that she was innocent, and she hadn't expected Jess and Rachel to believe her either.

He picked up the note she'd left him and reread it, then he looked down at the exposé in *Pure Dirt*. It was all one huge mess. One thing, however, stood out way above everything else – was heads and shoulders above everything else – and that was his absolute conviction that Evie didn't write that article.

Even at the very moment that he'd seen her name beneath the article, he'd known that she would never have written such a story. Someone had written about him and Zizi in a way that suggested a sexual relationship, and along with a photo they'd managed to find of the two them, plus a sensationalised account of him reading legal material he shouldn't have done, they'd made him look morally reprehensible as well as in breach of the Bar Code.

But that someone wasn't Evie.

At that moment, in a blinding flash of self-realisation that almost knocked him over with its force, he'd known that he loved her with every inch of his being, and that she loved him just as strongly. It had taken that filthy rag to make him see a truth that had been staring him in the face since that first day in Umbria.

Of course Evie didn't write that report. People who loved each other didn't act like that; they couldn't.

He pushed his drink to one side, threw the magazine across his study and stood up.

Panting slightly from the speed with which he'd rushed from his car, he knocked on the door to Evie's house, stepped back and waited. Footsteps could be heard coming to the door, and a moment later, it opened a crack.

'Since you're not Jess, and you're certainly not Evie, you must be Rachel,' he told the girl with long, brown hair who stood peering through the narrow opening. The door closed slightly. He heard the sound of a chain being undone, then the door opened wider again.

'And since you're obviously not here to sell us double glazing or to save our souls, you must be Tom,' the girl said cheerfully. 'And yes, I'm Rachel. Come on in. Jess warned that you might call or even come round.'

'Well, as you can see, I picked the "or even come round" option.' He gave her a slight smile and went into the house. 'It's good to meet you, Rachel, although I'd have preferred to do so under different circumstances.'

'Likewise,' she called over her shoulder as she went ahead of him into the sitting room.

Jess was on the sofa, reading a magazine. She looked up as Tom came into the sitting room and hastily made a move to stuff the magazine under a cushion.

'Don't bother, Jess. I've already seen it,' he said, and he sat down in the armchair. Rachel went and sat on the sofa next to Jess.

Jess leaned forward, an expression of sympathy on her face. 'I'm so sorry about the article, Tom.'

'Why, Jess? Did you write it?'

'Of course not,' she retorted indignantly.

'Then you've nothing to be sorry about, have you? What about you, Rachel? Did you write the article?'

'No, I most certainly did not. The first time I heard about your naughty past was when I read the story over someone's shoulder in the tube this morning.'

'So I've forestalled any more apologies from anyone here, I hope. And that goes for Evie, too, should she suddenly appear.'

Rachel and Jess exchanged glances. 'I don't follow,' Jess said.

'Be honest. In your heart of hearts, do either of you think that Evie could ever have sent that story to *Pure Dirt*?'

'Of course, we don't. She wouldn't do such a thing,' Rachel said at once. 'But as you've probably guessed by now, *Pure Dirt* did send Evie to work for you – the editor thought you'd been at it with a client and he wanted to see you struck off as payback for all the money you've cost them in the past. He hates you.'

'Then they'll be out of luck. It's not an offence for which I could be struck off – a barrister's self employed and can rather do what he likes. But any suggestion that he's having a relationship with a client obviously looks bad if that client's claiming that she's morally blameless and has been defamed. They'll be trying to claw back some of the money that the original case cost them.' He paused. 'And Evie's role in all this?'

'She'd only just started working for *Pure Dirt* when she was given the task of digging up some dirt on you,' Jess said. 'She was desperate to work for a magazine and that was all she could get. And she'd still got an idealised view of the job and thought she could do it without being nasty. Rachel and I really went on at her for not thinking it through, but happily she soon came to her senses. She was going to quit the job last Friday and tell you the truth that evening.'

So, he'd been nothing but an assignment in the beginning. It hurt, but it didn't change things. He knew Evie, and he knew their connection was real.

'Where does the agency come in?'

'Nowhere really,' Rachel said. 'Her editor's got a contact at the agency, and he told the editor that you wanted an Italian speaker. The contact was paid to recommend Evie for the job. The rest is history, as they say.'

'I think I get the picture now. You can be sure that I'll sort out the agency in the fullness of time, but for the moment, my focus is finding Evie.'

'What I don't get, Tom,' Rachel said, 'is why you're so certain that Evie didn't write the story. Jess and I know her really well, and we know that she could never do anything malicious to anyone – she's just not wired like that. But how can you be so sure that she wasn't involved, assuming that you told her everything that was in the article? They had to get it from somewhere.'

'I've known her for long enough to know she couldn't do that. You don't necessarily have to be with someone for years to know them. A day can be sufficient. And as for what you indirectly asked, reading a fax that I shouldn't have read was true, and that I'm friends with Zizi is true, but our friendship is platonic and has never been anything else, which Evie knows. That part of the article is a lie, and the whole thing has been made to sound ultra sensational.'

'You don't have to explain to us,' Jess cut in quickly. 'It's your business.'

'Not any longer, unfortunately. There's only one glaring omission in the article, and that's to do with the material faxed to me by mistake. Evie knows that I was very young at the time and that it was my first solo case, but they left out any reference to my youth and inexperience. I guess it would have made everything sound much less serious –

after all, a young barrister making a mistake doesn't sound as bad as an experienced barrister doing what he knows to be wrong.'

'They're such pigs at *Pure Dirt*,' Rachel said indignantly.

'Anyway, to move on – we're all agreed that Evie didn't write that story, aren't we?' he said.

Jess sighed. 'I wish she'd been here to hear you say that. I bet it would have stopped her from running away like she's done.'

'I wish she was here, too.' He looked from one to the other. 'I don't suppose you've had any more thoughts about where she might have gone, have you?'

Jess gestured helplessly with her hands. 'We haven't a clue. Believe me, we'd tell you if we had, but we've absolutely no idea at all. She's not even responding to my text messages.'

'Do you have any idea who dropped you in the shit, Tom?' Rachel asked. 'It's definitely not Evie, so it must be someone else.'

'Funnily enough, I'm less bothered about that than I am about finding Evie. But yes, I do have a pretty good idea who it must have been.'

'So, who do you think it was, then? Jess and I were talking about it just before you got here. We can only think of one person.'

'I don't like to accuse anyone without being sure, but I, too, can think of only one other person it could realistically be. It's probably the same person that you've come up with.'

'Accuse away,' Rachel said with a giggle. 'You're among friends. We think it must have been Gabriela – she and Evie have spent a lot of time together since Gabriela came to London. Too much, if you ask me – Gabriela was all over Evie like a rash.'

'But we can't see why she would do something that

would hurt you,' Jess cut in. 'From what Evie said, Gabriela really likes you. In fact, when you first met Gabriela, Evie was a bit jealous about how well you two seemed to hit it off. So why would Gabriela do that?'

Tom shrugged his shoulders. 'It's hard to explain, I know, but it must have been her. When I spoke to her just after Evie had disappeared, she emphasised that Evie had told her that she'd done something she regretted doing. That's significantly different from the messages the three of us got. There's no reason why Evie would have said two such different things.'

'No, there isn't,' Rachel agreed.

'As for why Gabriela did it,' Tom went on, 'I can only guess that she must have been very against Evie for some reason known only to herself, and she didn't want to see her happy. She must have thought that by breaking us up, she'd make her unhappy. She may well have overlooked the fact that she'd be hurting me in the process.'

Rachel looked anxiously at Tom. 'What do you think is going to happen about what the paper claimed?'

'The worst of the two attacks is, of course, the Zizi thing. *Pure Dirt* will probably go to the Court of Appeal and claim that Zizi having a candlelight dinner during the course of the trial with her barrister, who'd already been shown to be dishonest, is enough to suggest that their other claims could be true. They'll say that as she's diminished her reputation, their damages should be accordingly diminished. They'll want something financial out of this after all of their devious efforts.'

'You can bet they will,' Rachel said bitterly. 'Will they win, do you think?'

'My guess is that they'd settle. Going to court is always a gamble, and in this case there are too many uncertainties on both sides. I imagine that Zizi will probably have to give up some of her damages and pay her own costs, but not theirs. *Pure Dirt* may even get away with not paying any damages at all.'

'What about the fax thing?' Jess asked.

'As far as that goes, the Bar Standards Board will probably refer the matter to the Head of Chambers or to a Disciplinary Tribunal, and I'll be fined and reprimanded. I don't want to let myself feel too confident as it's a very serious offence, but I'd be surprised if I were to be suspended – it happened a long time ago. The fact that the revelation comes from such an unpleasant source should help me, too.'

'I certainly hope it won't be any worse than that,' Rachel said warmly. 'We both do. We'd hate to see that sleazy rag win.'

'By far the worst punishment for me is that I'm not going to be able to hunt for Evie until my current case is over. It opened today and I've got to be in court every day for two weeks – there's a limit to what the junior can be left to do by himself. Not only that, I've a full workload for the coming weekend; not only working on the present case, but I'm also preparing for a case that begins in a month's time.'

'That sounds heavy,' Jess said with a grimace.

'I'm used to it. But it means that much as I'm desperate to find Evie, I dare not let myself be distracted in the next couple of weeks. I want to do my best for my client – that's paramount – but I'm also determined to show *Pure Dirt* that their sordid little plan couldn't even lose me the case I was working on.' He paused, then added, 'Since I can't look for her at the moment, I think I'll hire a detective to find her.'

'I wouldn't, if I were you,' Jess said at once. 'She obviously needs time by herself to get over what's happened. Otherwise she'd have been in touch.'

'Jess is right, Tom. Give her some space.'

He hesitated. 'I don't know. I need to feel as if I'm doing something. If I can't do it myself, and I can't, the next best thing is knowing that someone else is doing it. I'm not good at sitting back and doing nothing.'

'But that could be the best thing for Evie,' Jess said quietly.

Tom sighed deeply. 'Maybe you're right. OK, I'll hold off on the detective; for the moment, anyway. Soon as the case is over, I'm going to concentrate on finding her. Till then, though, I'll be patient. That is, when I've done the one thing that I've got to do this evening – something that can't wait.'

Jess smiled at him. 'It wouldn't entail a trip to Holland Park, would it?'

Chapter Twenty-Six

The Moment of Truth

'Who is it?' Gabriela's voice came through the intercom seconds after Tom had buzzed the number of her flat.

'It's Tom. I was in the area and I thought I'd drop by on the off chance you were home. But just say if it's not convenient – I can always go away. I wouldn't want to impose.'

A little laugh sounded through the intercom; a slightly nervous little laugh, he was inclined to think.

'It's no imposition, Tom. I shall be happy to see you.' He heard the pleasure in her voice, but there was definitely a hint of wariness, too. His lips tightened. So there should be. 'Push the door now,' the disembodied voice instructed. 'I'm on the first floor.'

He pushed open the door and went into the entrance hall. Struggling to stifle the wave of anger that welled up in him, he made straight for the staircase. When he reached the first floor, Gabriela was standing in her doorway. She stepped forward as he approached, her wide smile not quite touching her eyes. Pursing scarlet-coloured lips in the air, she raised her face to him.

Steadying himself, he leaned down and kissed her on both cheeks. Musky perfume enveloped him.

'It's wonderful to see you again, Gabriela,' he said, straightening up and staring into her face. There was unmistakable nervousness in the depths of her jet black eyes. 'Wonderful,' he repeated, putting as much warmth and enthusiasm into his voice as he could muster.

'I feel the same,' she murmured, and he sensed her

beginning to relax. 'It's so lovely to see you again, Tom. But come – we must not stand here. Let me be very English and offer you some tea.' With a smile of invitation, she turned and led the way into the apartment and across the hall.

He closed the door behind him. His jaw clenched, he followed her into the sitting room. Pausing, he looked around. 'What a beautiful room,' he commented.

Huge pictures hung from the white walls, their muted grey and brown tones echoing in the profusion of light grey and lavender throws and cushions, and in the intricate shapes of musky grey sculptured glass that had been skilfully placed around the room for dramatic effect. 'You must have worked very hard to get it like this in so short a space of time.'

'I didn't have so much to do. The flat was already very beautiful, and in a style that pleases me. For the rest, I had help. You lent me Evie for a few days, did you not?'

'That's a name I'd rather you didn't mention, thank you very much,' he said tersely, and he sat down heavily on the sofa and started to loosen his tie. He stopped mid-action, his hand still on his tie for dramatic effect. 'It is OK to make myself at home, isn't it?'

'Of course, it is,' Gabriela said with a broad smile. 'You must look upon this as your second home.'

'You're very kind,' he told her. 'Or as my third home, to be more precise.' They both laughed.

He pulled off his tie, put it into his pocket and undid the top button of his shirt. Leaning back against the sofa, he smiled up at her. 'And I'm going to be even bolder than I've already been, and tell you that I could do with something stronger than tea. I rather think I need it, the way I feel.'

She laughed merrily. 'I have a very good single malt whisky. At least, I have been told that it's good. You must tell me if you agree with the recommendation. For me, I prefer to drink wine. There's a bottle of white wine in the fridge. Perhaps you will go and open it for me and bring it in here. You'll find a rather elaborate opener in the cupboard above the refrigerator.'

He promptly got up and went out to find the kitchen.

When he returned to the sitting room, an open bottle of wine in one hand and an ice bucket in the other, he saw Gabriela bending over the glass table. She'd obviously just moved one of the magazines from the top of the pile to the bottom and was hastily straightening them all.

'Here we are,' he said, putting the ice bucket on the table, and resting the bottle on the ice.

'Thank you, Tom,' she said with a smile, and went over to the white cabinet in the corner of the room.

He sat down on the sofa and watched as she took out a wine glass and a crystal whisky glass, followed by a decanter of whisky, and carried them on a pale wood tray to the coffee table. She placed the whisky glass and decanter in front of Tom, and the wine glass by the chair on the opposite side of the table. Putting the tray squarely on top of the magazines, she sat down.

'You're certainly right about it being an all singing, all dancing wine opener,' he remarked, raising himself slightly to pour some wine into Gabriela's glass. Then he rested the bottle back in the bucket, filled his glass with whisky and sat back on the sofa.

Gabriela picked up her glass. 'I think we should have a toast. To the first of what I hope will be many visits.'

'I'll drink to that,' he said, and he forced a smile to his face as he raised his glass to his lips. 'It's good to see a friendly face after the day I've had.' He took a long drink, then put the glass on the table. As he did so, his gaze slid along to the pile of magazines under the tray. He leaned across and removed the tray.

He felt Gabriela's eyes on him as he ran his fingers down the edges of the magazines, nudging them sideways to expose the issues that lay at the bottom. He heard her catch her breath as his eyes zeroed in on the letters visible on the magazine at the bottom of the pile. *Dirt* and EXPOSÉ glared back at them.

'I assume you've read the article,' he said flatly, sitting back and nodding towards the magazine.

'Yes, I have, Tom,' Gabriela said, a note of apology in her voice. 'I started buying the magazine as it was one of the things that Evie said I should read in order to learn about the English way of life.'

'The English way of life!' He injected a harsh note of bitterness into his voice. 'So that's how she describes the content of filthy rags like *Pure Dirt*, is it? Well in my book, using subterfuge and lies to uncover and expose the secrets of people in the public eye, secrets that are no one else's business, is the very opposite of the English way of life. There's something deeply sick about it, and about the people who are making their living by trying to destroy the lives of others. And that includes Evie Shaw. She really pulled the wool over my eyes in order to screw me good and hard.'

He leaned forward and picked up his glass of whisky. Out of the corner of his eye, he saw a flicker of triumph play across Gabriela's lips. It swiftly passed and she raised her glass, took a sip of her drink and set the glass down.

'I'm sure that Evie didn't mean to write the story,' she said, her voice gentle. 'The people at *Pure Dirt* will most likely have found her notes by accident and they themselves will have written the story. I cannot believe that Evie would ever give them anything unpleasant about you. She seemed to me to be very fond of you.'

'Well, that's what I thought, too, but obviously we were

both wrong. Much as I'd like to believe that it was all a mistake, as you're suggesting, I can't. This isn't Hollywood – it's real life – and in real life she wouldn't have jotted down what I'd said if she hadn't intended to make a story out of it. There'd have been no point. And what's more, if she had made such notes, she'd never have left them lying around – a reporter wouldn't be that careless. Every story means money to them and they'd jealously guard the facts that they'd gathered.'

'It did say that Evie was a new reporter. She will not yet think in the way that experienced reporters will think.'

'Even if you're right – and it's a sign of your very generous nature that you're trying to make Evie innocent in all of this – even if you're right and she'd left her notes lying around, no one would have been able to read them. Apart from the fact that her writing leaves a lot to be desired, it's virtually impossible for one person to make sense of another person's notes. The essence of notes is that they remind the writer of what was said, not that they record every detail. No, that story could only have been written by Evie – I told it to no one else.'

He sat back with a deep sigh.

'Oh, Tom, I'm so sorry for you.' Her voice shook with sympathy. 'I can see how much Evie's action has hurt you. Will you be in terrible trouble for these things you have done?'

'I may have to make some reparation for reading what I shouldn't have done – a fine and a reprimand for the business with the fax, maybe; hopefully not much more than that. As for Zizi, despite their insinuations, there's no proof that we had a sexual relationship – and there couldn't be as we didn't. Nevertheless, *Pure Dirt* will obviously try to get their damages reduced at the very least. No, one of the worst aspects of the whole thing for me personally is the way in which my colleagues will look at me after such an exposure. To be shown to have breached our code of conduct is humiliating, to say the least.'

'I wish I knew what to say that would help you. People who know you, Tom, will know that you are a good man – a man, though, not a saint. Zizi will have led you on, like many unscrupulous women do to powerful men. And as for reading forbidden material, you were a very young man, who was working alone on his first big case.' He stiffened. 'After all these years of great work, they will not hold these unimportant things against you. You must put this magazine story behind you and forget about Evie and her betrayal. Look only to the future now.'

'You're right, Gabriela,' he said very quietly, and he sat upright. 'I was extremely young when I read that fax and it was the first time that I'd ever gone solo. However, that information doesn't appear in the magazine article. Evie knew the facts, though, as I told her the full story. The only way you can have known them, and known about Zizi and me, was if Evie told you. You wrote the article for the magazine, didn't you?'

'I don't know what you are talking about, Tom.' Her mouth smiled. 'We are friends, are we not? Friends do not do things like that to each other. Evie was not your friend, but I am.'

'I used to think that that was the case, but I've clearly been proved wrong.' He looked across the table at her. 'Tell me, why did you do it?'

He watched the colour drain from her face. A harsh patch of red stood out on each of her cheeks. 'I don't understand what you mean,' she stammered.

'Oh, but you do. I didn't for one moment think that Evie wrote the story and gave it to the magazine, but if I *had* harboured any suspicion of her being guilty, it would have been swept away the minute you confirmed that she'd passed on what I told her in Italy.'

'I have confirmed nothing like that.' She attempted to laugh. 'You are not making much sense, Tom. Or perhaps I am not understanding your English very well. Evie was the reporter, not me.'

'I'm quite certain that you manipulated Evie into telling you what I told her. When I find her – which I will do – she'll tell me how. What I want to know from you now is why you did this. What on earth can have been your motive?'

Gabriela took a deep breath.

For a moment he thought that she was going to protest her innocence again, but then he saw her hesitate. A look of resignation crossed her face and she released her breath in a small sigh. Positioning herself on the edge of her chair, she gave an elegant shrug of her shoulders and spread out her hands, palms upwards, in a gesture of helplessness.

'It was on the spur of the moment, Tom. I was not thinking clearly. When Evie told me these things about you, and told me about the magazine, another person inside me took over. I can't say any more about it than that. Please believe me, I am so sorry for what I did.'

He stood up. 'Hardly a spur of the moment action, I would have thought. However, I have a feeling that I'm going to have to be satisfied with that as your answer, although it still doesn't explain why you wanted to hurt me.'

'Oh, no, I never wanted to hurt you, Tom.' She quickly stood up and started to move round the table towards him. 'Not you. I would never hurt you – I love you. It was about Evie. She does not deserve you. Who is she? What kind of family does she come from; what breeding does she have; what education? She is not the woman for you, and she would not have been the woman for my brother.'

'For Eduardo?'

'Yes, she would have been wrong for him, too, although he could not see this. The Montefiori family must unite themselves only with the best. I have known you are the person for me since Eduardo showed me your photograph and told me about your illustrious career. Oh, Tom, do you not feel in your heart that you and I are meant to be together?'

She stretched out her arms and put her hands on his shoulders. With a shudder, he pushed them away from him and stepped back from her.

'I now have your answer to my question, Gabriela. And my answer to your question is that I'm leaving this flat now, never to return.'

He walked past her, crossed the room in long strides and went out of the apartment without a backward glance.

Gabriela turned slightly and stared at the open doorway. His footsteps echoed around the stairwell as he bounded down the stairs, and then she heard the front door slam shut. She started to tremble. A moment later, an engine was revved up in the street below her apartment.

She spun round, ran to the window and reached it just as his black car started to pull away from the kerb in front of her house. Pressing her face against the window pane, she watched him drive around the central garden and turn down a road that led out of the square.

'Tom,' she whimpered as she saw him go, and she put her hand on the cold glass as if to stop him. 'Tom.'

Slowly she raised her eyes from the garden below to the brick gateposts that flanked the Victorian houses on the other side of the square, and higher still, beyond the jagged line of tiled roofs and chimneys to the pale blue sky above.

White clouds drifted slowly into view, bringing with them

the sound of three girls laughing in a bustling, crowded restaurant. She could see their faces smiling at her, faces offering friendship. One more face appeared, the face that had dominated her thoughts for so many months – a man's face.

But the clouds continued their leisurely pace across the sky, and they took with them the laughter, the smiles, and the faces – all of the faces. And there was nothing.

Month after month stretched out ahead of her, imprisoning her far from home, alone and friendless in an alien country. She turned away and looked back at her sitting room. Before her she saw emptiness. In her head, there was silence.

Chapter Twenty-Seven

Eureka (well, almost Eureka)

What a brilliant end to the week, Tom thought in jubilation as he walked into his house. Winning a case had never been as satisfying as it had been that afternoon. How he would have loved to have been a fly on the wall when those hacks at *Pure Dirt* heard what the jury's verdict had been.

Of course, there were still some loose ends to be tied up, such as the award of costs and the amount of damages, but the decision in favour of his client had come through loud and clear, and he hoped that those muckrakers hadn't missed a single word.

But even better than his victory over *Pure Dirt*, with the current case behind him and the preparation for his next case well under way, he could now get down to looking for Evie. He'd waited long enough to do something about finding her – he fervently hoped that he hadn't made a mistake in heeding the advice of Evie's friends about the detective – and he wasn't going to wait a moment longer. He couldn't wait to see her again. Just the thought of starting the search that would end with him holding her in his arms made him feel more excited than a schoolboy on the first day of the summer holidays.

He left the wheelie bag at the foot of the staircase, pulled off his coat and dropped it on the bottom stair – it would have to go to the dry cleaner's before he wore it again – hung his suit jacket over the rail, went into the drawing room, poured some whisky into a glass and carried the glass up the stairs to his study. Sitting down in his swivel chair, he leaned back and linked his fingers behind his head.

Where to begin his search, he wondered.

Looking back, he now wished he hadn't listened to Rachel and Jess, but had followed his instinct and gone ahead and hired a private detective. If he'd done that, he might already know where to find her and not be sitting in his study, staring at a glass of whisky, in a quandary about where to start looking.

He stared around the room, deep in thought.

Rachel and Jess would definitely have rung him if they'd heard anything so there was no point in ringing them that evening. Getting in touch with *Pure Dirt* was a non-starter. He could hardly ask them if they'd pass on Evie's details so that he could track her down. That would really make the editor's day.

He swivelled round in his chair and stared through the window at the walled garden below. The agency was going to be his only hope, and that was a very slim hope – they'd probably never even had her full details as the whole thing had been a set-up, a supposition rather borne out by the fact that no one had returned any of his calls.

But the agency was all he had.

Unfortunately, once again it was much too late on a Friday evening for there to be anyone on the premises so he'd have to wait until Monday morning before he spoke to them. There was no point in leaving yet another phone message. That meant that there wasn't a lot he could do that weekend, apart from visiting Rachel and Jess, which he'd do first thing the following morning. Even if they hadn't heard from Evie, it would be nice to be able to talk to them about her, and the three of them might even come up with something if they brainstormed some ideas about where she might have gone.

Also, he'd ask them for the contact details of Evie's parents in Australia, and then he'd call her parents. But there was no point in trying to get their number that evening because the time difference meant that he wouldn't be able to ring them until the following day. The girls were probably right in thinking that she wouldn't have gone to Australia, but she might just have phoned her family and given them some idea of where she was. It was a long shot, but any sort of shot was worth pursuing.

At the same time, he'd tell the girls that he was going to hire a detective at once. The more people looking for her, the better. As far as he was concerned, Evie had had enough breathing space in which to sort herself out, and she might be more than ready to be found, especially when she knew that the truth was out and nothing very terrible had happened. And he was desperate to see her.

So, Camden Town the following morning it was, and then the agency on Monday. Feeling better at having a plan of action, he swung back round to face his desk, finished his whiskey and went back downstairs.

He reached the foot of the stairs and stepped over his coat. There was a very good dry cleaner's in Camden Town, he remembered; he could drop it off on the way to visit Rachel and Jess. He rested his glass on the bottom stair and picked up the coat to check the pockets – he'd once sent a jacket to the cleaner's that had in its pockets the only copy of the many billable hours he'd worked on a case. He'd never made such a mistake again.

He checked the outer pockets – they were empty – then he dug deep into his inside pocket. His fingers closed around a small package – it was the present that he'd bought for Evie. He'd planned to give it to her on the Friday night that she'd finished working for him, as a way of marking the start of their new relationship. Not surprisingly, however, he'd forgotten about it in the turmoil of the last two weeks.

Getting exactly the thing he'd wanted for her had taken

some organising, but he'd managed it, and he'd been certain that it was going to have been worth every minute of the trouble he'd gone to when he saw the expression on her face as she opened it.

He took the package out of his pocket, unwrapped it and lifted out the piece of carved onyx. He stared at it with satisfaction – yes, Evie was going to love it. Just one problem, though – he had to find her first if he wanted to give it to her.

All of a sudden, his heart leapt, and he gasped out loud. What an idiot he was! He knew exactly where he would find Evie. It was all but staring him in the face.

He thumped the worktop with his clenched fist, and then, smiling broadly, he reached across to the telephone and pulled it towards him.

Chapter Twenty-Eight

And then there were two

Evie sat under the *loggia*, staring across the distant hills as the sun set over Todi.

The deep red sky, streaked with crimson and vermilion, was slowly fading into the black of night. As she gazed at the panorama in front of her, the first light of evening came on in the heart of the old town of Todi, followed by another light, and other, until the town was ablaze with silvery lights, an island of glittering diamonds adrift on a sea of darkening hills.

A little way down from the old town, just beyond the outer edge of the town wall, the ancient white stone of the large round dome of the Santa Maria della Consolazione shone pale in the night.

If only it was always that easy to see the light, she thought ruefully.

In her mad panic on that dreadful Friday in London, all she'd been able to think about was getting out of the city as fast as she could and going somewhere miles away where no one would find her. She'd been so sure that once she'd escaped London, she'd see clearly what to do about Tom and the mess she was in. It hadn't worked out like that, though, and she still hadn't a clue what to do next. And time was fast running out.

She pulled her yellow cardigan more closely around her shoulders, stood up and started to stroll through the spotlit gardens towards the paved steps that led down to the pool and the olive groves.

She couldn't imagine how she'd ever thought that coming

back to the house where she'd fallen head over heels in love with Tom, could help her to think clearly. She'd desperately missed him for every single minute of the two weeks that she'd been in Italy.

Every step that she took in his house reminded her of the steps she'd taken with him; the plastic glasses that she used were the glasses that she'd used with him; the bed she slept on was the bed she'd chosen with him; the lavender-scented Italian air she breathed was the air that she'd breathed with him.

He was on her mind every second of the day, surrounded as she was by all her memories of him.

If anything, she was even more confused about what to do than when she'd left London. It should be a simple choice – either move to Italy and take the job with Eduardo, or turn down Eduardo's offer for a second time and return to London to try to convince Tom that no matter what it looked like, she didn't write that story. So why couldn't she decide what to do?

Was it fear that was stultifying her?

The magazine article was only one of the things she'd have to answer to Tom for. Even if she managed to convince him of her innocence – and it was a bloody big *if* – she'd still have to convince him that it was a temporary aberration that made her agree to work for a fetid rag like *Pure Dirt* in the first place, and then she'd have to explain why she'd passed on to Gabriela what he'd told her in confidence. Was she afraid that a failure to convince Tom would mean the end of all hope, and it was that trace of hope that was keeping her going?

How could she have been so stupid as to have been taken in by Gabriela that easily! And how could she have been so silly as to let herself get so drunk that evening that she blurted out something that she'd had no intention of ever telling anyone? And then what happened afterwards ... how could any woman be as scheming and manipulative as Gabriela? And why?

It must have been Gabriela who dropped off the story that Wednesday morning. No one else – not even Rachel and Jess – knew what Tom had told her. It made sense of why Gabriela had always been there, no matter which way she turned, watching over her, making sure that she rang the editor on the Tuesday night, and not on the Wednesday morning.

Gabriela must have phoned her on the Wednesday afternoon to check that she hadn't spoken to anyone at *Pure Dirt* during the day. She must have wanted to make sure that she didn't learn about a story being delivered until it was far too late to do anything about it. Gabriela would assume that she'd panic on the Friday as soon as she found out, and get out of London fast, which is what she'd done.

If she'd been able to think more clearly, she might have come up with a better plan of action than running away. She could have challenged Gabriela on the Friday, and stayed on that evening to tell Tom what had happened. But her head had been all over the place and she'd been in a frantic state. All she'd been able to see in her mind's eye was Tom's face when he learnt the truth about their trip to Italy, and she'd been overwhelmed by the anguish she'd felt.

And she'd been certain that Tom wouldn't believe her.

Why would he? He'd have thought that in the hope of hanging on to him and his lifestyle, she was trying to put the blame on a charming woman, who had absolutely no reason at all to want to hurt him. Gabriela would come across as innocence itself and would deny that she'd ever been told Tom's story, and it would be impossible for her to prove that she had.

No, in the state that she'd been in on that fateful Friday, she'd latched on to the only constructive thing that had rushed into her mind – Eduardo's offer of a job that would take her miles away from the trouble she'd caused.

Gabriela would probably be horrified to know it, but unwittingly she'd helped her – she'd told her that Eduardo was attached to someone else. If it hadn't been for that, she would never have moved back into Eduardo's life again. Even if she hadn't fallen for Tom, Eduardo would never have been her type and it wouldn't have been fair to have given him false hope.

As she'd run from Tom's house to Hampstead Tube Station, she'd phoned Eduardo to ask him if the offer of work was still open. He'd been audibly surprised to hear that she was considering taking the job after all, but he'd quickly recovered and told her that the position was still hers if she wanted it.

Not only was there a job for her, he'd assured her, but the first items of Tom's furniture were to be delivered in a couple of days, and he'd just started looking for someone to be at the house. If she wanted to be that person, he need not look for anyone else. Such an arrangement would help them both.

She'd instantly said no, that it wouldn't be right. But Eduardo had insisted. The co-operative was excellent, he'd said, but it was disorganised and the furniture was unlikely to be delivered all at once. It would be so much easier for him to know that there was someone at the house in the day. And if she was going to be there all day, she might as well stay on in the evening.

What's more, he'd added, there'd been a robbery last week in an empty second home owned by Americans, so it was a good idea to have someone living in Tom's house as much as possible.

The thought of going back to Tom's house had been irresistible, and she'd been willing to let Eduardo persuade her. She'd stay there, she finally agreed, but only until the furniture had all been delivered.

One of his cousins had some apartments in Todi, Eduardo had told her, and he would make sure that she had the first one that became available. In the meantime, he was sure that Tom would approve of their arrangement.

She'd hastily cut in that she'd prefer Tom not to know that she was in Italy, and Eduardo had agreed not to tell him. He'd also reminded her – and there'd been a smile in his voice as he'd said it – that Tom would find it rather difficult to understand anything he told him, unless he happened to be with Gabriela at the time.

And nor should he tell Gabriela where she was, she'd quickly begged. As Gabriela and Tom were friends, she'd added to soften her words, it wouldn't be fair to ask her to keep a secret from him.

If Eduardo had thought the whole thing very strange, he hadn't said so. All he'd said was that he'd pick her up from Rome Fiumicino later that evening – she must let him know her time of arrival as soon as she'd booked her ticket – and he'd take her straight to Tom's house. She wouldn't need to hire a car as he'd find her a car. After all, she was going to be working for him so she'd need transport.

'*Grazie mille, Eduardo,*' she'd whispered gratefully into the phone. She'd entered the tube station, and the line had gone dead.

When he'd met her at the airport, he'd clearly seen that she was in a real state and wouldn't be able to cope with questions, so their journey had passed in friendly silence. He'd left her at Tom's house, saying that he'd come up the following day and they'd go and get some provisions and collect a car for her – but that she was to have a holiday before she started work. That was an order, he'd added, and he'd kissed her lightly on the forehead and driven back down the mountain road.

The following evening he'd taken her out to dinner and told her that he could sense that something was troubling her, but that he wasn't going to pry. However, if at any time she felt like confiding in him, he would be happy to help her in whatever way he could. The most important thing was that she sorted out her problems before she tried to do anything else.

She'd thanked him and added, without thinking, that his fiancée was dead lucky to have him.

Oh no, she'd screamed inwardly. Gabriela had stressed that no one should know what was on the cards for Eduardo until the arrangement had been formalised. Wanting to kick herself for making such a slip, she'd started to apologise for what she'd said, but she'd seen the amazement on his face and her words had died away.

What fiancée? He didn't have a fiancée and never had done. He had only ever met one woman he'd have wanted to bear that title, but regretfully he knew deep in his soul that her heart belonged to someone else. He'd glanced quickly across the table, then looked back down at his plate.

She must have misheard Gabriela, she'd said hastily, and she'd furiously twirled her tagliatelle on to her fork.

That lying bitch, she'd thought angrily. While that lie had done her a massive favour – she would never have contacted Eduardo without it – Gabriela had landed poor Eduardo in a situation that could cause him a lot of unhappiness.

Her sandals hit a patch of hard earth, and she came back to the present with a jolt.

She stopped walking and looked around her. She was standing in the middle of two rows of olive trees. It was the very spot where Tom had first kissed her, she realised.

She put her fingers to her lips. There might never be any more such kisses. A sharp pain ran through her.

How the hell was it possible for someone to hurt so much and for so long, she thought in despair, and she turned round and started to make her way back along to the house.

As she walked, she thought she heard an engine coming up the mountain road, and she stood still and listened. But she couldn't tell where the noise was coming from as the hills and trees were distorting the sounds of the night. The sound died away, and she started walking again.

Leaving the shadowy groves behind her, she went up the slope to the illuminated pool and walked slowly all the way round its edge, staring down at the cool, clear water, remembering the time she'd sat there with Tom. She'd have one last swim in the morning before she left, and then she'd go back to London.

Back to London.

It was the first time she'd let those words come into her mind, but the moment she'd done so, she knew that that was what she wanted to do more than anything else in the world. Being in Umbria had given her the breathing space that she'd needed, but she was ready to go home. And she now knew what she was going to do.

Of course she hadn't been able to find peace of mind in Italy – she'd never find that until she knew that she'd done everything in her power to make Tom believe that she hadn't betrayed him. Maybe she wouldn't succeed in convincing him, but she wouldn't know until she tried, and hiding away in Italy was not trying.

There was no way she was going to let Tom go without a massive fight, and not only was she going to fight for him, she was going to win. The thought of not being with him for the rest of her life was unthinkable, just unthinkable.

She started to run towards the house. Late though it was, she had to start packing.

Hurrying through the arched glass doors into the sitting room, she pulled the shutters closed behind her, locked the glass doors, switched off the spotlighting and ran across the room to the hall. With every step that she took, her excitement grew. With luck, the following night she'd be home.

Passed the wide stone staircase that led up to Tom's bedroom, she paused for a moment and stared up at the landing. If only he was up there in his room, waiting for her, she thought in a moment of intense longing. If only. Then she tore herself away and continued across the hall to the bedroom she was using.

She pushed open the door. A thin shaft of moonlight cut into the darkness, sending tall shadows into the far corners of the room and up to the wooden rafters, and she went over to the lamp that stood on the bedside table nearest to her and switched it on.

The lamplight bathed the centre of the room in a warm golden glow. She stood next to the lamp and looked slowly around the room, trying to lock an imprint into her memory so that she could take it with her when she left. Her gaze came to rest on the centre of the bed, and she drew her breath in sharply.

In the middle of the white sheet lay a small black scorpion. The beam of the table lamp was bouncing off its hard shell, and it shone with ebony lustre.

She took a hesitant step towards the scorpion, leaned toward it and peered intently at it. It was motionless – there was no movement at all.

She went closer still to the bed.

Small though the scorpion was, she could clearly see that neither of its claws was moving, nor were its legs, nor was the tail – not even so much as a fraction of an inch. And the shell looked hard, unusually hard. She looked at it from different angles. She could almost swear it was a stone fossil or lifeless, but that wasn't possible – it had obviously managed to make its way to the centre of the bed.

She took a step back, picked up the corner of the sheet and lightly shook it. The scorpion rolled over a couple of times and came to a stop. It lay absolutely still.

Tentatively she stretched out her arm and touched the back of the shell. It *was* made of stone. Her heart stood still. She straightened up and her hand flew to her mouth. Where had it come from and how had it got on her bed?

And then she knew.

She let out a long sigh of absolute joy, and her face broke into a smile of sheer happiness.

'Well, aren't you going to ask me to sleep with you, Evie?'

His words came from behind her.

She spun round to face the door and he was there, in the doorway, one arm resting casually against the side of the door, the other holding a jacket which dragged on the floor. There was a dark shadow along the square line of his jaw.

'Tom! Oh, Tom!'

She flew across the room and into his arms, tears falling down her cheeks.

'My Evie.' He buried his face in her hair. 'Don't you ever do that to me again. The last two weeks have been a bloody nightmare.'

'I won't. I promise I won't.' She hugged him tightly. 'I don't think I've ever been as miserable as I've been since I left you. I couldn't bear it if I lost you.'

'You're never going to lose me, Evie, you can be sure of that. I intend to be here at your side for the rest of your life. That is, if you'll let me.' His put his finger under her chin and raised her face to look into his. 'It's all very simple really. I'm sure you love me, and I know that I love you and want to marry you.'

Her tears died away.

'But that article in *Pure Dirt*, and what I did, not that I did it ...'

'Ah, how I've missed that Evie logic,' he murmured, stroking her hair. 'I never for one minute believed you wrote the story. I knew you could never have done a thing like that, not to me, not to anyone else.'

'But I'd pretended to be someone I wasn't, and you knew that I must have told Gabriela everything you told me. I was drunk – it was the Wagamama night. She kept filling my glass with wine and more wine. She must be the one who sent the story to *Pure Dirt*.'

'I guessed you'd told her, and I guessed she'd passed it on. Technically, though, I'm not sure that I ever asked you to keep it to yourself. But even if I had, I knew you must have been somehow tricked into telling her – you aren't the sort of person to do the dirty on anyone, so you wouldn't be expecting anyone to do the dirty on you. But she's actually done us a favour.'

'She has?'

'The whole shebang has made me realise how much I love you. I have done since the day we got here. I was just too blind to see it. Which reminds me, you haven't answered my question yet.'

She giggled. 'This sounds like a conversation we've had before. What question are you talking about this time?'

'I seem to recall asking you to marry me.'

'You mean "I love you and want to marry you" is a question? I know I wasn't an ace reporter for long, but isn't that more of a statement?' She looked up into his face, her eyes opening wide in mock bewilderment. 'Or don't you think?'

He smiled down at her.

'I think that I want you to be the last thing I see before I close my eyes tonight, and the first thing I see when I open them in the morning. Tonight, tomorrow, and every day for the rest of our lives. I want to make an honest woman of you, Evie Shaw. So, will you marry me?'

'Of course, I will. Honesty is always the—'

His lips silenced hers before she could reach the full stop.

About the Author

Liz was born in London and now lives in South Oxfordshire with her husband. After graduating from university with a Law degree, she moved to California where she led a varied life, trying her hand at everything from cocktail waitressing on Sunset Strip to working as a secretary to the CEO of a large Japanese trading company, not to mention a stint as 'resident starlet' at MGM. On returning to England, Liz completed a degree in English and taught for a number of years before developing her writing career.

Liz has written several short stories, articles for local newspapers and novellas. She is a member of the Romantic Novelists' Association. Her debut novel, *The Road Back* won a Book of the Year award in 2012. Her second novel *A Bargain Struck* was shortlisted for the 2014 Romantic Historical Novel of the Year Award.

Follow Liz on:
Twitter: @lizharrisauthor
Facebook: https://www.facebook.com/liz.harris.52206
Web: www.lizharrisauthor.com

More Choc Lit

From Liz Harris

The Road Back

Winner of the 2012 Book of the Year Award from Coffee Time Romance & More

When Patricia accompanies her father, Major George Carstairs, on a trip to Ladakh, north of the Himalayas, in the early 1960s, she sees it as a chance to finally win his love. What she could never have foreseen is meeting Kalden – a local man destined by circumstances beyond his control to be a monk, but fated to be the love of her life.

Despite her father's fury, the lovers are determined to be together, but can their forbidden love survive?

'A splendid love story so beautifully told.' Colin Dexter, O.B.E. Bestselling author of the Inspector Morse series.

Visit www.choc-lit.com for more details including the first two chapters and reviews, or simply scan barcode using your mobile phone QR reader.

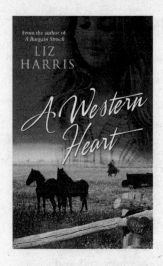

A Western Heart

Wyoming, 1880

Rose McKinley and Will Hyde are childhood sweethearts and Rose has always assumed that one day they will wed. As a marriage will mean the merging of two successful ranches, their families certainly have no objections.

All except for Rose's sister, Cora. At seventeen, she is fair sick of being treated like a child who doesn't understand 'womanly feelings'. She has plenty of womanly feelings – and she has them for Will.

When the mysterious and handsome Mr Galloway comes to town and turns Rose's head, Cora sees an opportunity to get what she wants. Will Rose play into her sister's plot or has her heart already been won?

Visit www.choc-lit.com for more details including the first two chapters and reviews, or simply scan barcode using your mobile phone QR reader.

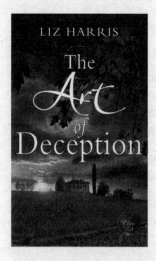

The Art of Deception

Jenny O'Connor can hardly believe her luck when she's hired to teach summer art classes in Italy. Whilst the prospect of sun, sightseeing and Italian food is hard to resist, Jenny's far more interested in her soon-to-be boss, Max Castanien. She's blamed him for a family tragedy for as long as she can remember and now she wants answers.

But as the summer draws on and she spends more time with Max, she starts to learn first hand that there's a fine line between love and hate.

Visit www.choc-lit.com for more details including the first two chapters and reviews, or simply scan barcode using your mobile phone QR reader.

Introducing Choc Lit

We're an independent publisher creating
a delicious selection of fiction.
Where heroes are like chocolate – irresistible!
Quality stories with a romance at the heart.

See our selection here:
www.choc-lit.com

We'd love to hear how you enjoyed *Evie Undercover*.
Please leave a review where you purchased the novel
or visit: **www.choc-lit.com** and give your feedback.

Choc Lit novels are selected by genuine readers like yourself.
We only publish stories our Choc Lit Tasting Panel want to
see in print. Our reviews and awards speak for themselves.

Could you be a Star Selector and join our Tasting Panel?
Would you like to play a role in choosing which novels we
decide to publish? Do you enjoy reading romance novels?
Then you could be perfect for our Choc Lit Tasting Panel.

Visit here for more details...
www.choc-lit.com/join-the-choc-lit-tasting-panel

Keep in touch:
Sign up for our monthly newsletter Choc Lit Spread for
all the latest news and offers: www.spread.choc-lit.com.
Follow us on Twitter: @ChocLituk and Facebook: Choc Lit.

Or simply scan barcode using your mobile phone QR reader:

Choc Lit   *Twitter*   *Facebook*
Spread